RED DIRT HEART 2

N.R. WALKER

COPYRIGHT

Cover Artist: Sara York
Editor: Erika Orrick
Red Dirt Heart 2 © 2014 N.R. Walker
First edition: August 2014

All Rights Reserved:

Warning

Intended for an 18+ audience only. This book contains material that maybe
offensive to some and is intended for a mature, adult audience. It contains
graphic language, explicit sexual content and adult situations.

Trademark Acknowledgments:

The author acknowledges the trademark status and trademark owners of the
following wordmarks mentioned in this work of fiction:

- Land Rover: Land Rover
- Skype: Microsoft Corporation
- Land Cruiser: Toyota Motor Corporation
- Akubra: Akubra Hats Pty Ltd., Ian Dixon Pty. Limited

- Harvey Norman: Harvey Norman Retailing Pty Ltd
- Driza-bone: Driza-bone Pty. Ltd.
- Nutella: Ferrero S.p.A.
- *The Price is Right*: Freemantle Operations B.V.
- Woolworth's: Woolworth, LLC
- McDonald's: McDonald's Corporation
- Domino's: Domino's IP Holder LC
- Google: Google Inc.
- Justin: Boot Royalty Company, L.P.
- MC Hammer: Burrell, Stanley K.
- Wranglers: Wrangler Apparel Corp.
- RM Williams (RMs): R.M. Williams Pty. Ltd.
- *The Mummy*: Universal City Studios LLC
- *The Godfather*: Paramount Pictures Corporation
- Bundaberg Rum (Bundy): Bundaberg Distilling Company Pty Limited

DEDICATION

For those who took a chance on me years ago, and for those who are with me still,
Thank you.

INFORMATION PRIOR TO READING AND GLOSSARY

Size matters - Sutton Station, while fictional, is based on a working property in the middle of Australia and is three hours drive to the nearest town. Sutton Station is 2.58 million acres (10,441 square kilometres). In comparison, the largest ranch in the USA is King Ranch at 825,000 acres (3,340 square kilometres). Sutton Station is the third biggest station in the Northern Territory and is classed as desert. Sutton Station is approximately the same size as Lebanon.

The Northern Territory is a federal territory in between Queensland and Western Australia. It's like a state, just don't call it that to someone who lives there.

Australian Terminology Glossary:

Station: Farm, ranch.
Paddock: Large fenced area for cattle; a pasture.
Holding yard: Corral.
Swag: A canvas bedroll.
Ute: Utility pickup truck.

Motorbike: Motorcycle, dirtbike.

Akubra: Australian cowboy hat.

Scone: American sweet biscuit, usually eaten with cream and jam.

Pub: Bar/drinking venue, usually serves meals.

Trolley: Shopping cart.

Car park: Parking lot

Driza-bone: Oiled coat farmers wear to protect from rain and wind.

RED DIRT HEART 2

Welcome to Sutton Station:
One of the world's largest
working farms in the middle of
Australia — where if the animals
and heat don't kill you first,
your heart just might.

CHAPTER ONE

FOUR DAYS. FOUR BLOODY LONG IT-WASN'T-LIKE-THIS-BEFORE-HIM DAYS.

LEANING AGAINST THE KITCHEN COUNTER, I looked at my watch for the twentieth time and sipped my tea.

"He won't be much longer," Ma said.

I pretended not to know what she was talking about, and she pretended not to smile. Ma was trying to get dinner ready, and I was under her feet and in her way. I put my still-full cup in the sink and sighed. "It makes no sense," I said. "I spent twenty-six perfectly capable years without him, how can four days be so fu—" I stopped short of swearing and tried again. "How can four days be so bloody long?"

Ma smiled her eye-crinkling, that's-so-cute smile. "You miss him. It's only natural," she said. "Can you lift this tray for me?"

I carried the old heavy cooking tray of roast beef to the centre table where Ma usually cut it for serving. "But still. Four days. It's pathetic," I mumbled. "And they're late!

How long does it take for them to come in from the southern fence line? It shouldn't take them this long."

Ma ignored my whining and asked me to get the platters down from the shelf. Then she asked me to get the plates and set the table. I knew she was just keeping me busy and getting me out from under her feet. I'd annoyed her enough for the most of the afternoon. And possibly some of yesterday as well. Day three hadn't been much fun either.

Travis had been gone for four days. Four freakin' days. Four days when time stretched thin, draggin' its sorry self forward. Four days of keepin' myself busy, four days of being a miserable disgrace.

He was fixin' fences on the southern line with Ernie, Bacon and Trudy. I wasn't surprised the fencing needing doing; it was too many years of sun and rust in the making. There was a stretch of fencing a few kilometres long that needed restumping and rewiring. It was a big job and about a hundred kilometres from the homestead. It wasn't worth coming in each night for. We kept in constant radio contact, and George flew fresh supplies down to them on the second day, similar to what we do when droving cattle.

When Travis said he'd join the others for the job, I'd said I could go too. We were in bed, and Travis rolled us over so he was on top of me and laughed at me. "Can't you live without me for four days?" he'd asked.

"Don't be stupid," I'd shot back at him. "Of course I can."

He'd grinned in the darkness, kissing me with smiling lips. "You totally can't."

"Don't flatter yourself," I'd replied.

"You'll be useless without me," he'd goaded, pinning my hands above my head and nudging his nose to mine. "You'll see."

And the smug bastard was right.

"You know," I told Ma as I pulled out the tray of condiments from the dry store pantry. "You know what I hate the most? I hate that he has to be right *all* the time. It really pisses me off."

"Hm   mm," Ma   hummed   in   that   sure-it-does-honey tone.

"And I hate that he thinks *he'll* be the one to decide whether or not he goes fencing for four days, when I said the others were more than capable. I mean, I'm not his keeper, but I am his boss."

Ma said nothing, just looked at me as she stirred the pot of gravy. She had one eyebrow raised in a 'course-you-are-honey kind of way.

"And he didn't seem to think leaving me for four days was a problem. He volunteered to camp out for four days rather than be with me, for shit's sake. So what does that say about me?"

"Charlie," Ma chided.

"And you know what else I hate? He leaves his towels on the bed. I really hate that. How hard is it to hang it back up again? It's not hard. At all. And he grinds his teeth when he sleeps. I *really* hate it when he does that. And what the bloody hell is that letter from my old uni addressed to him for—"

Then we heard the sound of motorbikes and the old ute pulling up at the gates near the shed.

And my chest got all tight and my stomach knotted with butterflies.

Ma burst out laughing. "Hm mm. I can tell by your smile just how much you hate all those things."

"They're back," I stated the obvious.

Ma nodded toward the front of the house. "Go." When

I got to the hall, Ma said, "Charlie?" I turned to look at her. "Try not to give too much away, honey. Then he'll know he was right."

I walked out the front door into the cooling air. It was almost winter now, the days were shorter and the nights chilled off quickly. The sunset had gone from its usual array of oranges and reds to darker purples before it became night.

Two bikes and the ute came in from the southern paddocks and pulled up at the shed. The engines died, and I'd only made it as far as the front porch when the silence was cut by the sound of laughter. Either Travis had said something funny, or they'd made a joke about me waiting for him on the veranda like a lovesick schoolgirl.

I just couldn't bring myself to care.

Travis came up from the shed grinning, just like usual, and bounded up the veranda steps. His tanned skin high-lighted his blue eyes and his wide smile, and the red dust covered his jeans and shirt from riding one of the dirt bikes.

Travis had been here for six months, his knee—from where he'd injured himself and got himself lost for a night—was almost good as new. He pulled his hat—my old hat—off his head and smiled. "Evenin'."

Of course I was smilin' right back at him. I was just glad the light was fading so he couldn't see the blush that heated up my cheeks when he looked at me like that. "Evenin'."

I wanted so bad to touch him, wrap my arms around, kiss him. But I couldn't. The others were still at the shed, and we were in clear view of all who were looking.

"You totally missed me," Travis said. He bit his lip, and he looked at my mouth like he wanted to kiss me too.

"Don't flatter yourself," I said. I tried for nonchalant, but it was barely a whisper.

He laughed, and then his smile faded and all he did was look at me. We just stood there, not speaking, just staring, for the longest minute.

He swallowed loudly. "Did the mail come today?" he asked.

"It did." I nodded toward the front door. "There's quite a few for you. It's all on our bed."

Our bed.

It still felt weird to say it.

I followed him when he walked inside the house and hung his hat on the hook next to mine. He hesitated in the hall, looking between me and the kitchen, then he snatched up my hand and pulled me into the bedroom.

He turned, and in one fluid motion, he slid his hand around my neck and pulled me in for a kiss.

A four-days-gone kind of kiss.

It was urgent and certain and warm, and it was everything I needed.

He wrapped one arm around me, pulling us together, and he sighed as our bodies melded into each other.

"Boys!" Ma called from the kitchen.

Travis groaned and took a step back, ending the kiss. "You better go out there," he said. "I better get cleaned up and try and get rid of this," he said, adjusting himself.

I eyed the bulge in his dirty jeans. "I could help you with that," I said.

"You *will* be helping me with this later," he said, readjusting himself again.

Then I remembered something. "Trav," I continued, nodding pointedly toward the pile of mail on the bed, "care to tell me why the University of Sydney has sent you something?"

His eyes shot to the envelopes and parcels. "Um, maybe later."

I picked it up, but he took it off me and threw it back on the bed. He walked out the door and headed toward the bathroom. "Don't touch it, Charlie."

"Trav," I whined. "I've waited all day."

At the bathroom door, Travis laughed. "Answer's still no."

Then Ma called out from the kitchen. "Charles Sutton."

"Saved by the bell," Travis whispered. Then he bloody grinned and shut the door.

"I could just open it and read it," I said to the bathroom door.

"You could," he called out. I heard the bathroom tap turn on. "But you won't."

I huffed at him, which might have been a growl, and stomped off into the kitchen where Ma was waiting. "Why are men so frustrating?" I picked up a fork and threw it into the sink.

Ma barked out a loud laugh. "Honey, that is an age-old question. Must be twice as bad for you two." She was struggling with a heavy pan, so I snatched up a tea towel and lifted it from the stove to the table for her.

I huffed again and opened the dry-store pantry, probably with more force than was completely necessary. "*I'm* not frustrating at all. He is." I carried the tray of sauces out and put them on the kitchen table. Ma was looking at me, biting her top lip.

"What?" I asked. "I'm not!"

She turned back to the sink, I guessed so I couldn't see her smile. Her voice gave her away. "I take it he wouldn't tell you what was in the envelope?"

"No."

Travis appeared in the doorway, looking all clean and smelling even better. "Has it been bothering you?" he asked, not even trying to hide his smile.

"All day," I admitted.

His smile became that eye-crinkling kind as he walked into the kitchen. He put his hands to my face and kissed me. It was something he only ever did in front of Ma. The kitchen was neutral territory, where anyone was free to speak their minds. The other station hands, my employees, never came into the kitchen, and we never touched—let alone kissed—in front of them.

"Go get cleaned up," he said. "I'll finish setting the table." He pecked his lips to mine again and pushed me toward the door. "Go." When I was halfway up the hall, he called out, "And don't touch the envelope."

After I'd washed my hands and face, I went back out to find George, Bacon, Trudy, Billy and Ernie at the dining table. Travis was there too, of course, and as we ate, they were talking about their four days on the southern fence line.

Travis looked tired, though he was still all smiles. I had no doubt he'd been up before the sun each day, and his bed being a swag on the ground hardly made for sound sleeping. Winter was the best time to get the most work done; the nights were cold but the days were merely warm compared to the scorching heat of summer. And Travis loved to work. He loved being busy, he loved being productive, and he didn't stop all day.

They all talked about their weekend off, how they were leaving for the Alice in the morning. There was the usual excitement and bullshit about who was doing what.

Before dinner was finished, Ernie said, "There was a

large mob of roos getting into the top south paddock too. Makin' a real mess."

I pushed my empty plate away. "How many?"

Travis shrugged. "About twenty."

I looked at George. "We might take a look this weekend."

I could tell George was making plans in his head before dinner was cleared away, and I knew we'd sort it out tomorrow. But tonight I had other things on my mind.

I wanted Travis in my bed. And I wanted to know what the hell he was up to with that envelope from my old uni.

When everyone else was gone and the house was quiet —and after Travis had deliberately avoided it for as long as I could stand—I dragged him into our room. He shut the door behind us and laughed when I handed him the envelope.

"Please open it." I wasn't above begging.

Travis ignored me and picked up the largest brown box first. The label was in his mother's handwriting, so I tried to be patient while he ripped into that one first. His mum had sent over his favourite hoodie. He'd come over here in the heat of the summer fully intending to stay for just four weeks. He had no winter clothes, except for what he swiped of mine. I'd ordered him some more shirts and jeans online, but somehow I ended up with those and he just kept on wearin' mine.

His mum had also sent him some biscuits.

"Cookies."

"Biscuits."

"Cookies."

"They're biscuits."

"They're cookies. It even says so on the package." He held it up to show me. "And these are my favourites. I've missed these." He ripped into the packet and shoved a biscuit in his mouth. He moaned and his head lolled back as he chewed. "They're so good." He unfolded the handwritten note from his family, and I waited as he read it. "Mum sends her love," he said as he kept reading. I stood and waited as patiently as I could until he was done. Travis looked at me then and held the packet of biscuits out to me. "Want one?"

I shook my head. "Trav."

The next to be opened was the small brown box. We ordered all sex supplies online, and they were delivered in discreet plain cardboard boxes. I'm sure George and Ma knew what was in them when the mail was collected, but it sure beat asking for either of them to pick up flavoured lube when they went to town next.

He ripped the box open and upended it onto the bed. "Oh look, lube," he said. "Lots of lube. If you play your cards right, I just might let you use these on me."

"Travis," I said. "Please."

"It really bothers you, doesn't it?" he said, picking up the large white envelope that had indeed bothered me all damn day. He was looking at it, turning it over in his hands. His smile was gone.

"Why won't you tell me what's in it?"

"I don't want you to be mad at me."

"Trav, what did you do?"

He bit his bottom lip and finally looked at me. He swallowed hard and handed me the envelope. "I might have contacted them, and I might have inquired about gettin' you re-enrolled to finish your degree."

I stared at him for a long while and slowly took the envelope from him. "You what?"

"You always said you wished you'd finished, and I was

here one day and you were out, and I thought it might be a real good idea, but now I'm thinking it probably wasn't."

I opened the bloody envelope and pulled out the papers inside. *Mr Charles Sutton, we are pleased to offer...*

"How did you do this?" I asked. "It's all in my name."

"I might have pretended to be you. It was just emails and an online application, but I asked the mailing directions be to me." He shrugged. "I told them Travis was the station manager and all mail was addressed to him. You'd be surprised, actually. It wasn't that hard to do."

"Travis."

"Don't be mad."

I shook my head at him. "How can I do this? I can't just go back to Sydney!"

"No, it's for you to finish it by correspondence. They do everything online. You might have to go Sydney for the final exams, but that's not for a while yet and it'll just be one weekend, and I thought maybe you and I could go..." He was rambling and nervous, and he looked a little scared. He shoved another chocolate biscuit in his mouth and talked around it. "I just finished the course last year, and I can help you. I'm sure there's probably one or two of my assignments you could use, which isn't terribly legal and probably borders on plagiarism, and all of my stuff is still in the States, but between the two of us it won't take long—"

I put the envelope, which was incidentally a University of Sydney enrolment pack, on the bed and reached out and took Travis's hand. "Why didn't you tell me?"

He swallowed his mouthful. "I didn't want you to get mad." The corner of his lip drew down. "Are you mad? You've said a few times that you hated not finishing your degree," he added. "And I thought I could help you finish it. I don't know... I'm sorry, it was a good idea at the time."

"I'm not mad," I said with a sigh. The truth was, I did hate that I'd left it unfinished.

Travis smiled, kind of. "You don't hate me?"

I snorted out a laugh. "I don't hate you. But maybe it's something you could have mentioned or we could have talked about."

"We did talk about it," he said. "The other week I mentioned my graduation and you said you regretted not graduating."

"That wasn't really discussing going back to college."

"Well, it kind of was."

"Uh, no, it really wasn't."

"Are you sure you're not mad?"

"I'm not mad."

"I think you should kiss me," he said. "Because then I'll know if you really are mad and just saying you're not, or if you're really not."

I chuckled and pecked his lips with mine. But he shook his head. "Nope. You're mad. I knew you'd be mad."

"I'm not mad!"

"Yeah, you kind of are."

"No, I'm not. I should be, but I'm not."

"Yes, you are," he kept going. "I can tell by the way you kissed me."

"Is that right?"

He nodded, totally serious. "Yep. That was an I'm-mad-but-trying-to-pretend-I'm-not kiss for sure."

I grabbed him and pushed him back onto the bed, squashing the rest of the mail under him, and I landed on top of him. I pushed the hair off his forehead and kissed him softer and slower until his eyes fluttered closed. He tasted of chocolate. "Am I still mad now?"

Travis smiled and licked his bottom lip. The man had mischief in his eyes. He nodded. "Definitely."

So I kissed him again, hard. I held his face and plunged my tongue into his mouth until he gave in. I could always feel the moment he gave in; his body melted into mine, his legs opened for me, his hands held onto me and he moaned.

So then I kissed him some more.

When he was breathless and wanting, I pulled my mouth from his. Travis was kiss-drunk, all dazed eyes and swollen lips. I leaned up off him and pulled his shirt over his head, then took mine off. I leaned over him and he put his hand to my chest, stopping me from kissing him again.

"So you'll do it?" he asked.

I didn't remember him asking me to do something to him. "Do what?"

"Finish your degree."

"I'd rather finish you instead," I offered. I rolled my hips into his, feeling how turned-on he was.

He gave me a slow smile and raised his ass a little, still not letting me kiss him until I answered. "Charlie."

I snorted out a laugh. "You're blackmailing me?"

He grinned without shame. "What do you want to do more? Me, or your degree."

I growled at him and pinned both his hands above his head on the bed. "Both," I told him. "I'll do both."

He smiled victoriously and hooked one leg around my thigh. "I knew you would." I leaned in to kiss him, and he stopped me again. "Charlie?"

"What is it?"

"Would you hurry up?" He grinned. "It's been four days."

CHAPTER TWO

WHEN THINGS START TO GET COMPLICATED

I SLEPT SO WELL. Despite the late hour, we actually fell asleep; with him beside me in our bed, I slept like a baby. I was up before the sun, just like always, and after the dogs were fed, I came back inside to find Travis throwing his duffel bag on the bed.

"What are you doing?"

He was a little startled. "Oh." He looked to the bag, then back to me. "Well, I thought because everyone was heading into the Alice, I was hoping... maybe we could go too."

"Oh."

"I just thought we could have a night in town, that's all."

"What?" I scoffed. "I can't go."

"Yes, you can," he said simply. Like it was just ever so easy to leave for a weekend.

"Trav, I can't just leave."

"Are George and Ma not capable of looking after this place?"

"They're very capable," I shot back, then realised I'd just helped his side of the argument.

He smiled. Kind of. "I want to get some stuff in town too."

"Like what?" I asked. "If you want something or need something, you just have to say. We can order most anything online."

"Well, we'd need to pick this up," he said, giving me a quick glance. "I was thinking of doing up Ma's vegetable garden."

"She has a veggie garden."

"That's not a vegetable garden," he said flatly. "It's a dry patch of baked clay. It's not elevated enough, there's no water retention or filtration. How on earth she grows anything in it is a miracle."

I was wounded. "George and I built her that."

His eyes widened. "Please tell me it was before you studied agronomy."

"It was," I said indignantly. "I was about sixteen."

"Oh, thank God. Because if it was afterward, I'd be seriously worried about what you spent three years at college doing."

I smiled at him. "I told you what I spent three years doing."

"Hmm," he huffed. "Yeah, every gay man in Sydney."

"Not every *gay* man," I replied cheerfully. "I'm pretty sure some were straight."

He snarled at me, and I laughed, but it was short-lived. I touched his duffel bag, feeling the worn canvas. "Trav, you can go into town if you want."

"I want you to come with me."

"I can't."

"You mean you won't."

"Trav, I can't just leave. I can't just leave the responsibility on someone else."

He sighed.

"Don't be mad."

"I'm not mad," he replied quietly. "I'm disappointed."

I had no comeback for that.

He reached out, took his duffel bag and quietly put it in the corner of the room. "George said he's heading out this morning. He's gonna look for that mob of kangaroos we spotted."

"Travis."

"I think I'll head out with him for the day," he said, giving me a tight not-happy smile.

Now it was my turn to sigh. "Maybe we could head into the Alice next weekend or the one a fortnight after. When it's all hands on deck—when everyone else's here—maybe we could go in town then."

"Maybe," he replied. Then he smiled a little more genuinely. "Small steps, Charlie."

"I'm sorry."

"Don't apologise. I *could* go in with the others if I really wanted to."

"You could," I agreed. Now I felt guilty. "You know, maybe you should go in with them. Have a weekend away."

"I don't want to," he said simply. "I want to go with you. And now you've said we will?" He smiled. "I'll hold you to that."

———

"JUST YOU AND ME AGAIN TODAY," I said to Ma as I handed her a cup of tea. Travis and George had gone out looking for roos for the second day in a row and would be back around the same time everyone else came in from the Alice.

"What's your plan for the day?" she asked.

"I'll take Shelby out into the eastern paddock and check on those yearlings." I sipped my tea. "Then this afternoon before everyone gets back, I'll look over some books."

"You and Travis looked cosy on the couch last night."

"He made me... study."

"It didn't look like a great deal of studying going on."

I hid my smile behind my cup of tea. "Well, it was my first day."

"Hm mm." Ma pushed her cup of tea away. "You right to get yourself some lunch today?"

We hadn't even had breakfast. "Of course," I told her. "You feeling okay? You're not all bright-eyed, bushy-tailed like normal. You were a bit quiet yesterday too. Everything okay?"

"Yeah, I'm fine. Just a bit under the weather. I think I might be getting a cold," she said dismissively. "Winters get colder as you get older, didn't you know that?"

"Ma, you should have said something earlier."

"I'm fine," she repeated. "But given everyone's out for the day and it's just you and me, I might take it easy. I'm allowed a morning off, aren't I?"

"Of course you are," I answered. "Go in and sit in the lounge room. Put your feet up. I'll make you some toast."

"You don't need to do that."

"Ma. Go in and sit down," I said, my tone serious. "Now." Then because it was Ma, I added, "Please."

I ushered her out of the kitchen and got busy. Toast, juice and water later, I took out the full tray into the lounge room. I pulled one of the side tables over to her seat, grabbed her latest crossword book, and made sure she was comfortable.

"I don't have to head out this morning," I told her. "I can

stay around the homestead. In fact, I'm sure the dirt bikes could do with a service."

"Charlie, I am fine," Ma said. She was getting mad. It was a tone I knew well.

"Ma, if you're not feeling well, I can look after you."

"I don't need a babysitter."

"Ma."

"Charles Sutton."

Bein' full-named was the line-crossing. I sighed and made myself busy restacking the fireplace with fresh kindling. "If you get cold, throw a match on this, okay?" I stood up and walked to the door. "I have the satellite phone if you need me. And I will be back at lunchtime, and I'll make *you* lunch."

She did roll her eyes and ignore me, but she didn't argue, so I considered it a win.

I kept my run out east to check on the yearlings fairly short. I kept my promise and made it home by lunchtime, but Ma was up and about in the kitchen. She looked better.

"Here you go, love," she said, handing me a plate of sandwiches and fruit.

There was enough for two, so I put it on the kitchen table and poured two juices. I loved days like this, when it was just me and Ma and we'd sit at the kitchen table and talk.

It had been far too long.

We talked about the coming muster, the winter cattle drove, and what we'd need to organise. It was still some weeks away yet, but Ma loved to be prepared.

It was late afternoon when I heard the familiar sound of the two utes coming down the driveway and knew everyone was back from their weekend in town. Everyone would go to their own houses—Sutton Station had three workers' homes—and freshen up for dinner.

It wasn't long after that I heard mutterings from the veranda. Figuring someone was coming in to see me, I got up from my desk to meet them.

I had only got as far as the hall when Billy came in the front door. He looked uncharacteristically nervous, and his usual half-a-face smile was gone.

"Billy, you okay?"

"Sure, boss," he said. He pressed down his shirt and looked around the hall.

"Billy, whatever's bothering you, just say it."

"My cousin got into some trouble," he said. "If it's no problem, Mr Sutton, I was hoping she could stay here."

"Where is she?"

"She's here, boss. I brung her back with me already," he said.

"Is she okay?"

Billy looked as unhappy as I'd ever seen him. He spoke quietly. "The other fellas were talkin' 'bout... wantin' to take turns, if you know what I mean, Mr Sutton. I take her with me so they not... do that."

"Is she okay, Billy?" I asked, immediately concerned. "Has she been hurt?"

"She's okay," he answered. "She was scared, and no one was lookin' after her. But no one touched her if that's what you mean."

I breathed a sigh of relief. "It's fine, Billy. She can stay. Can I meet her?"

Billy looked back at the front door. "Nara?"

An Aboriginal girl walked in, about as frightened as a baby rabbit. She was maybe fifteen years old, had long untidy hair, dark skin and scared, scared eyes. She kept her eyes on Billy, no doubt waiting for his cues.

"She can stay in my place, if that's okay," Billy said. "Now that Fisher's gone, we got the room spare. She won't be no bother, Mr Sutton."

I waited for the girl to make eye contact with me. "Nara? Is that your name?"

She nodded.

"You can stay here," I told her. "But I'll have no trouble. You'll be expected to work to earn your keep. Have you had a job before?"

Nara shook her head. "No."

"Did you go to school?" I asked.

She swallowed hard, and her eyes darted to Billy, before she looked back at me. "I wanted to, but I look after my family instead."

It was common here in the Outback Aboriginal communities for older girls to assume the role of carer for younger siblings. "Well, you start work in the morning. We'll discuss station rules tomorrow. But generally, you do what either me or Billy tells you, okay?"

She nodded again and gave me a timid smile. Billy gave a pointed nod toward the door, and Nara was quick to walk out of it. Billy gave me a genuine, relieved smile. "Thank you, Mr Sutton." I'd known him for years, and I'd never seen him so... uncertain. I knew he had a big family, but he'd always kept his private life exactly that. For him to bring Nara here, to ask if she could stay, meant he had genuine concerns for her.

"Billy, is she really okay?" I asked. She certainly didn't look okay.

"She will be now," he said quietly. He walked to the door.

"Billy?" I asked. He stopped and turned to face me. "Are *you* okay?"

"I'm good, Mr Sutton. I do appreciate your sayin' she can stay. She won't be no trouble."

"I know she won't," I replied. It was a warning as much as it was a reassurance.

After he'd gone, I stood in the empty hallway for a minute, then joined Ma in the lounge room. She'd obviously borne witness to the whole conversation.

"That was nice of you," she said.

"That kid looked scared as hell."

"She did."

"Was I too hard on her?" I asked. "I don't want anyone comin' here thinking they can do what they please, so I had to say something, but jeez, she looked ready to run."

Ma gave me a reassuring smile. "She'll be fine. Let's give her a day or two to settle in, huh?"

Then because it was a night for what-the-fucks, Trudy and Bacon knocked on the open lounge room door. "Can we see you for a minute?" Trudy asked.

Ma stood up. "Um, I'll just be heading to my room," she said, leaving my two station hands standing rather awkwardly in the doorway.

"Come on in, guys," I said, cautiously curious as to what the purpose of this visit could be. I snatched up the remote and turned the TV off. "What's up?"

I should have known what was coming when they sat on the lounge together.

"Well," Bacon started. "We wanted to let you know that we've been seeing each other for a while now."

I'm sure I blinked like an idiot. "Huh?"

"Me and Craig are together. We're... a couple," Trudy

explained, looking embarrassed. I had never seen her blush. Ever. "Have been for a while."

I was dumbstruck. It even took me a minute to realise that Craig was Bacon's real name. I think I laughed. "Um, I'm not sure what to say."

"We didn't want to hide it anymore," Trudy added.

"How long have you...?" I asked, not really sure how to ask that question.

"About a year," Bacon said. He was smiling, but he looked nervous. He reached over and took Trudy's hand.

"It's just now," Trudy said, "now with things with you and Travis, we thought you might..." No one had ever, *ever* talked about my relationship with Travis. Well, not to me anyway.

Bacon squeezed her hand. "We weren't sure if we should say something. We didn't want you to tell us it wasn't allowed, or maybe one of us would have to go."

"What?" I asked. "No. No, that's not... I wouldn't do that." The truth was, a year ago, I probably would have. But now, now that I was living and working with my boyfriend, I could hardly blame them for doing the same. "I know you won't let it interfere with your work." There was another warning-cum-reassurance. I was getting good at them.

Bacon shook his head. "We won't."

Trudy quickly added, "I'll kick his ass to the kerb before I lose my job."

I laughed at Bacon's expression. "I don't have a problem with it," I said. "In fact, I'm sorry you felt you couldn't say something earlier. I appreciate you telling me now."

"Travis said you wouldn't mind," Bacon said, and from his immediate oh-shit face, I knew he wasn't supposed to say that.

"Travis knew?" I asked.

Trudy swallowed hard. "He was with us fencing last week," she said, as though that explained it. "He said you'd be fine with it. Just told us to be honest, that's all."

"Did he now?"

"Don't be mad at him," Trudy was quick to add. "We asked him not to say anything, and he agreed it would be best coming from us."

"We just wanted you to know," Bacon said. "Nothing changes. Everything is just like it was when it comes to work."

I nodded and gave them a smile. "I know it is. And thanks for telling me." They took that as their cue to leave, and when they got to the door, I stood up and said, "Hey." Trudy and Bacon both stopped and looked at me. "Um, I guess I should thank you both as well. For not bein' bothered about me... and Travis. I, uh, I appreciate that it can't have been too easy, but you stood by me and that means a lot and I should have told you thanks before now."

I always rambled when I was nervous.

Both Trudy and Bacon smiled at me. It was probably the most least-boss thing I'd ever said to them. "He's a good guy," Trudy said. "Hyperactive or something—he can't sit still for too long—but he's a good guy."

I laughed at that, and after they'd left, I sat back down on the lounge and sighed.

Well, that was weird. Actually, this whole evenin' had been weird.

Next, I heard the bikes come in and chatter from the shed. When the front door opened, I expected Travis. But it was George.

"Hey," I said, greeting him.

"Charlie," he said with a nod.

"Um, just so you know," I said. "Billy's cousin will be

stayin' with us for a while. So if you see a kid wanderin' around, that's who it is."

"Fair enough," he said. Not much fazed George. He looked me over. "You okay there?"

"Weird day," I answered cryptically.

George laughed, like he knew something I didn't, but without another word, he disappeared down the hall.

I sat back on the lounge and ran my hand through my hair. What a fucking day. First Ma being unwell, then Billy and his cousin, then Trudy and Bacon... Jesus. I was wonderin' if anything else could possibly drive this day further into shitville, when I heard Travis walk up the veranda steps. The front door opened and he stuck his head around the door frame. He looked excited and a bit nervous.

"Trav?"

He stepped out, and it was then I saw he was holding something. His hoodie, the one his mother had sent him, was a bundle in his arms. Travis grinned and pulled the fabric back to reveal two big ears and two big brown eyes.

Oh, crap. Travis was holding a baby red kangaroo.

CHAPTER THREE

SHITVILLE. POPULATION: ME

"TRAVIS," I asked quietly. "What are you doing?"

He grinned and walked into the room, still holding a bundle of big ears and curious brown eyes. "Well, her mother met an untimely end," he said, the corner of his mouth pulling down. "And when we went over to cut the carcass for dog food, this little one was there."

"Travis," I said, shaking my head. "We can't keep a kangaroo."

"Why not?" he asked.

"Because they're a pest. They demolish crops for our cattle. You were out there to cull them, not keep them."

Travis's smile faded. "But it's just a baby. I have no problem with eradicating pests, but I couldn't just leave a defenceless baby out there. She would have either starved to death or dingos would have got her."

"Or you could have shot her... it. Whatever. You could have shot it."

Travis's mouth fell open. He looked... horrified. "I couldn't just shoot her!"

"Red kangaroos can open a grown man from sternum to

stomach, Trav. Let alone what they do to working dogs." I shook my head. "You can't keep her."

Travis looked down at the joey he was holding for a long while, and when he finally looked back at me, he had that stubborn, determined I'll-do-what-I-damned-well-want look in his eyes. "Well, I *am* keeping her. At least until she's big enough to fend for herself."

"Travis," I started.

"No, Charlie," he said flatly. "No." With that, he turned and walked into the kitchen.

I stood in the empty lounge room, not sure what alternative fucking reality I'd stepped into today. My boring, quiet, nothing-ever-happens life was getting rather not-boring. I scratched my head and considered following Travis, but figured he needed time to calm down and see reason. Sure, baby kangaroos were cute and fluffy, like all baby animals. But so were baby foxes, baby rabbits and even baby rats. And we sure as hell weren't keeping any of those.

A pest is a pest.

And little baby kangaroos grow into big full-grown kangaroos, and red kangaroos were dangerous. They'd been known to attack and seriously injure or kill working dogs and even people. I just wouldn't risk it.

So, deciding I didn't want to argue with him anymore—and getting my head around everything else that had gone on this afternoon—I went to bed.

I stayed awake, waiting for Travis, for as long as my eyelids would allow.

I woke up alone.

I HEARD voices from the kitchen—it sounded like Travis and Ma—and given that he obviously didn't want to see me, and not particularly feeling like conversation or worse, being ignored, I grabbed my hat off the hook and walked out the front door. I wasn't technically avoiding Travis, but I had dogs to feed and shit to do before breakfast. Anyway, he was technically not talking to me first, and he didn't sleep in our bed...

...my bed.

The bed. What the fuck ever. He didn't come to bed last night.

I made myself busy in the shed for as long as I could. Well, until Ma called me for the second time to come eat breakfast. I put my hat on the hook and sat my cranky arse in my seat at the head of the table, next to Travis.

I didn't look at him. I didn't acknowledge him. I guess the others could sense my mood because there were quiet looks between them with quick glances at me and Travis. George, of course, either didn't pick it up or didn't care. He gave his orders, short and direct, and before I could get up and leave, Travis hooked his foot around mine in that under-the-table-foot-holdin' thing he did.

I untangled my foot from his and stood up before my erratically thumping heart stopped me. I carried two empty trays into the kitchen, where Ma was. "How are you feeling this morning?" I asked. "I should have asked before now, sorry."

"Better, I think," she said, putting her hand on my arm. "You okay, Charlie?"

I didn't make eye contact with her. "Sure, why wouldn't I be?"

Then, like he took his perfect-timing cue from a stage director, Travis walked in. Which, of course, was my cue to leave. I didn't look at him either.

"Charlie," he said quietly as I passed him.

"Busy," I called out from the hall. I grabbed my hat and let the front door slam behind me. So busy is what I made myself. All fucking day.

I spent some time with Billy and his cousin, Nara. She looked a lot better all showered and in clean, presumably borrowed, clothes. We talked for a while, I gave her the standard station rules, and tried to find out a bit about her. As it turned out, she couldn't ride a horse or motorbike, she couldn't read or write all that great, and I had no clue what I was going to do with her.

"'S'okay, boss," Billy said. "She be my shadow 'til she picks it up."

It was obvious Billy wanted his cousin to stay, but I was short on patience and long on not-in-the-fucking-mood. I took a deep breath and tried to get my shit together. It wasn't this kid's fault my boyfriend slept on the couch. "Sure, Billy," I said. "Nara, you listen to Billy, okay? We'll see where you fit in over the next few days."

She nodded nervously. "Sure. Thanks, Mr Sutton."

Nara looked about ready to bolt, and I couldn't help but wonder what this kid had been through and what had really happened to make Billy give her refuge. I tamped down my mood and gave her a smile, trying to make her feel welcome. "It might not be terribly exciting for you," I amended. "But these are good people. If Billy's not here, you can come to me. If you'd rather not, Ma is usually around the house somewhere. You go talk to her. She won't mind one bit."

Nara nodded, and Billy gave me one of those half-his-face smiles. I clapped my hand on his shoulder and left them to it, deciding I'd spend the day with Shelby instead of waiting around for Travis to not speak to me. I called Shelby over, saddled her up and headed north before anyone could come out and question what I was doing.

I just needed time. Time to clear my head and time to breathe. I hadn't spent a day riding by myself in six months, since Travis arrived, and after spending so long by myself before he got here, it was nice to have some time alone.

Maybe that's why he'd volunteered to have four days fencing. Maybe he needed time away from me...

I tried not to think about that while I rode. Shelby felt good under me, fluid and familiar, and I was sure by the way her chin and ears were up that she felt good out here too. I think she missed this as much as I did.

"Been a while, hey, girl?" I said to her. "Is it good to be out here, just us, like it used to be? Or do you miss Texas riding alongside us?" No one really understood why I talked to my horse like she was human. I just always did. "I like it when Travis and Texas come along. Well, okay, I don't like it. I love it. But it's kinda nice when it's just us, yeah?"

She didn't answer, of course.

"You like Texas, yeah? He's a nice horse, started out a bit silly, but most young guys do. We can't help it. But Travis seems to have sorted him out just fine. He's a good stock horse. Travis also seems to think it's all *his* doing," I said. "But we know it's not. It's because you and Texas spend so much time together—because Trav and I spend so much time together—that Texas learned good manners from you." I leaned down and gave her neck a rub. "But we won't tell them that."

The winter desert took on different colours than it did under the summer sun. The ground was still as red as ever, but it was... softer. Maybe it was the different sunlight, or maybe it was the cooler air, crisp and clean. There was no blistering sun scorching everything it touched, and the air didn't burn your lungs.

Winter had its own woes in the desert, but the cooler

days and cold nights were my favourite. Especially now that I had a tall Texan body in my bed to keep me warm...

"Ugh." I groaned out a sigh. "I'm entitled to be mad at him." Then I growled. "Well, okay then. Maybe I'm not. Maybe I overreacted. But kangaroos are pests. They eat our crops, we shoot them. That's just how it is. And then he didn't come to bed. He slept on the couch... or in the spare bed or... I don't even know where he slept, but it wasn't with me. And what's up with that?"

I sighed dramatically and pulled Shelby to a stop.

"So maybe I overreacted. But he did too." I huffed. Or growled. Or something. "And what's with the silent treatment? You don't just ignore someone..." Even as I said the words out loud I remembered Travis had tried to speak to me this morning, and it might have been me that was ignoring him...

I sighed, long and loud. "How the hell am I supposed to know what I'm doing? I don't have a freakin' clue! I don't have experience in this shit. I don't know what it takes to make relationships work."

Shelby shifted her weight and twitched her ears, which was horse-speak for "go home and apologise you idiot."

I pulled hard on the right rein, turning Shelby around. "Yeah, yeah. Righteo, I'm going."

It was possible I grumbled most of the way home.

I rode Shelby back at a walkin' pace and was unsaddling her at the shed when Ma found me.

And I mean *found me* like how an angry piranha finds a bleeding swimmer.

I could tell by the look on her face she was pissed off. "Hey. What's up?" I said weakly.

Ma raised her pointer finger at me. "You left without water and a phone. It was stupid, Charlie. You know damn better than that. You've known better than that since you were four years old. If you want to hide out in the desert all damn day, then go right ahead, but you tell someone where you're going, and you take supplies."

Man, she was pissed off. Her anger was a little surprising, then I remembered that she hadn't been well. "I'm sorry," I told her. "And I wasn't hiding..."

She raised one eyebrow at me. "You gonna give him the silent treatment?" she asked.

"He started it."

Yep, I said that. I was officially eight years old.

Ma didn't even bother replying to that. She huffed instead. "Charlie, I love you dearly." She stopped and looked at me. "But you need to grow the hell up."

I'm sure my surprise was clear on my face, because she sighed, resigned. "He's been worried about you."

"I needed some time to clear my head."

"That's what I told him."

"I didn't mean to make anyone worry. I should have said where I was going. You're right. I do know better than to just leave. Sorry."

Ma was quiet for a while. "Don't fight over the little things, love," she said, softer this time. "But I suggest you go find him before it becomes a not-so-little thing."

I nodded, knowing what I had to do, and picked up the saddle off the fence. "I'll put this away and go find him."

I didn't have to go far. I put Shelby's saddle away and found Travis inside the house. He was hanging one of my old flannelette jumpers off the lounge room door handle. When I looked closer, there was a rather suspect kangaroo tail poking out of it. Ah Jesus, he was using a sweater as a pouch for the freakin' joey and hanging it off the bloody door.

He kind of shrugged me off and mumbled, "I need to wash my hands," as he brushed past me. I followed him down the hall to the bathroom and stood in the doorway while he finished at the sink.

Travis turned around, and leaning against the bathroom vanity, he folded his arms across his chest. It was defensive, as was his tone. "Just say it, Charlie."

My mouth opened and... shut again. I didn't know what to say. "I don't want you to be mad at me."

"But I still can't keep her?"

I didn't want to fight about the kangaroo again. But I couldn't find the words. I shook my head. "Travis..."

"Is this Charlie-my-boyfriend talking or Charlie-my-boss?"

"That's not fair."

He stood up straight, pushing off the bathroom counter. "Well, I'm not asking. I'm telling you. I'm not getting rid of her. She's completely defenceless. If I go dump her somewhere, she'll die anyway, and I can't—I *won't*—do that."

I put my hands up and pressed them against his chest as he tried to walk past me, stopping him. "It's not about the kangaroo."

He searched my face. "It's not? Then why are you so pissed at me? You brushed me off this morning and rode off not telling anyone where you were going. George said you weren't headed to the lagoon, because you went north, not east."

I shrugged. "Well, it *was* about the kangaroo, but then it wasn't. I don't know why. I just needed some time or something." I was now fisting his shirt so he couldn't leave or to keep me from leaving. I wasn't sure. "But I came back..."

"You came back..." Travis prompted at my unfinished words.

"Shelby thought it was a good idea." I wanted to give myself a facepalm for saying that out loud, but decided to play it cool.

"She did, huh?"

"Yeah. She thought I probably overreacted." I let go of his shirt, but neither of us moved.

"She's a smart horse."

"She thought you overreacted too."

Travis was now trying not to smile. "Did she?"

"Yep. But she thought the walk out through Arthur creek might clear my head, and that I should probably come back and apologise."

"She really is a smart horse."

I nodded and took a deep breath, looking to the floor between us. "She wanted to know why you didn't come to bed last night..."

And there it was. The real reason.

Travis slid his hand over my chest and up to my neck before lifting my chin so I looked at him. "I had my dinner, and then when I was feeding Matilda I must have fell asleep. Charlie, I didn't mean to. I'm sorry."

"Matilda?"

"The joey."

"You named it?"

"Of course I did."

"Matilda?"

"Yeah, you know that Australian song 'Waltzing Matilda'?"

"*I* know it," I answered. "Just don't know how *you* know it."

"Google."

"Of course."

"Were you really mad about me not coming to bed?" He

seemed amused. "I thought you were pissed off because of Matilda."

"It's no big deal. Just stung, that's all," I admitted. "And I didn't know how to deal with you not wanting to speak to me, so I left before you could tell me you didn't want to speak to me, because thinking it is one thing, but hearing it is something else…"

Travis leaned in and kissed me. Probably to shut me up, but I didn't care. It was the warmest feels-like-home kiss I think we'd had.

Travis slowed the kiss, pulling on my bottom lip with his own, then he nudged my nose with his to make me smile. "And you left this morning without talking to me," he whispered. "And you moved your foot away from mine under the table this morning."

"I'm sorry I did that. Your foot-holdin' thing is one of my favourite things," I said quietly.

"Foot-holding?"

I nodded. "Foot-holding and nose-nudges. It's what you do."

Travis laughed and kissed me again.

I pulled back a little so I could see his face. "I, uh… I'm not too good at this talking-about-stuff stuff."

"I'm no expert either," he said. Then he smiled like he was as relieved as me. "But let's agree that no one rides off into the desert alone, okay?"

I rolled my eyes. "I've been riding off into the desert alone for twenty years."

He ignored me. "And no one goes to bed alone. That should be a new rule. No one sleeps on the couch."

"I like that one better."

"It's not that I missed you. It's just that the couch is really not that comfortable."

I smiled at that and breathed in his warmth, his smell. "I don't like fighting with you."

"Did you just smell me?"

"I can't help it. I missed it... how you smell. You. I missed you."

Travis smiled a just-one-corner-of-his-mouth kind of smile. "I don't like fighting with you either."

I looked at him for a long while. His light-brown hair was longer now and messy, his blue eyes matched his shirt. Well, it was my shirt, but I'd long given up protesting his what's-yours-is-mine policy when it came to my wardrobe. "I can't believe you called the bloody kangaroo Matilda."

"You called my horse Texas." He shrugged. "Anyway, it suits her. She's cute. Wanna see her?"

I had a much better idea. "Maybe later." I pulled him against me by his shirt and walked us backward into the bathroom. "I think we've got about ten minutes before—"

"Charlie?" Ma's voice interrupted.

"Before that?" Travis asked with a laugh.

I sighed and readjusted myself. "Coming, Ma."

Travis snorted. "And not in a good way."

Reluctantly, I headed back out to the kitchen with Travis right behind me. Ma was at the sink. "Hey, Ma. What's up?"

She turned around and smiled when she saw us. "I'm glad you boys are... talking," she said, looking suggestively between us.

"Did you need something?" I asked. She looked better than she had, but it wasn't often that she asked me to do something for her.

"Can you go out to the yard for me?" she asked. "I need eggs, spinach and carrots." Then she turned back to the sink. "I would go myself, but I'm a bit behind. I spent the morning worrying where in the desert a certain twenty-six-year-old man-child was."

I walked over and kissed her cheek. "I'm sorry, Ma."

She tried not to smile and kind of failed. "Go on, the both of you." She ushered us out. Just as we got to the back door, she added, "And bring in some more firewood!"

Travis and I stepped off the back veranda and walked toward the back area of the main yard. Between the sheds and the water tanks was where we kept some chickens in a large wired-in coop and where Ma grew her vegetables.

It was where we kept the four kelpies, each with its own kennel, and when they weren't working, they were chained or on a run. If we left them off to roam as they wanted, they'd naturally want to round up the cattle, and when we didn't want them rounded up, it usually didn't end well. The dogs also served as a good deterrent for any dingos that might come in looking for a free meal of live chicken.

I opened the door of the chicken coop and went in, collecting what looked like a few days' eggs in a bucket. Travis was on veggie duty and when I was done, I walked over to the raised vegetable beds. He hadn't collected anything. Instead, he was digging in the first row.

"Trav, whatcha doing?"

He looked up at me. "What the hell do you call this?"

Well, I thought that was pretty obvious. I looked at the rows of spinach, carrots, potatoes and corn. "Not sure what you call this back home, but here it's called a veg-e-ta-ble garden. You feelin' okay?"

Apparently he didn't like me sayin' words slow like he was stupid. He glared at me. "Charlie, we need to fix this. This is bad." He let some of the soil fall through his fingers to prove a point.

I put the bucket of eggs down at my feet and looked

over the garden beds. Truth be told, I never really paid much attention to it. Ma grew seasonal stuff, and we tried to be as self-sufficient as we could, but he was right. It was in pretty poor shape.

"Well, yeah. It's pretty bad," I agreed.

"We can redo this whole area. It's going to need new beds, new soil," he said, panning his hand across what was there already. "We will reuse what we can. These old rail sleepers still look good." He kicked the wooden edges of the garden. "We could go into town and get it all."

"We could," I hedged. Although I meant it like a question, I'm pretty sure Travis took it for gospel, because he grinned. "Trav," I started to protest or to put in a disclaimer of some sort, but he ignored me.

"Here," he said, stuffing spinach into my arms. "Hold this."

"Trav," I said again but almost dropped the spinach. "Wait... just... hang on... Trav." I kept almost dropping the bloody spinach, and then I almost kicked over the bucket of eggs, and he kept loading carrots on top of the spinach.

"I'll take the eggs," he said brightly, picking them up and swinging the bucket and skipping inside like little Red fucking Riding Hood. Where I, on the other hand, juggled, almost-dropped, caught and juggled again armfuls of spinach and carrots all the way back inside.

I made my way to the kitchen, dumping the vegetables in the sink. Travis was standing with the fridge door open, drinking from a bottle of water. Ma was at the stove, not even seeing how I struggled with what Travis had made me carry. "It's alright, Trav," I said sarcastically. "No need to help."

He grinned behind the water bottle. "I carried the eggs."

"Thanks, boys," Ma said, probably more of a shut-up-thanks than a thanks-thanks. Then she added, "Travis was just telling me you're both heading into the Alice for the weekend."

I looked at Travis. "Oh, are we?"

He swallowed the last of his water, closed the fridge door and just kept on smiling that shit-eating grin. "Yep. We'll leave in the morning."

CHAPTER FOUR

A WEEKEND AWAY TOGETHER. WHAT COULD
POSSIBLY GO WRONG?

I DROPPED the duffel bag down in the foyer at the front
door and walked into the kitchen. It was before breakfast,
and in fact, Ma didn't look like she'd been up long. But it
was Travis who took my breath away.

He was sitting at the kitchen table like he'd done two
hundred times. But this time he was holding the kangaroo
like it was a baby, feeding her a bottle of milk. Travis looked
up at me, and knowing I wasn't a fan of this bloody new
addition, I could see in his eyes that he was ready for me to
say something not altogether pleasant.

I looked from Travis's eyes to the big brown eyes of the
kangaroo and how it had the longest eyelashes I'd ever seen
and even had its little hands up on the bottle Travis was
holding. I sighed and felt whatever fight I had in me about
the joey drain out of my body. "Do you have to be so cute?
I'm trying to be mad at you."

Travis finally smiled, slow and wide. "She *is* cute,
isn't she?"

I walked in and kissed the top of his head. "I wasn't talking about her."

Travis laughed, and Ma smiled at us. "I told him to use a bottle from the poddy calves supply. It's a bit big for her, but better than nothing," Ma said. "Can I make you a pot of tea, love?"

"How about you sit down and I'll make us both one," I said. It was still well and truly dark outside and cold, so when I sat down and handed Ma her tea, her hands automatically went around the cup. I'd learned not to come right out and ask if she was feeling okay, because she usually replied by ripping my head off. Instead, I hedged around it. "I'll stoke up the fire before I leave," I said. "And there's plenty of wood beside the mantel. I told Bacon to keep an eye on it if you get low, and he'll bring some more in."

"Charlie, you don't have to babysit me," she started to say.

"And Trudy will make sure you don't lift anything too heavy," I said. "I told her that you'll be too stubborn to ask and that you'll tell her she's just in your way. I told her to be in your way as much as possible, so if you want to yell at someone about that, yell at me, not her."

Ma sighed. "Charlie."

"And I asked Nara to take care of Matilda while I'm away," Travis added. "She can keep her here in the house all day and just come in to feed her every four hours, but she can take her to her place overnight so it's easier to do the night feeding."

Ma looked at both of us, probably realising that arguing with the two of us at the same time was pointless. I also knew damn well the second we walked out the door, she'd do as she pleased anyway and she was looking much better this morning. But at least she knew we cared, and the others knew to keep an eye on her.

"I feel better," she said, looking at her untouched cup of tea.

"Good," I said. "Then don't overdo it, and you'll *be* better."

She smiled, but it was a would-you-shut-up-about-it-already kind of smile. She changed subjects. "So, Trudy and Bacon, huh?"

"Yeah." I nodded. Then I remembered something. I gave Travis a pointed stare. "And you knew about it and never told me?"

Travis was about to reply when Matilda conveniently fussed with her bottle. "Well, would you look at that," he said, holding up the nearly empty bottle and ignoring me completely. "You was a hungry girl this morning," he said to Matilda in a baby voice. He stood up, still holding the kangaroo like a baby, carried the bottle to the sink and mumbled something about fixing her pouch as he walked out the door.

I stared at the now-empty doorway, then looked back at Ma. "Do you two take avoiding-answering-questions tips from each other? Because you both have it down pat."

Ma laughed and stood up. "You two better hit the road."

"You just did it again."

Ma patted my shoulder. "Have some fun this weekend, Charlie. Let your hair down a bit." She took my not-quite-finished cup of tea. "Oh, Charlie," she said, remembering something. She opened the fridge and handed me a paper bag. "Take these for a breakfast on the road."

I looked in the bag to find some of my favourite Ma's-breakfast-egg-and-bacon-pie things. "Oh, yummo." I kissed her cheek. "Thank you, Ma."

"And there's a thermos of coffee on the counter for Travis." She handed me the insulated bucket of coffee. "You know how he likes that stuff with his breakfast."

I smiled at her. "I do." I stood there, a little unsure of leaving for the weekend. "You have my mobile number, and I told George to call me if I'm needed. For anything, okay? I don't mind."

She was ignoring me again, already pulling trays of bacon out of the fridge. "Now hurry up and get out of my kitchen. I have breakfast to organise."

————

"I CAN'T BELIEVE I'm doing this," I said, looking over at Travis. I was driving, heading along the highway into the Alice. The sun was just coming up, and we'd already been travelling for an hour.

Trav leaned down into the bench seat of the old ute and stretched his long legs out the best he could. "You're allowed to have a weekend off."

"I could have ordered everything online or over the phone," I added.

"Yes, you could have," he countered simply. "And I know you'd be quite happy to spend every day of forever on Sutton soil, but I need a weekend away."

"What?" I turned quickly to look at him. "Why didn't you say something earlier? If you're sick of being there, you should have told me."

Travis snorted, smiling his you-missed-the-obvious smile. He shook his head at me. "I'm not sick of being there, but one weekend out of every six months isn't asking too much."

"Oh."

"I want to go out and have a few drinks *with you*, and have dinner *with you*, and I want to eat some Mickey-dee's and—"

I cut him off. "Eat some what?"

"Mickey-dee's," he explained. "You know, McDonald's."

"Macca's?" I stared at him. "Really?"

"Yes, McDonald's." He shook his head. "Do you really call it Macca's?"

"Do you really call it Mickey-dee's?"

"Yes, we do, and truth be told, I never ate a great deal of it before, but because I *couldn't* have it for six months, now I want it. I'll probably regret even considering it about twenty minutes after eating it, but yes I want Mickey-dee's."

"Macca's."

"I'll use words like ute and mozzie, and I'll even call a cell phone a mobile, but I draw the line at using the word *Macca's*."

I laughed at that. "We don't shorten *every*thing."

"You're the only person on the planet to call me Trav."

I smiled at him as I drove, my eyes darting between the road and him. "Trav suits you."

"Anyway," he went on, ignoring me completely. "As I was saying, we can go out and have a drink and a dance."

"Dance?" I said, probably an octave higher than normal. "I don't dance."

"Yes, you will."

"No. I won't."

"You will dance with me," he said lightly in that you-should-know-better-than-to-argue-with-me tone that I hated. And loved.

"Wanna know what I want most of all?" he asked,

looking out the window. "I want to stay somewhere that has showers we can both fit in, and that has enough water that we can spend half an hour in the shower together, and I want to spend Saturday and Sunday morning in bed with you until lunchtime."

"Now that I can do."

He was quiet then, smiling at the passing scenery. It was growing lighter as purples turned to blue across the horizon as the sun came up. "Hey, did you wanna drive?" I asked.

"I've told you before," he answered simply, "you sit on the wrong side of the car, and you drive on the wrong side of the road. No, I don't want to drive." Trav then sprawled out some more so he was almost lying down across the seat with his head on my shoulder and his feet up on his window. He pulled his hat—my old hat—down over his eyes and smiled. "Now shut up and let me sleep."

———

I BOOKED us into a double room in one of the nicer hotels in town, so when the lady behind the counter spotted Travis outside at the old truck, she didn't seem to think anything of it. I even joked with her that I'd take the queen-sized bed and he could take the single.

There was always that stabbing fear that someone would know. They'd somehow be able to tell we were *together*. I know Travis didn't give a shit if people knew...

But I did.

I wasn't ready for that. I wasn't ready for Sutton Station to die a homophobic death because other farmers wouldn't trade, buy, sell or even talk to a gay farmer.

Travis said he understood. And at home, when it was

just us, or even if Ma and George were around, we didn't have to hide anything. We were free to be us. We kept our private life in the homestead and were completely professional when we were working, and the last six months had been pretty fucking awesome.

But this was our first weekend away, together, as a couple. And I'd be lying if I said I wasn't a bit scared.

"You okay?" Travis asked. He was looking at me a bit funny. "You've got your overthinking-shit face on."

I couldn't help but smile at him. "Yeah, it's all good." I threw him the hotel room key and grabbed our bags from the back of the ute. "We can offload our stuff here and head straight to the co-op."

Travis opened the hotel room and walked in first. I followed him in with our overnight bags to find him staring at the bed. "Or we could stay here for a while first."

I threw our luggage into the middle of the big white soft-looking queen-sized bed. "That's why we need to go to the co-op first," I told him. "I know if stay here, we'll never make it to the store before they shut."

Travis sighed, and his tone was deeper. Huskier. "I'm sure we could get all the gear we need in the morning."

I was very familiar with what the change in his voice meant. "I'm sure you won't want to get out of bed in the morning either," I said.

"You mean I actually get to sleep in?" he said. "Later than six o'clock? No dogs to feed, no horses to water and feed before the sun comes up. Ma's not here yelling at us to get our lazy bones outta bed. Jeez, it's like a vacation!"

I know he meant no harm, but his words kind of stung. I smiled at him, but it was an effort. "I guess."

He put his hand on my hip. "Hey, I didn't mean anything by it," he said. "I was just joking."

"I know," I replied, still trying to smile. I knew he was joking, but the truth was, he'd just described every morning of my entire life like it was a bad thing. I needed to change the subject. "Come on, let's go clean out my bank account at the co-op."

And we very nearly did. Well, not quite, but I needed to replace all the fencing wire we'd used the other week and buying over two kilometres of fencing wire wasn't exactly cheap. The poor kid behind the counter thought I was joking when I ordered it, then Travis thought the kid behind the counter was joking when he told us the price.

The manager came over—an older guy named Brian who I'd known since I was a kid—calling me by name when he saw me and shook my hand. I introduced Travis as one of my station hands, and we talked for a while—about the farm, about my old man, who Brian had known all his life, then about the weather and what was news in the town.

Eventually we got around to ordering everything else we needed, and I signed off on our account, organised everything to be trucked out to the station on Monday and we were done.

When we climbed back into the ute, Travis was quiet. "You okay?" I asked.

"Yeah," he said quickly. After a while it must have got the best of him. I thought he might have been pissed off that I introduced him as staff, but it wasn't that at all. "That was a lot of money. And I know it's not my business to be asking, but can you seriously afford that?"

I threw the ute into reverse and backed her out of the car park with a laugh. "You worried the account won't clear?"

"No, no," he said, shaking his head. "I knew it was gonna cost a lot, but Jesus, it was thirty grand! If I had of known it was that much, I wouldn't have added all that garden stuff on for Ma."

"A few bags of soil, some aggregate pipes and some old railway sleepers hardly made a dent in that amount of money," I told him. "Plus, Ma will love it. You're right, you know. I should have done it years ago."

He ran his hand through his hair and shook his head. He said nothing for a while as I drove through town, but as I pulled into the hotel drive, he looked at me. "Charlie, you don't have to answer this and you can tell me to mind my own business, but is Sutton Station doing okay? I don't know why I never thought of the financial implications of what we do. You take care of all that or send it off to your accountant or whatever, I don't even know, and it's none of my business"—he cringed—"but you'd tell me if things weren't great, wouldn't you?"

I parked the ute and turned off the engine. "Trav, things are fine. We had a pretty good season."

"I have some ideas on diversification," he said quickly. "We could set up some smaller yards—"

"Trav," I said, cutting him off. "You don't need to worry. It's all fine. We work on a four-year cushion, like most farmers here do. The money we're spending today was earnings from four years ago. It allows for a few years of drought, or tough times. We still watch what we spend, of course, and we budget and plan everything. It's the only way you can survive out here." Then I added, "Some aren't so lucky and work year to year, but like I said, we're doin' okay."

He nodded but didn't seem too placated. "I just don't want to be a burden."

"A burden!" I scoffed. "Travis, please."

"Okay, so maybe that was the wrong word," he amended. "But I just wanna help out if I can."

"You already do, Trav. More than you know," I said and opened the door to the ute. "Now, about that shower for two..." I looked back at him with a smile. "Wanna waste some water with me?"

CHAPTER FIVE

GREEN REALLY IS MY COLOUR

FRIDAY NIGHT in Alice Springs was hardly Oxford Street in Sydney. The pub was like any other country drinkin' hole I'd been in: footy and horse racing on the wall of TV screens, regulars at the bar and guys playing a game of pool that nine times outta ten became a midnight bar fight. It certainly wasn't a bar where we could... well, it certainly wasn't Oxford Street.

I thought Travis might be disappointed, given he was so open with who he was, and I was not. But he said he was fine. "I just want to see you drunk."

I sipped my first beer and made a face as the bitter taste hit my tongue. "Well, I don't think you will."

"Are you nervous?" he asked. "What are you nervous for?"

I sipped my beer again. It still didn't taste any better. "I'm not nervous," I kind of lied. "It's just been a very long time since I've been out or even had a beer, for that matter."

"How does it taste?"

"Like crap."

Travis laughed. "After a few, they'll taste great."

"After a few, I'll be on the floor."

"I happen to like you on the floor."

"Travis," I warned quietly.

He swigged his bear, completely unfazed, and nodded toward the wall-mounted flat screens. "What game is that?"

"Footy."

He rolled his eyes in a thanks-for-your-help kind of way. "What kind? Is that rugby?"

I shook my head. "Aussie rules." Then I amended it. "Australian rules."

He watched the screen for a while with his head tilted. "It makes no sense."

I laughed. "And gridiron does?"

He whipped his head around to stare at me. "Are you dissin' my football?"

"Did you want me to start on baseball instead?"

Travis's mouth fell open. "You wouldn't!"

"For starters, you guys got the cricket pitch all wrong."

His nostrils flared and he drank another mouthful of beer as he turned back to the game on TV. "How the hell can they play football on a round field? That's bullshit."

I laughed at him. "And hockey! You guys should try playin' it on grass, not ice."

He ignored me for a while, mumbled under his breath a little and continued watching the footy. Well, I think he was actually watching the tall, fit and lean players in their tight shorts and sleeveless shirts because his head tilted. There might have been drool. "You know," he said lightly. "This game ain't all bad."

I hid my smile with a sip of beer. "Told you it was better than gridiron."

He smiled at that. "I'm hungry," he said, changing the subject completely. "What have they got to eat here?"

I took the menu off the table and handed it to him. Two bowls of buffalo wings and four beers later, the football on the TV was forgotten. I didn't give a shit about the tall, sexy-as-hell football players on the telly. I was more interested in the tall, lean and fit American who was whipping my ass in a game of pool.

He was only winning because I was drunk.

And because he was flirting with some girls who giggled at his accent and I can't play pool when I'm pissed off. Or drunk, apparently.

Okay, so maybe *he* wasn't flirting. *They* were flirting and being all girly-giggly every time he said something, so of course, he kept saying something. And then he was being all adorable and laughing, and what I really wanted to do was push him against the pool table and kiss him until he made that moan-whimper-breathless sound that buckles my knees. But I couldn't do that. Not here.

I wanted to be pissed off at him, but he was just bein' polite. He would look at me all sexy-like, then deliberately play his shots in front of me, leaning over the pool table, deliberately shoving his arse in my face.

Okay, so I couldn't play pool when I was turned-on either. I stayed sitting on the stool drinking my beer, thankful my jeans hid my lengthening dick.

And then if I thought it couldn't possibly get worse, it did.

One of the girls came over and smiled at me. "I was just saying to your friend over there that we should play doubles," she said. She was being all suggestive and shit. I mean, I'm gay, not stupid. I know suggestive when I see it: the smile, the tilt of the head, the twinkly eyes and the boob-wiggle.

And the plus side was that I no longer had a hard-on.

"Sure," I said, standing up. "Why not!"

She looked genuinely pleased, somewhat relieved and a lot like the cat that caught the canary. She stuck out her hand for me to shake. "I'm Brandi. With an i."

I shook her hand, then resisted the urge to immediately wipe the remnants of her limp, soft grip on my jeans. I couldn't help it. I like hard, rough hands. Callused, scratchy hands.

Travis's hands.

"Nice to meet you, Brandi with an i," I introduced myself right back to her. "I'm Charlie."

Her smile got wider just as Travis and the other girl came over. He was grinning, but his eyes were what-the-fuck kind of cautious. "So, we're playing pool?" he asked.

I held my finger up. "One condition," I declared. "I get to pick which team I'm on." I laughed at my own awesome joke. "Me and Trav against Brandi and..."

"Maddy," the other girl introduced herself.

"Guys against girls!" I added.

So we played pool for a while, and the girls were pretty cool. We bought them a round of drinks and made them laugh. Not that I'd probably tell Trav any time soon, in case he wanted to do it again, but I had a good time.

Well, I *was* having a pretty good time, until Maddy got a bit closer to Trav and it started to grate on me. She was a nice girl, and she meant no harm. But he was here with me.

I must have been watching them talking, and when Maddy put her hand on Travis's arm, I cleared my throat. But they didn't hear. Then Brandi giggled in my ear. "I think Maddy likes Travis."

"Travis is spoken for," I said.

Well, they heard that. Travis's eyes darted to mine, and

then because me, Maddy and Brandi were all staring at him, he said, "I am. Very spoken for."

I chugged back some of my beer to hide my smile.

Then Travis said, "And my girlfriend gets kind of jealous."

I almost choked on my drink.

"Gives me the silent treatment," he went on to say. The fucker was boasting.

"Aw," Maddy said. "Doesn't sound very mature."

Travis burst out laughing. "That's what I said!"

"Do you have a girlfriend?" Brandi asked me.

"I sure do," I told her.

Travis snorted. "She's really cool. Patience of a saint."

"She's a pain in my arse," I deadpanned.

Travis laughed at that. "She's a fucking good sort, though. Smart, too."

By this stage, the two poor girls were utterly confused. It was pretty obvious there was something we weren't telling them. I stood up off my stool. "We'd better get going, but I'd love to buy you girls another drink. You've been great company and even let us win a game of pool."

I threw a twenty on the bar and gave the barman a nod toward Brandi and Maddy. "For the ladies."

I grabbed my jacket from my bar stool and headed toward the door. I looked back to see Travis being all charming and shit, still making the two of them giggle as he walked out.

He fell into step alongside me, and we walked the block to the motel in silence. When we finally got into our room, Travis fell backward onto the bed with a laugh. "You were so funny tonight."

I stared at him. "What do you mean funny?"

"You were totally jealous," Travis said. He was thoroughly amused. "Of girls, no less."

"She was touching you."

He just laughed some more. "They were fun. Nice girls, no harm, no foul."

I grumbled under my breath at him while I toed out of my boots. Travis pulled at his belt, unbuckling it but leaving it on. He sat up on the bed and pulled his shirt over his head. "You can't play pool for shit."

"I'm out of practice," I replied. I walked over so my thighs pressed against the bed next to his legs. "And I ain't your girlfriend."

Travis burst out laughing, so I grabbed his leg closest to me and rolled him over, pulling him to the edge of the bed. He was bent over it and I was directly behind him. He chuckled into the quilt cover. "Let me undo my jeans," he mumbled.

I don't know if he was expecting me to get lube and start prepping him, but I didn't. As soon as his jeans were undone, I pulled them down his thighs, dropped to my knees and spread the cheeks of his arse.

And I ran my tongue up the line of his perineum and over his hole.

"Holy shit!" he cried. He wasn't laughing now.

I smiled as I did it again. Only this time I flicked my tongue over his hole, then again and again, before pushing my tongue inside him.

Travis moaned and his whole body arched, so I gripped his hips to keep him still and started to fuck him with my tongue. Normally it wasn't my favourite thing to do, but after five or so beers, I wanted it. And by the way he moaned and gripped the quilt, spreading his legs even wider for me, I was guessing Travis wanted it too.

As I worked him, he uncurled one hand from the quilt and slid it between him and the mattress. The way he was rocking back in time with my tongue left no doubt in my mind that he was fucking his fist. The sounds he made confirmed it.

"Fuck, Charlie," he panted. "You need to fuck me now, please."

I stood up and undid my jeans, pulling my aching cock out of the denim confines. I slid the tip of my cock up and down his crack, smearing precum over his hole. Then I leaned over him, letting him feel the length of me pressing against him. "I wanted to do this over the pool table," I whispered, kissing down his shoulder and spine. "When you bent over the table to take a shot, I wanted to fuck you right there."

"Holy shit," he whispered.

I smiled at how much he liked dirty talk. I pulled back, only to grab the lube and smear it up and over my dick, and then after a generous squirt on two of my fingers, I pushed them inside him.

"Do it, Charlie. Please. Would you just hurry up? I need your dick inside me," he said, almost begging. "I need you to fuck me."

So I gave him what he wanted. I pushed the blunt head of my cock inside him and slowly sunk into his welcome heat. Travis arched again, fisting the quilt as I breached him. Holding onto his hips, I slowly leaned over him, giving us both time to adjust, and whispered gruffly near his ear, "Is this what you want?"

He nodded quickly, and when I held still for too long, he started to rock back onto me. He wanted me to fuck him, so that's what I did.

I thrust into him hard, keeping him pinned to the bed

with my weight. I rolled my hips, pushing harder and deeper inside him with each pass, up to my balls in his arse. I nipped his shoulder blade, making him jerk and moan.

"Feel good having my cock buried in your ass?" I rasped out, barely holding back my orgasm.

"Yes, fuck, Charlie," he cried out. His whole body flexed and jerked, and he moaned long and low. I swear, every inch of his body succumbed to pleasure.

I rammed into him over and over as his orgasm barrelled through him. Travis bucked and shook underneath me as he came, sending me right along with him. Every inch of me inside of him surged and swelled as I pumped my seed into his arse.

I collapsed on top of him. Neither of us spoke for a while, until our breaths evened out some. We were hot and sweaty, though neither of us moved. I guessed he loved the contact as much as I did.

It was only when I slipped out of him that he moaned and squirmed underneath me. "So, um, jealousy gets you hot, huh?" he murmured with a chuckle.

I rolled off him and dragged his still-pliant body into the crook of my arm. He nestled in, despite the smeared mess on his abs and all over the quilt. I was already looking forward to the water-wasting we'd be doin' shortly.

"I wouldn't call it jealousy."

Trav snorted. "Um, you were totally jealous."

I huffed and pressed my lips to the top of his head. "She kept touching you."

He laughed, all lazy-like. "Oh, Charlie. If letting girls touch my arm is gonna make you fuck me like that, I'll do it more often."

I growled at him. "You wouldn't dare."

"For your tongue in my ass, I totally would."

I rolled us over and dug my fingers into his ribs, managing to smear cold cum over both of us. "I think we need to go waste some water."

"Does it involve douching and jealous rimming?" he asked, all smiling-eyes and smug-smirking. "Because I'm all for that."

"I wasn't jealous."

"You were just fucking my arse with your tongue to prove, what?" he asked. "That my arse belongs to you and no one else?"

"Exactly."

Travis laughed in an oh-good-because-that's-not-jealous-at-all way.

"Shut up."

———

I WAS awake before the sun was up, but when I tried to get out of bed, a strong arm slid around me and held me still. Travis nuzzled into my side and mumbled something that sounded like "sleep in."

I was always up before sunrise and for the last six months, so was Travis. But not today. He planted his face on my chest and was soon snoring softly. So with a can't-beat-him-join-him mentality, I rolled onto my side, nestled a still-sleeping Travis into my arms and closed my eyes.

I don't know how long I slept again for, but something in my brain was telling me to wake up. Something else—the dreaming part of my brain—wanted to stay right where I was. I was having the best sex dream: hot, slick, consuming and so very, very good.

Then from under the covers, Travis chuckled, and my dream spun into reality as I jolted awake. Only I wasn't exactly dreaming, because Travis's chuckle became a moan as he slid his mouth back down my shaft.

"Jesus, Trav," I said, my voice croaked with sleep.

He swirled his tongue up my length and sucked on the head before releasing me. "You don't like waking up with your dick in my mouth?"

I laughed, still sleepy, ran my hand down my stomach and gripped my hard-on. "You finished talking?" I asked. Travis gently scraped his teeth across my cock, and I got the message. So I asked a bit nicer, which was more like a tone a rung up from begging. "I love waking up with your mouth on me. The feel of your tongue, your lips... God, what you do to me..."

He licked me from base to tip, in the way he knew drove me crazy, and I swear he was smiling when he took me into his mouth again.

It wasn't long until he worked me into a sheet-grabbing, back-arching, holy-fuck-yelling frenzy. He drew the pleasure from every fibre in my body, shooting liquid fire through my bones. He cupped my balls and moaned as I came, drinking down every drop I gave him.

I felt as though I was made of molasses. I couldn't even lift my fucking arm. I felt the bed dip on either side of me as Travis crawled up my body and pressed his lips to mine. He laughed as my eyes fluttered open, trying to focus on him.

"You okay in there?" he asked with a chuckle.

"I am *so* much better than okay."

He sat back so he straddled my stomach, showing me his hardened cock. "How long will you need before it's my turn?"

I considered telling him when I could feel my legs and arms again, considering they were still heavy and spongy. But then I looked at his gorgeous cock jutting proudly onto my chest with the head swollen and glistening precum. I licked my lips. "Feed it to me," I whispered.

Travis quickly shuffled up, his knees either side of chest, and leaning against the headboard, he did exactly as I'd asked.

I was pretty sure of one thing. We really should sleep in more often.

CHAPTER SIX

REALISATIONS AND REALITY CHECKS

EVENTUALLY WE SHOWERED and made our way downtown. The main street of Alice Springs was no thriving metropolis, but we found a coffee shop and had ourselves a late breakfast.

Trav ordered the biggest breakfast they made and some fancy coffee. He was oddly excited, or just very happy. I tried not to smile at him, looked at the girl behind the counter and just held up two fingers. "Make that two."

He snatched a couple of newspapers off a nearby table and found a table at the back of the shop. He slid into one seat and pushed one newspaper across the table, presumably for me. He flicked through *The Australian* until he found the world news page. "You know, technology is great and all. It's instant and gratifying and I can pull up any newspaper from anywhere around the world in a few seconds, but there's nothing quite like sitting in a coffee shop and reading an actual newspaper."

I turned the Alice's local rag, *The Centralian*, over to the stock price section. "Makes you wonder how long actual newspapers will be around for," I noted. "People'll stop buyin' them eventually, when they can get it all online."

Trav looked up from the newspaper in front of him. He seemed to consider my words. "True. Shame, though."

I looked at what he was reading. It was the international news page, and I guessed he was looking for American-related news. It got me thinking. "Did you want to start ordering a newspaper to be delivered to the station? It will just come with the mail on Mondays and Fridays," I explained. "My dad used to do it, but with the internet, I never saw the point."

He seemed to consider it, just as the waitress brought over two coffees. Travis smiled at her, lifted the cup straight to his lips and sipped it. His eyes closed slowly, and he hummed at the first taste, or maybe it was the aroma, but I made a mental note to buy him a coffee machine. It'd be worth every damn cent just so I could see him look like that.

"God that's good," he murmured. "I've missed good coffee." His gaze snapped to mine. "I mean, the station coffee is good. Don't get me wrong. I'm used to it now, I guess."

I laughed and sipped my coffee. I had to agree, it was so, so much better than the crap we drank at home. I was more of a tea drinker, but since Travis arrived, I'd taken to coffee. "It's okay, Trav. I agree. This is so much better."

Our breakfast arrived, and as we ate, Travis read the paper and I searched up coffee machines on my phone and found one of the department stores in Alice Springs stocked a popular brand.

"What are you smiling at?" Travis asked, his mouth half-full. He'd been watching me as I looked at my phone. "Your food'll go cold. Eat it while it's hot. It's good."

I pushed my phone away. "Nothing in particular," I told

him. I started to eat the plateful of bacon, eggs, tomato, sausage, beans and toast, ignoring the side-eyes he was giving me.

When we had eaten far too much, we hit the footpath and walked up the street in the warm winter sun. "Where are we going?" he asked.

"Up here," I said, pointing to the Harvey Norman store.

"What are you looking for?"

"You'll see," I said. When we got to the store, I held the door open and followed him through.

A salesman met us on the furniture floor. "Can I help you, gentlemen?"

Travis looked at me and waited with the salesman for me to answer. I couldn't help but smile. "Coffee machines?"

We followed the guy into the electronics section, and he waved his hand at a whole row with two dozen types of coffee machines and looked at me. "Were you after percolating, filtered, brewing or pods?"

I blinked slowly. "Um." I looked at Trav for some help. "I have no clue."

"Is it for me?" he asked, genuinely surprised.

"Of course it is," I said. "You're the one that drinks it."

The salesman looked at us both, taking in my worn jeans, old dusty boots and hole-ridden hat, then looked Travis over. And I was pretty sure he knew. Like we had *boyfriends* written all over us. He gave us a small, forced smile.

Travis didn't see any of it, he was too busy looking over the rows of coffee machines. "We're three hours outta town," Travis said, not even looking up to see if the guy was even still there. "Which one would be easier to buy and store coffee for?"

They discussed coffee machines, and I kind of

wandered off, finding myself in front of the huge flat screen TVs. I certainly didn't plan it, but two girls seemed to find me. They were customers, probably twenty years old, and we got to goofing off in front of the camera that put us on the biggest screen on the whole floor. We were just being silly buggers, and I figured it couldn't hurt if the salesman thought I was more interested in the two girls than I was in buying a freakin' gay coffee machine with my boyfriend.

"Charlie!" Travis called out.

I spun around to look at him and tried to act like I wasn't just trying to walk like an Egyptian, making the girls laugh. Travis raised his what-the-actual-fuck-are-you-doing eyebrow at me.

I left the girls without so much as looking back and walked over to Travis and the salesman. "Did you get their phone numbers?" Travis asked. He sounded joking, but there was a sting in his stare.

"Nah, must be losing my touch," I joked.

"Or they saw you dance," he deadpanned. "Really? 'Walk Like an Egyptian'? That the best you got?"

"Well, I can't be MC Hammer without the pants," I said, not really meaning to say that out loud.

Travis snorted out a laugh, though I think he was trying to be pissed off. With a God-help-me sigh, he turned back to the sales guy, ignoring me. "I'll take this one," he said, patting a box on the shelf.

I picked up a few boxes of the coffee pods that went with it and handed over my credit card before Travis fished his wallet from his back pocket. Travis was quiet throughout the whole transaction, and when we'd collected our goods and left the store, he still hadn't spoken.

I was carrying the bag with the coffee pods in it, he was carrying the box, and we headed back down the street toward where we'd parked the ute. He was back to being pissed off. "Trav, what's wrong?"

"I can't believe you were flirting with those girls."

"What?" I asked, incredulous.

"You so were."

"I've never flirted with *any* girls," I replied. "*Ever*. Sweet mother of God, how could *that*"—I pointed back to the store —"what I did back there, be classed as flirting?"

He stopped walking. "Why did you walk off in the store?"

"I don't know anything about coffee machines," I answered lamely. I sucked at lying.

He took a deep breath and exhaled slowly, probably because he knew I wasn't telling him the truth. Then he did the waiting thing, which usually made me talk.

"I didn't want the sales guy to think we were, you know, a couple."

Travis blinked, his mouth opened then he blinked again.

"I'm not like you," I admitted quietly. "I'm not as brave as you. Just to be out and don't give a fuck. I wish I was. But I'm not. I have to think of my business, and it's different for me. I wish it wasn't."

Travis's shoulders slumped and he sighed, defeated. My admission just made him feel guilty.

So then I said, "I don't want you to feel bad. I just wanted you to have a coffee machine. You love coffee and I should have done it months ago. It wasn't until I saw your face and you made that sex sound when you tasted that coffee this morning—"

"Sex sound?"

My face grew hot, and I knew I was blushing. "Yeah.

You kind of hummed-moaned-sighed the way you do when you're..."

He raised one eyebrow at me, and one corner of his mouth lifted in a smirk. "Is that right?"

I nodded. "It's my favourite sound."

Travis was smiling now, and he shook his head. He started to walk again, and I took a few quick steps to catch up to him.

"I'm sorry," I told him. "I was a dick."

"Yes, you were. But you're *my* dick." He stopped walking and tilted his head. "That didn't come out right."

I laughed at him, and he put his hand on my shoulder and then the bastard pushed me into a street sign.

————

WE SPENT the afternoon at the local museum, and then we went to the movies. I wanted Travis to see some local artwork, in particular Aboriginal art pieces, and I also wanted him to do something as simple as watch a movie— something the isolation of the station didn't allow us to do as often as he'd probably like.

We went out for dinner, to an Italian restaurant, which I thought would have a menu of food he might have missed in the last six months. And he ordered a bunch of stuff I never would have: fancy cheeses and mushrooms, seafood and pasta, and cakes and coffee of course.

I wanted him to experience as much as he could.

I didn't want him to miss anything and regret his decision to stay. Or worse, resent me.

And the truth was, the sinking realisation was, that as much as I wanted to show him, to give him, to let him experience in these two pathetic days in Alice Springs... all I wanted to do was go home.

————

"THERE'S a lot to be said about aqua therapy," Travis said huskily. His hair was still wet, but his body now mostly dry. He was lying face first on the bed, his arms spread out and his ass still slightly raised. He hadn't moved. There was smeared lube on his hips from where I'd gripped him, and over his ass cheeks and down his crack, from when I'd been inside him.

We'd got back to the hotel from dinner last night, too full of food and coffee to contemplate sex. We sure made up for it this morning. Chuckling, I leaned over him and kissed the back of his neck. "Aqua therapy?"

"Hm mm."

"Just how many showers are we gonna have?"

"A lot." He stretched out and moaned. "You taste better wet."

I laughed and lightly smacked his arse. "Go have another shower. I'll pack our stuff into the ute. We better get going."

He sighed longingly. I didn't know if it was an I-can't-wait-to-go-home sigh or an I-don't-want-to-go-back kind of sigh.

Before I could ask him, he rolled off the bed and walked slowly to the shower.

"You okay?" I asked him, pulling on my jeans. "Are you sore?"

He looked at me over his shoulder. "If by sore you mean feeling very well-fucked and completely sated, then yes."

"Are you sure?"

He rolled his eyes and shut the bathroom door. Since we'd got back to our room after dinner, there was a change in him. He was quiet. He wasn't his usual talkative-smiling-charming self. He seemed... distracted.

Unhappy.

Trying not to overthink it, I packed everything up, and by the time Travis was out of the shower, we were all but ready to go.

Shopping.

Grocery shopping to be exact. It was its own special kind of hell. But I figured it was something we'd never done together, and maybe that would make it bearable.

But when I pulled up in the parking lot at the super-market to get Ma's long list of shopping, instead of walking into Woolworth's, Travis walked the other way.

"Where you going?" I called out.

"Just over here," he answered. He kept on walking to the park at the end of the complex. It was just a small park, some kids had graffitied the seats and the play equipment was kind of broken, but there were big maple trees that Travis headed straight for. He sat down on the dirty park bench, and by the time I got over to him, he was pulling off his boots. He looked up at me and smiled, then took off his socks and put his bare feet on the grass.

The longish green grass.

I sat down beside him. "Trav, you okay?"

He gave me a bit of a smile. "Sure. Why wouldn't I be?"

"You've just been a bit quiet, that's all," I said, avoiding making eye contact, looking at his feet instead.

"I just wanted to feel grass under my feet." He shrugged. "Didn't realise I'd miss the feel of grass."

Then it dawned on me. Travis was homesick.

I swallowed down the lump in my throat and could

barely form the words. They were a whisper at best. "Do you want to go home?"

He sighed. "We'd better get Ma her shopping first, or she'll have our hides."

He didn't understand. "No, I meant *home*, home." I cleared my throat and took a deep breath. "As in Texas?"

He shot me a look. "What?"

I felt a bit sick at the thought, but that voice in my head that knew this was inevitable at some point was loud and clear. I didn't want to hear it, I didn't want this to end—ever —but I had to know. "Home. Do you miss it?"

He didn't answer for a while. I could feel his eyes on me, burning into me, but I couldn't look at him.

"I'll understand, Travis," I whispered. "Just say it."

"Charlie," he said softly. "Look at me." He waited for my eyes to meet his before he continued. "I won't lie to you. Yes, I miss it. I miss my family."

I nodded and took a deep breath, trying to keep it together. "I don't blame you," I said. My voice croaked, and I bit my lip to stem the burning in my eyes. I couldn't bear to look at him, so I looked out at the car park instead.

"Charlie."

I shook my head. I couldn't do this. Not here, not ever. I wanted to stand up and walk away, but I couldn't seem to move.

"Charles Sutton, you can stop that right the fuck now."

I looked at him then, and his face went from pissed off to oh-hell-no when he saw that I was fighting tears.

He kind of laughed, but he put his arm around my shoulder and pulled me into him. "No, no, no, Charlie, no. I'm not leaving."

I lifted my head from his shoulder and looked at his face. "But you miss home."

"Yes, I miss my folks, but that's only natural. I don't want to go home, maybe for a visit sometime, yes. But not for good." His eyes were soft and he smiled. "Charlie, you're just waiting for me to tell you it's over, aren't you?"

I swallowed hard. "Well, I wouldn't blame you."

"Well, you know what?" he asked. "You're stuck with me. I've told you that. A hundred times."

"Aren't you sick of it, though? Even just a little bit?" I asked. "The heat, the dust, the monotony of it all. Being so far away from everything. I know it's not an easy life."

He smiled but looked out to a passing car. "You know what *does* bother me, Charlie?"

"What?"

"The fact I keep telling you I'm staying, that I love it here, that I love you," he said quietly, "and you don't believe me."

I wanted to take his hand. I wanted to reassure him with a touch. But I couldn't. My hand wanted to move, but my hammering heart wouldn't let it. "I do believe you."

"Then why do you always think I'm leaving?"

I shrugged. "Because I would understand if you did." I looked back out across the car park again. It was easier than looking at him. "I do believe you. I'm sorry if you think I'm doubting you. Because I'm not. I doubt me."

"How?"

"That I'll fuck it up, or the fact I'm not technically out," I admitted. His eyebrows furrowed in that what-the-hell-does-that-mean way he did. "Well, this weekend... I booked us into a twin room so the lady behind the counter wouldn't know, I wouldn't dance with you, I walked away from you in the stupid electronics store, and I wouldn't hold your hand at the movies and that's not fair on you." I shrugged again. "I'm trying, Trav, but it's not easy for me.

I wanted this weekend to be a bit special and I kinda failed."

"I never asked you to hold my hand at the movies," he said, obviously confused.

"I know you didn't. But I wanted... I wanted to hold your hand," I admitted quietly. "And I couldn't do it. Even in the darkened cinema. In case someone saw it... I hate that I can't... like right now. I want to do something as simple as hold your fucking hand, and I can't."

Travis stared at me for the longest time. "Charlie. You didn't fail. This weekend's been great. And don't ever apologise."

Before I could lose my nerve, I asked him, "Are you happy? Here with me?"

He didn't answer. Instead, he just kind of smiled and shook his head in a frustrated I-can't-believe-you're-so-fucking-stupid kind of way. "Charlie, do me a favour?"

I nodded. "Sure."

"Take your boots and socks off."

"What?"

He looked pointedly at his bare feet. "Boots and socks. Take 'em off."

I considered arguing. I considered telling him it was the middle of town, in the park next to the supermarket, and that taking my boots off probably wasn't strictly proper. But it was Travis, and it was kind of pointless to argue, and considering how this conversation was going, I didn't dare. So I took off my boots and socks.

"Doesn't that feel good?"

"Um..."

"The grass," he said. "Under your feet."

It was like soft paper and... green. "I guess."

"Of all the things, I didn't think I would miss this."

"Grass?"

Travis looked at me and grinned. "Weird, huh?"

I thought about it for a long moment. "I guess not. Not if you were used to it before."

He smiled wistfully and sighed. "Charlie, I can see how hard you're trying this weekend."

"I want you to be happy."

He smiled more genuinely this time. "I know you do. And I am."

"But?" There definitely sounded like there was a 'but' looming.

"I've loved this weekend here with you. No work, no anything. Just us."

"And?"

"And all you want to do is go home."

"No I don't," I lied.

He raised his eyebrow again. "You really are a terrible liar."

"I've loved being here with you," I said quickly. Then I shrugged and opted for honesty. "I just feel very... out of place."

"Can I tell you something?"

I nodded, really not wanting to hear what he had to say.

"You don't belong here." He smiled at my expression. "You belong on Sutton Station. It's a part of you. The vastness, the open spaces, the red dirt."

"It's who I am."

He smiled. "It's who I love."

I looked at him then, really looked at him. He laughed and shook his head. He sat like that for a little while longer, wiggling his toes in the grass. I sat with him of course, but as soon as he said, "Come on, we'd better get this shopping done," I was quick to put my old boots back on.

CHAPTER SEVEN

WHERE THE WANNABE-SUNDAY SCHOOL TEACHER
WANTS TO PERFORM AN EXORCISM ON TRAVIS IN
AISLE SEVEN.

GROCERY SHOPPING with Travis was fun—well, as much fun as we could have in Woolworth's. It was such a domestic thing to do, an everyday thing, that most couples probably took for granted, even whinged about. But at the risk of sounding like a lovesick schoolboy with hearts in his eyes, it was the first time we'd ever done it.

I tried to put our earlier conversation about homesickness to the back of my mind and just enjoyed this trivial, domestic chore for what it was.

We had a trolley each and a rather long list of stuff to get. At the station we were pretty self-sufficient, and we did online orders and had things delivered, but there was always things that got missed, and whenever someone went into town, they were given a list of stuff to get.

Our trip was no different. We could have split the list and done it in half the time, but we didn't. We went, side by side, down each aisle. By the third aisle we were having a sliding contest, which I totally won.

"You cheated!" Travis cried.

I laughed at him. "It's not cheating just 'cause you can't steer straight."

"Straight never was my forte," he said, smiling at some old biddy who was scowling at us. I think it was the same little old lady he almost collected in aisle two. "Plus I have a wonky wheel."

I laughed and threw a jar of Nutella into my trolley.

"That's not on the list," he pointed out. "Ma won't approve."

"Ma won't know about it," I said quietly. "It's only for... private consumption."

A slow smile on Travis's face became a grin. "Should we add small paintbrushes to the list? You know, body art?"

"A basting brush, maybe?" I asked with a shrug.

Trav laughed. "Add it to the list." He leaned on the trolley until his feet were off the ground and he coasted into aisle four. "I'm going to see what other goodies I can find."

After I'd collected ten kilos of flour, three kilos of sugar and two boxes of UHT milk, I found Travis in the personals aisle. He was up the far end, so on my way to him, I threw in a bunch of shampoos, conditioners, soaps, deodorants and toothpastes into my trolley. That was when I realised what he was looking at.

Lubes.

Fucking hell.

He turned over an orange bottle in his hand, reading the label, and when I got beside him, he looked up at me and smiled. "This one tingles!"

"Jesus, Travis."

"Or there's grape flavour." He made a face. "Why the hell someone decided *that* was a good idea, I'll never know."

"Trav, we're in a supermarket," I whispered. "I'm sure we don't need to discuss this here."

He looked around at the people in the aisle, who were mostly minding their own business, and he shrugged. "They don't know it's for us," he said quietly.

I knew what he was saying, but jeez, I was barely comfortable being out in public where anyone might think we're a couple, let alone discussing personal lubrication in the middle of aisle seven.

Small steps and deep breaths, Charlie.

I sighed and became extremely interested in the other side of the aisle, which thankfully, was razors and shaving cream. I added a few packs of both, and then spotted the cold and flu stuff and thought I could get some to help Ma shake her head cold.

I added some lemon-sipping stuff, Echinacea tablets and then I threw in multivitamins for women, because well, Ma's a woman, and I'm a guy and it made sense to do that.

I looked back at Travis, to show him what I picked out for Ma, when I noticed he was looking toward the end of the aisle, holding up a bottle of lube and showing it to someone. I followed his line of sight and saw the little old lady he nearly collected in aisle two—the same lady who eyeballed him in aisle three—was staring back at him.

Then Travis held the lube like he was showcasing it on *The Price is Right*. He even turned, giving her a view of the bottle from left and right. "Silicone based, lasts three times as long," he said, loud enough for her to hear, in a phoney salesman's voice.

"Jesus, Travis," I hissed at him. "What are you doing?"

He hiss-whispered, "She's being all evil-grandma, and I figured if there's anything in this store she needs, it's this!" He held up the lube. "I just need to find the dildo section so she can go fuck herself."

I rubbed my temples. "Trav, they don't sell dildos in Woollies."

"Woollies?" he asked, obviously confused. "Is that a euphemism for cock-socks? I didn't ask for those."

"Woolworth's," I explained.

"See? You *do* shorten everything. Woollies? Seriously?"

"Yes, Woollies. What's wrong with that?"

"It sounds like socks or thermal underwear."

"Can you put down the lube?" I asked.

He glanced back over at the lady with the demon-glare and gave her a blinding smile. I risked a quick look. Jesus, she was coming straight toward us.

She was all of five foot tall, three foot wide and had hair that oddly resembled a grey helmet. Fucking hell, she was even wearing pearls. Her vitriol was aimed right at Travis. "You're a hooligan, young man. I should have you reported," she said, her tone full of contempt. "You almost hit me back there, young man, and then you continued to parade around in a reckless manner."

I blinked, stunned that she was saying this shit, and that she was serious.

Trav, on the other hand, smiled. "Can I interest you in a survey on personal lubricants?" He grabbed a pink bottle and held it up for her. "Strawberry flavour, perhaps?"

She put her hand to her heart and pressed her thin lips into a frown. "Well, I've never..."

"Well, you should," Travis said. Then he smiled his best you-can't-not-like-me smile. "My name's Travis, and I'm a sociology and psychology major, conducting an experiment on secularisation of consumers and emotive behaviours in confrontational advertisements. I'd like to thank you for taking part, somewhat unknowingly." Then he laid on his accent extra thick and tipped his hat. "I meant no offence, ma'am. Just playin' a part for my end-of-year thesis. And if I don't say, you played your part perfectly."

The woman blinked, clearly not expecting this from him. "I, um, well, I..." she stammered.

I was stunned, yet somehow not surprised at all.

Travis, still grinning, tilted his head just so. The woman had traded the demonic look in her eyes for a confused, dazed look. "Your reaction was textbook upstanding citizen, concerned and not afraid to speak up. Well done."

He wheeled his trolley around and left her staring, open-mouthed and absolutely silent. I gave an apologetic shrug and followed Travis. When I caught up to him, he was looking in the baby product section.

"What the hell was that?"

Travis looked at me. "What was what?"

"What you just said to that lady?" I whispered. He smiled, of course. "You're not a major in sociology or psychology."

He laughed. "She doesn't know that. It's a tactical self-defence manoeuvre. I've always done it. Someone starts yelling, change direction. Simple."

"Simple? How was that simple? She's still in aisle seven stuck on the word secularisation."

He laughed again. "You liked that word?"

I shook my head at him. "You're unbelievable."

"I know, right!" he said proudly. "You know, when I was high school, I got called into the principal's office for making a fart bomb in science."

"A fart bomb?"

"Yep. One part ammonium sulphide, lime sulphur and sulphuric acid," he said.

"Of course it is."

"Anyway, the principal started yelling, so I stood up all

concerned, asking him if he felt okay. I told him he didn't look well, and I thought he should sit down. I asked him if he was on blood pressure medication, and called out really loud for his secretary to come in." He smiled as he spoke. "Anyway, he sat down pulling at his tie, the receptionist called 911, and my lecture and subsequent punishment was forgotten."

God, he made me laugh. "You're unbelievable."

With his lips curled in a smile, the way they always were, he pulled a baby bottle off one of the hooks. "What about this one?"

"What on earth for?"

"For Matilda."

Oh, the fucking kangaroo. "What's wrong with the poddy calf bottles you've been using?"

"They're too big, and she chokes a little because the flow's too fast."

"Seriously?" Oh dear God. He was serious.

"What would the equivalent be?" he asked. "This says for one month old, but it's not like baby humans and baby kangaroos are the same."

"I'll be in the toilet paper aisle," I said, leaving him to find whatever freakin' baby bottle he wanted.

When he caught up to me, he had quite the collection in his trolley. "I'll pay for these separate."

"Three bottles?" I asked. "I think I can afford that." Then I actually looked at what he'd chosen. "Is that a nappy bag?"

"The diaper bag?"

"What the hell do you need that for?"

"What if I need to take warm bottles with me?"

I stared at him with my mouth open, dumbfounded. I tried to think of something to say—something funny, something reasonable, something, anything. In the end, I sighed. I knew once he'd decided on something, there was no going back.

"Can you get the extra soft toilet paper?" he asked, obviously moved on from the nappy bag conversation. "You know, considering, you know—" He looked around to see no one could hear us. "—what you actually do to my arse, I'd appreciate some soft ply."

I picked up some wet wipes and showed him. "Like these?"

He smiled slowly and looked at me like I'd just given him a bouquet of flowers. "Aw, you're so sweet."

It made me laugh, and I looked around, disappointed that the crazy-lady from aisle two, three and seven wasn't there to see it. I threw a few packs of them into Travis's trolley just as my phone rang.

It was Greg Pietersen, my closest neighbour. He ran Burrunyarrip Station, which was 250 kilometres east of Sutton Station. I'd helped him muster in some cattle earlier in the year, and he'd come over to help search for Travis when he was lost in the desert. I answered the call. "Greg?"

"Charlie," he answered warmly. "I hear you're in the big smoke."

He must have called home first. "I am. In the middle of Woollies, actually."

He scoffed into the phone. "Sounds... interesting."

"Well, we just had a wannabe-Sunday School teacher want to perform an exorcism on Travis in aisle seven."

He laughed loudly. "How is he going? The knee heal up okay?"

"Yeah, he's okay. When he's not offering little old women surveys on personal lubricants."

"What?"

"Never mind," I answered quickly. "What can I do for you?"

He had to stop laughing first before he could talk. I held the phone out until he was able to speak. "I've joined the Board of the Northern Territory Beef Farmers Association. And I was actually hoping you'd join me."

I stopped walking. "Join you with what?"

"On the Board," he explained. "As a director."

"A what? With all those old farts. The median age is eighty. You've just notched it down a decade."

He laughed again. "Not quite, but that's exactly my point," he went on to say. "They need shaking up."

"They need bringing into the twenty-first century."

"Exactly. That's why I want you. The industry needs young blood, not these old-generation farmers who refuse to accept it's a different game these days."

I ran my hand through my hair. I was flattered— honoured, actually—that he was asking me, but I just couldn't. "Ah, Greg, I wish I could, but I kind of can't right now. I have a lot going on. I've actually just signed up to finish my degree. I'm doing it externally, but still, I have assessments and shit." I didn't bother explaining about Billy's cousin coming to stay or the fact that two of my employees had hooked up. He didn't need to hear my staff problems. "Plus we're coming into the winter muster. I'm all out of spare time."

He sighed, and it sounded an awful lot like disappointment. "Look, don't decide right now. We're having a Territory Farmers meeting next month, and the Annual General Meeting to decide the Board isn't until well after mustering season. It's a few months away yet. Think it over. I'll be in touch."

When I clicked off the call, Travis was standing in front of me. "What was that about?"

"He wants me to run for Director of the Beef Farmers Association."

"That's awesome. You should do it."

"I told him I can't."

"Why?"

"Because some arsehole signed me up to finish my degree, that's why," I said. "Plus I have mustering in three weeks."

"*We* have mustering in three weeks."

I ignored him. "Trudy and Bacon have hooked up, that poor kid Nara looks about ready to run any given minute, and someone is up every three hours doing night feeds for a joey."

"And?"

I sighed. Okay, it was more of a huff. And when he was still looking at me like "Is that all you got?" I looked around to make sure no one was within earshot. "And I need to spend time with you," I whispered.

He raised one eyebrow. "Need? Like a charity kind of need?"

I snorted. "No. Need like *I don't know what I'd do if I didn't* kind of need."

He grinned something special. "And you think you're not romantic."

Before I could blush myself stupid, I pushed my trolley and headed for the checkout. "I never said that." Then I stopped dead and turned to him. "Wait! Did you say that?"

He threw his head back and laughed. "You're far too easy." He pushed past me with his trolley. "Come on, we'd better hurry and get this stuff home, or Ma will send out a search party."

————

IT WAS WEIRD GOING HOME. I'd always had a sense of warmth, of familiarity, a sense of centre, when I drove home. Normally, like I was out of alignment or off kilter until we turned off the Plenty Highway, every kilometre we got closer to home I'd start to feel like my world was righted.

But it was different this time. It wasn't that I didn't want to go home, because I really did. I just didn't want my time with Travis to end. There had been some realisations this last weekend, and I needed to get my head around them.

By the time we'd unloaded everything and Travis had set up and tried out his coffee machine, it was later in the afternoon and I found myself in the kitchen with Ma.

It wasn't that I wanted someone to talk to exactly... Anyway, she knew me too well. "What's got you hanging around me for, hun? You need to talk about something?" She studied my face. "You look a mix of relaxed and depressed. What happened?"

I couldn't look at her. Before I lost my nerve, I swallowed hard and told her what I'd equally expected and dreaded. "I think Travis wants to go home."

CHAPTER EIGHT

WHEN IT RAINS, IT POURS

MA WAS IMMEDIATELY CONCERNED. "What do you mean?"

"I think he's—I *know* he's homesick. I think he wants to go home, as in America."

Ma was quiet for a little while, and then her eyes narrowed. "You think? Or you know?"

"He said he was homesick. He admitted it."

"Of course he is, love. That's only natural. He's a long way from home. But did he say he wanted to leave, or are you assuming?"

I shrugged. "Does it matter?"

She sighed, a sound of relief. "Of course it matters, Charlie. Goin' off assuming the worst, without actually talking about it, is a recipe for disaster. You said he admitted it?"

I answered with a nod, still looking at the floor. "There's so much he misses because he's stuck out here. Coffee, going out, having fun, takeaway food, green grass."

"Is that why you bought him the new coffee machine?"

I looked at her then and gave her a sad smile. "It doesn't really compare, but I had to do something."

"Well, he's awfully pleased with it. I think you did great!"

I tried to smile, but it didn't feel right. "He sat down in the park in the middle of town with his bare feet in the grass," I said, almost a whisper. "I can't compete with that."

"Compete?"

I felt stupid for admitting this stupid shit. "Yeah. He's all green grass, and I'm more of a red dirt kind of guy."

Ma put her hand on my arm. "Oh, hun. You need time to adjust. It's been a huge life change for both of you.

I was frowning and feeling a dozen shades of self-pity. "Well, I learned something else from our weekend away."

"What's that?"

"That it was great. That I loved it," I admitted. "And that I can't go back to the way it was before him. Without him." Then I whispered, "If he were to leave, I'd never get over it."

Ma sighed. "I'll tell you one thing too, Charlie. You're both as stubborn as each other. You need to talk."

The sound of the back screen door slamming put a stop to our conversation, and we waited for whoever it was to arrive at the kitchen door. I knew by the footfalls who it was before I saw him.

"Look who I found!" Travis said, his grin made my heart stutter. He was holding Matilda like she was a human baby, not a joey. She was snug in her makeshift pouch; all that was protruding was the end of her tail and her too-big ears and bright-brown eyes.

"You *found* her?" I asked. I couldn't help but smile at him.

He looked so damn happy. "Well, I had to find Billy

first, then together we found Nara, who did a mighty fine job looking after her. And *then* we found Matilda." He looked down at the bundle in his arms. "I think it's afternoon tea time, though. And I thought I could try one of her new bottles."

I turned to Ma. "He thinks the poddy calf teats have too much flow, so he bought some—"

Ma cut me off. "I saw them." Then she looked at Trav. "Her special formula is in the fridge."

Travis opened the fridge door with his foot and shuffled around, trying to hold Matilda and get the milk at the same time. It was almost comical, until he looked around and shoved the bundle of kangaroo into my arms. "Here. Hold her."

I was gonna object, until I looked down and two big brown eyes with the longest eyelashes ever looked back up at me. I huffed instead, and Ma pretended not to smile.

"It's not funny," I mumbled.

"'Course not, love," she said, biting the inside of her lip, still trying not to smile.

Travis took one of the new bottles from the steriliser and busied himself heating the milk then pouring it into one of the new bottles. When he was ready, he took Matilda from me. Once she was settled back in his arms, he tentatively put the new teat to her mouth.

Ma and I kind of leaned in to see how she'd take it, and lo and behold, she took right to it. Travis grinned at us, and I'd be lyin' if I said it didn't make my heart thump funny. He had this way of making me love him just a little bit more by doing the simplest of things. The littlest of things.

Maybe she caught me staring at him, or maybe it was the way he looked right back at me in a way that made the world disappear, but Ma blushed. "You boys go along now," she said softly. She cleared her throat and spoke louder. "I need my kitchen, or there'll be a riot come dinner time."

Ma pushed us out the door, and I followed Travis to the lounge room. He sat down on the sofa, still holding the bundle of baby kangaroo like a real baby, watching her feed. Realising I was just standing there watching him watch her and not doing anything at all productive, I wiped my hands on my jeans. "Well, I'll be in the office, then," I announced.

Trav gave me a smile that seemed to grow wider the longer I just stood there. I made myself walk out, sat my arse in my office chair, shook my head at Travis being all cute and making me stupid, and checked emails. There were the expected emails from the bank, the phone company, the feed supplier invoices, the transportation company reminder and the Alice Springs co-op confirming the order we'd made, which was being delivered tomorrow.

There was also an email from Greg.

I opened it, and had only read the first line before I sighed. *Have you reconsidered my offer? The Northern Territory Beef Association board nominations close in a few weeks.*

I hit reply and tried to think of a polite way to tell him, my friend, to sod off. I wasn't interested. With everything going on at the farm, I simply didn't have the time, and even if I did have the time, I lacked the inclination. To put it bluntly, I didn't fucking want to. I'd help him out with anything else, *anything*, but not this. I'd already told him no once, but that didn't seem to work. I just didn't know how to phrase "not fucking likely" in a way not to piss off my closest neighbour.

I closed the emails instead of answering at all and opened the weather tab. I checked it every day to see the forecasts, short and long term. I remember my father would scoff at the weatherman on TV. He said if a farmer didn't know what the weather was doing by the way the animals were behaving, he wasn't a real farmer.

I mean, that's kind of true. Ants and birds and horses were a good an indicator as any barometric instrument, but my father also wasn't a farmer in the age of the internet. I looked at the usual information, on percentages, pressure, forecasts and figures. And from all indicators, besides the cloud cover over Western Australia, we were getting rain. Lots of it.

Then I heard Travis, somewhat muffled through the wall. "Nara, come in."

Nara was so soft-spoken I could barely hear her, and if she came into the house, it must have been for something important. Not that I was eavesdropping, but I'd barely got more than two words out of that poor kid—so I was totally eavesdropping.

"Isn't she the cutest thing ever?" Travis said. Nara must have said something, because then Travis said, "No, you did a great job looking after her! You can babysit her anytime."

I heard her soft murmur but couldn't make out the words.

Travis laughed. "Nah, I'll do tonight. You should get more than three hours of straight sleep tonight. I've had two nights off."

It was quiet for a second, and whether Nara spoke I wasn't sure. I could hear Travis's voice easily when he spoke next. "Well, I'll need your help tomorrow."

I heard her this time. "What for?"

"We're making a start on rebuilding Ma's garden," he told her. "We're expecting a delivery tomorrow sometime, and I'm gonna need all the help I can get."

I stood up from my desk and walked as quietly as I

could to the lounge room door. I wasn't surprised that if anyone on this station could get a conversation out of Nara, it'd be Travis. And I was curious.

And nosey, and possibly a little bit jealous. Not crazy-jealous, but niggly-jealous, that she'd approach Travis to talk openly, yet look like she'd rather bolt into the desert when I spoke to her.

I stood in the doorway and Nara, whose eyes went wide when she saw me, went to stand up. I put out my hand, palm forward. "You can stay. Please, stay. I was just in my office," I said with a smile, trying to be as non-threatening as possible. Then I looked at Travis. He was still sitting with Matilda and an empty bottle at his feet. "Trav, I heard you mention the garden. I just checked the weather. We're expecting rain this week, so you might want to put off starting it..."

"Or start extra early," he prompted. "I know you don't get much rain out here, but it's only water, Charlie. It won't hurt me." He looked at Nara and gave her a dramatic roll of his eyes. I'm pretty sure he was trying to show Nara that I wasn't someone to be afraid of. "Plus, Nara's gonna help me."

I think she was going to protest. She blinked a few times and shook her head. "I, um—"

Trav nodded in that of-course-she's-helping-me way that meant Nara didn't have a choice. He only had to smile and most people did what he wanted. "Yeah, I can't do it all by myself."

It was obvious Nara didn't know what to say—her mouth opened and closed a couple of times—so she nodded instead. I smiled at them and left them to it. "I'm going to find George."

I found George at the back of the shed by the stables.

He was mucking 'em out, not payin' me any mind. "Surely someone younger around here can do that?" I asked.

He groaned when he stood up straight and held the shovel out to me. "Yep. Here he is."

"Someone younger, and someone who's not me," I said, but took the shovel anyway. I started where he'd left off while George stretched out the kinks in his back. "Why aren't you using the longer-handled shovel?" I asked him as I continued to shovel hay and shit.

"I was using that one out the yard and thought I'd just start on this in here," he said. "Then I kind of didn't stop."

I laughed at him. "You're a glutton for punishment. Your back will remind you of this for a week." Then I stood up and looked at him. "Not that you're too old for this."

He smiled, slow and warm. "I *am* too old for this."

"Never," I disagreed. I started shovelling again as I told him, "Just checked the weather channel. They're sayin' there's two inches of rain coming this week."

"I know."

I looked up at him, mid-shovel. "Your bones tellin' you that? Or arthritis, old man?"

"The internet, smart arse."

I barked out a laugh and kept mucking, scraping the shovel on the stable floor to pick up the last of the straw. I leant the shovel against the wall and walked over the pile of clean bedding hay. "Well, you know what two inches rain means?" I asked.

"Arthur Creek comes down. It'll be impassable."

"Yep. And we're drovin' in two weeks."

"Yeah, I know," he said in that casual, ever-patient way he did. "We could head 'em east and bring 'em down above the ridge line."

I nodded. "Sounds like we'll have to."

George gave a hard nod, no doubt already making mental plans. "We can do a flyover tomorrow and peg out the best route."

"Oh, that reminds me," I told him. "We're getting a delivery tomorrow. Travis wanted to build Ma a new veggie garden."

"Really?"

"Yep," I said, spreading another layer of hay. "He said it was disgraceful and a complete miracle that she could grow anything."

"He said that?"

"Yep."

"We built that."

I looked at him and laughed. "That's what I said!"

George chuckled. "You'll go and spoil her," he said. "Makes me look bad."

"I'll tell her it was your idea."

George laughed at that. "Then she'll *know* you're lyin'."

I walked over to the side gate. "Speaking of spoiling our girls," I said, giving a waiting Shelby a scratch on the fore-head. "You can smell fresh hay, can't you, girl?"

All out of patience, she snorted and threw her head down, making me laugh. I took my hand off the metal latch on the gate. "You stomp your foot and I'll make you wait."

So, of course, she stomped her foot.

I unlatched the gate anyway, and Shelby pushed it open so she could walk into her stable. George laughed behind me. "You were never gonna make her wait."

"She's spoiled bloody rotten," I grumbled. Then I spoke up to Texas. "Come on, you too. God forbid you get left out."

"Are you picking on my horse?" Travis asked, walking over. He was smiling, as usual.

"Picking on him?" I scoffed. "You mean, spoiling?"

Travis's grin was all white teeth and smiling eyes. "Ah, so you're trying to get him to favour you? You giving him sugar or something too?"

"No, but that's a good idea" I said, pretending to consider it. "Except for the fact that Shelby would kill me if I gave Texas sugar and not her."

Trav shook his head, then looked me over and stated the obvious. "You're all sweaty."

"Mucking out stables will do that."

Trav looked genuinely alarmed. "Oh, I could have done that." He headed toward the stables.

"I have arms and legs. I'm not completely useless," I said, following him. "Anyways, George started it. I felt bad, so I finished it."

George, who was looking on, spoke slowly and patiently, just like always. "Made him think my back was crook. He did the whole lot while I watched."

Travis collected a horse brush off the shelf and started to stroke down Texas's neck. "I just got caught up talkin' to Nara."

"Everything okay?"

"Yep. She looked after Matilda just fine while we were gone. Did night feeds and everything."

"She seemed happy."

Travis eyed me cautiously. "Oh, please tell me you're not jealous!"

My eyes darted to George, who just shook his head and laughed as he walked back toward the house. "No," I hissed. "Jeez, no."

"She's a kid," Travis said, back to brushing down his horse. "And she's a she."

I snorted quietly. "I'm just glad she talks to someone,

that's all. She seems to be settlin' in okay." It was a fishing-for-answers question.

Travis nodded. "She's much happier here. That's all she's really said about it."

I played with Shelby's mane for a bit. "She seems scared of me."

"I think she is a bit." Travis shrugged. "She's jumpy. Wherever she came from can't have been too good. She's settling in, though. Give her time."

He was right, and we both knew it. "She likes you, though."

"I asked her to look after Matilda to make her feel needed, appreciated," he said with a shrug. "Same with the garden tomorrow."

"It's a good idea. Very thoughtful," I told him. "But I could help you with it, if you want. I mean, it'll take a few days, I'm guessing, and it's gonna rain so the quicker the better..."

"You, mister academia, will have your nose in textbooks."

"What?"

"Your university degree? Remember?"

Shit. "Oh, the one you signed me up for without my permission?"

He grinned without shame. "That would be the one."

"I don't really have the time..."

He stood in front of me with his serious face on. "Four days of rain is plenty time for you to do some assessments. Anyways, you'll be stir-crazy after four days of rain."

A flood of memories swirled through my head. "Remember the last time we had four days of rain?"

Travis laughed, a warm throaty sound. I think it was part-groan. "I won't ever forget it. I was laid up in bed with my sore knee." He leaned in real close so I could feel his breath at my ear and whispered, "And we *switched*."

I remembered how he was flat on his back with his bandaged knee, and I straddled his hips and eased myself onto him. I could feel my cheeks heat as the memory warmed my blood. My voice was gruff. "Well, you couldn't move much... so it was only fair."

Travis leaned his face against mine, our eyes were closed and my breath quickened. He did that nose-nudgin' thing—barely a touch—and a ghost of a kiss. My heart thundered and my knees went weak.

Then I remembered where we were.

I took a step back and shook my head, more for thought-clearing than a no. "We shouldn't be doin' that here," I said, all out of breath.

Travis, lookin' kiss-drunk, glanced around the shed. "Ain't no one here but us."

I cleared my throat. "It's not that," I clarified. "I can't think straight when you do that, and I"—I readjusted my dick—"might throw you down on the hay."

Travis smiled at that. "I'm sure Shelby won't mind."

"I will. I just put clean hay down."

He snorted. "Yeah well, if it's any consolation, you smell like sweat and horseshit."

"You didn't seem to mind just now."

"I happen to like how been-workin' smells on you," he said, goin' back to brushing down Texas. "So maybe over the next few days I'll get to see what been-studyin' smells like on you instead."

———

THE NEXT MORNING AT BREAKFAST, where me or

George usually ran through everything that needs doin' that day, this time it was Travis who spoke. Normally we'd just say what needed to be done, and he'd just get stuck in and do it, but this time he told us.

"Delivery from the co-op should be around half-nine this morning. All the new fencin' gear is coming, but we're also redoin' Ma's vegetable garden. I was thinkin' me and Nara could make a start, Billy too if you want?" Travis looked at Billy—more of an offer to stay close to his cousin than asking for his help.

Billy looked to me, probably preferin' to take orders from me. I just shrugged. "Not up to me, apparently."

Travis either didn't pick up on my shot at him, or he didn't care. "But we got two or so hours before the truck gets here"—he looked at me then George—"so unless you need me for anything, I'd like to get started on the garden."

I tried to think of something that wasn't funny or inappropriate and came up blank. I shrugged instead. George was tryin' not to smile. He said, "Well, I was thinkin' we should probably head up to Arthur Creek. If the forecasts for rain prove true, the water should come down by Wednesday. Gives us three days to get the first of the herd south of the river. Me, Ernie, Trudy and Bacon can do that easily enough. It'll make it easier come musterin' time."

Travis must have known I was about to say I'd join them, or maybe it was how my face lit up at the thought of spending the day on Shelby out in the desert as opposed to being stuck inside studying. "Charlie's got an assessment due," he said quickly. Everyone just kind of stared at me, at him. So Travis added, "He's gonna finish his university degree."

I kicked his foot.

"Ow, don't kick me," he said.

I ignored him and the way everyone was tryin' not to smile. Except for Billy. He was just straight-out grinning right at me. I took a deep, calming breath, and explained, "It was decided—not that *I* decided, mind you," I added, aiming a glare right at Travis, "that I could finish my uni course, while someone here"—I narrowed my eyes at Travis again—"not long finished *his* degree and should probably do the whole thing for me. Because it was *his* idea, and he didn't ask *me* before he pretended *to be* me and signed me up."

Travis lifted his coffee cup to his lips, probably to hide the fucking smile. "I really do like my new coffee machine, thanks."

I made a huff-snarly sound that made George laugh and stand up. He clapped his hand on my shoulder. "Right. That's everyone sorted." He looked at Trudy, Bacon and Ernie, who I think were all a little confused and a lot amused by seeing this side of me and Travis. "We'll take the Land Rovers and leave in half an hour," George told them, back to business. They all nodded and cleared out. Travis walked out with Billy and Nara, leaving the room empty and quiet, while I resisted the urge to bang my head on the dining table.

"You had enough to eat, love," Ma asked. I hadn't noticed her come in, with my head on the table and all.

I looked up at her. "He's really impossible."

She chuckled and sat down in what was normally George's chair. "They all are."

I sighed. "He's so infuriating."

"And the worst part," she added, "is that they're normally right."

"That's the worst part!" I cried.

Ma gave me a few moments to sigh again and run my

hands through my hair a few times before she started to clear some of the plates. "Leave it. I'll carry them in," I said. Then I changed subject completely. "Want a cup of tea?" I asked. "If you put the kettle on, I'll clean up in here and then you and I can have a cuppa."

She patted my hand and smiled, but she left me to pack and stack plates and trays. By the time I was done, the pot of fresh tea was made.

The first thing she asked was how Matilda was going. I told her that she liked the new bottles better, according to Travis.

"Is he still doing the night feeds?"

"Yep. Twice a night. He doesn't complain, says he doesn't mind one bit," I said. "But he gets back into bed and puts his cold feet on me."

Ma laughed, but her smile soon faded. "Travis is so taken with her."

"I know," I said quietly. "It'll be hard on him when he has to get rid of her."

She nodded sadly. I didn't have to explain to her how dangerous full-grown red kangaroos could be. "It's a shame."

"It is," I agreed with a sigh. "I don't want to make him unhappy."

"I know you don't. He knows that too," she said. Then when I didn't say anything, she prompted me. "Things between you okay?"

"Yeah, I mean they are." My shoulders sagged. "I agree that we need to talk more, but we just haven't yet. Not really. He Skyped with his mum last night, and then his sister and brother turned up and they got talking for ages. He was telling them everything he's been doing, and he showed them the kangaroo."

"And?"

"I think he misses them more than he realises."

"Did you talk to him about it?"

I shook my head.

"Why not?"

"Well, it was late when they got done." I let out a long sigh and whispered the truth. "I don't want to talk to him about it because what if he says he wants to leave?"

"You know, Charlie, I love that you can tell me these things. I wouldn't change that for the world. But you're telling the wrong person. You need to tell him all this."

"It's easier to tell you."

Ma laughed. "Why?"

"Because you won't break my heart." I meant to think that, but I'm pretty sure I said it out loud.

Her eyes softened. "Oh, love. I wish you could see the way he looks at you."

"What?"

"The way Travis looks at you. Like you went and hung the moon."

I smiled into my tea cup. "Really?"

She shook her head in wonder and quite possibly a bit of so-God-help-me-you're-so-stupid. "Do me a favour, hun?"

"Sure."

"When you get into bed tonight, try talking instead, 'kay?"

I'm sure I turned a dozen shades of red. I coughed out my embarrassment. "I'll um, try?"

Ma patted my hand. "Well, it's been a great little chat, but you can't put off hitting the books forever." She gave a pointed nod toward the door. "Go on. The sooner you start, the sooner you'll be done."

So I sat in my office, read my emails, sorted payments

and knew I'd reached my limits of putting shit off when I started the filing. With a petulant sigh, I opened up the email, and using the login they sent me, I signed in to the university's online student profile. I'd read through this briefly with Travis the other day, but I hadn't really *read* it. He was skimming through it, and I was kissing down his neck not really looking at the screen at all. He'd grabbed a textbook and sat me on the sofa, tellin' me to read, read, read, but it only took about ten minutes before he was loungin' there with me and we were whisperin' sweet nothings that had less than zero to do with agronomy.

So I read through it properly now. After sorting out what was important, what was bullshit, I went through my core units and added assessment dates to my calendar.

My first assessment was due in three weeks, the same time as the winter muster. And my second assessment four weeks after that. I read through the list of textbooks I was expected to read and group discussions I was supposed to join in on and I could feel my blood pressure rising at the thought of it.

I was officially swamped. And my first assessment on meta-analysis being a promising approach in agricultural and environmental sciences made me want to scream or sleep or quit. I couldn't decide.

Thankfully, the sound of an approaching truck was much more appealing.

We offloaded the fencing gear first. All wire, mesh, droppers and star pickets were taken to the far shed, and then the truck backed up and dropped a few cubic metres of organic soil, some drainage pipes and gravel where Travis was pulling apart the old garden beds.

I was surprised by how much he had done. He'd only been busy for two hours, but he had all of the crops harvested, which Nara was now sorting through and cleaning, and he was moving old railway sleepers with a crowbar.

Dumping the new soil meant having to move it twice, but Trav wanted to do it properly. He wanted to remove all the old good-for-nothing soil first, then run aggregate and drainage lines and reharvest the water seepage for its nutrient value.

I was starting to think he just loved to work. Always busy, always smiling. He was happiest when he was doing some, the more constructive the better.

As soon as I'd signed for the delivery and the truck left, Travis picked up the crowbar again and continued to lever out the old sleepers. He was jimmying either end a little at a time and straining to do it. The muscles in his arms were taut, his face was red, and even in the cool winter air, he was sweating.

"Here," I said, grabbing hold of the crowbar. "I'll help you."

"You're supposed to be studying," he said, still trying to pull down on the crowbar to move the old sleepers. "What the hell did you put these down with?" he asked. "It's like friggin' concrete."

I took a better hold of the bar and helped him. "Baked clay, remember?" I said, rocking the crowbar back and forth and pulling on it as hard as he was. It was starting to move. "Jesus, I think the timber sleeper has petrified."

Trav snorted out a laugh, but the sleeper finally gave in and rolled as we levered the crowbar underneath it. "You can help with these," he said, kicking the other offending sleepers. "But then you have to go back to your books."

We both held the crowbar under the next sleeper and started the process all over again. "I remembered something," I told him, putting my back into the work. "About my uni degree."

"What's that?" he said, his face reddened as he strained, pushing down on the crowbar.

"That I hated it."

He laughed this time and moved the crowbar to the other end of the sleeper. We both pushed down on it again until the old timber moved some. "You know," I said, looking up the clouds rolling in. "If you wait for the rain, these railway sleepers will move a helluva lot easier. They'll basically slide in the clay."

He didn't even look up. He kept working the crowbar, a bead of sweat running down the back of his neck. "I want the drainage pipes down before the rain comes. I can do the rest in the rain, but I need to see how the water runs so I can get it right."

I smiled at him, though he didn't see. Maybe it was just as well he didn't see the you're-so-fucking-adorable look on my face. I think the dogs might have seen it from where they were chained up, because they started to bark. "Oh shut up," I grumbled.

Travis stopped pushing down on the crowbar. "You okay? Having conversations with yourself again?"

"I don't have conversations with myself," I defended myself. Then because I can't lie for shit, I added, "It's more in my head than with myself."

Travis laughed, and when I looked over at Nara, she was looking at us. She was smiling a little. "He's making fun of me," I told her.

"Well, you don't make it difficult," Travis said.

"You wanna do this by yourself?" I asked, just as the stubborn sleeper moved. We both bent down, picked up either end of the timber log and moved it to the other pile of already-moved sleepers.

Travis walked over and grabbed the crowbar. "Well, actually, yes."

I grabbed it out of his hands. "You'll bust yourself trying to do this on your own."

So the next four sleepers we jimmied, prised and moved without speaking. Once they were stacked out of the way, Trav picked up a shovel. Oh dear God, he was gonna try and move this by hand.

"Hold on," I said with maybe more frustration than intended. "You can't move it by shovel. Let me bring the smaller tractor around. It'll take fifteen minutes instead of five hours, and it'll save your back. Or your knee. You've only gotta turn on it wrong once, and you'll be back on crutches."

I didn't wait for him to argue, I just walked off toward the machinery shed. There was no way I'd let him do that job by hand. He could argue all he damn well wanted, but those clouds weren't getting any better.

I drove the tractor with the small bucket around the other side of the house and came in to the deconstructed vegetable garden from under the big tree. "Where do you want the old stuff?" I yelled out over the roar of the engine.

He pointed toward the way I came, so I didn't hesitate. I scraped and bucketed as much of the old, deteriorated soil as I could. I think once Trav saw how the tractor struggled to scrape the bottom section, he realised there was just no way he could have done it by hand. He still hadn't stopped, though. He was shovelling and turnin' soil anyway, stopping to feel it in his hands every now and then.

Forty minutes later and the area was cleared. I cut the engine. "Anything else need doing?" I asked.

"Don't take it too far," he said, walking over to the tractor. He grabbed hold of the rollbar and stepped up onto the foot rest. "Have you got an auger for this tractor, maybe eight inches?" He held out his fingers a good eight inches apart.

I smiled and said, "I know what eight inches is."

He rolled his eyes. "An attachment, for digging holes and trenches?"

"Yes, we have an auger."

"Can you get it?" he asked. "Or you want me to?"

Just then, Ma opened the back door. "Boys, lunch."

I hadn't noticed Nara wasn't outside, but when we walked inside, I was surprised to find her in the kitchen. She was standing in front of the table, which was covered in carrots, corn, spinach and potatoes, all the vegetables she'd harvested and cleaned from the old garden. Her hair was pulled back in a tidy ponytail and she was smiling proudly.

"Wow," I said. "That's a lot of food."

"We'll prep it all, blanch it and freeze it," Ma said. "That's this afternoon's job, isn't it, Nara?"

The girl nodded. She looked genuinely happy. It was very good to see. "Oh, good," I joked. "Because I thought I was having the world's biggest salad for lunch."

Travis snorted behind me, and Ma rolled her eyes. "Your lunch is on the table," she said, waving her hand in the general direction of the dining room. Then she looked us both up and down. "But don't even think about sitting at that table until you've cleaned up."

I hung my hat on the hook as we walked toward the hall that led to the bathroom, and Travis did the same. I scrubbed my hands and face with soap and water, and when I was bent over the sink, Travis put his hands on my hips and rubbed himself against my arse. I might have wiggled a bit for him and widened my stance.

"Oh Jesus," he groaned.

"You started it," I said, standing fully upright. I wiped my face on the towel and stepped aside, making room for him.

Travis kept his eyes on me but leant over as slowly as he could, sticking his ass out as far as possible. He gripped the countertop and rocked forward, giving a low moan, and his eyes rolled.

"Ugh," I groaned, having to readjust my cock. "You don't play fair."

He burst out laughing and started to wash his hands. "But I win, every time."

Still holding the towel, I twisted it and towel-flicked his arse. "Ow!" he said, scrubbing his face with soap. "Ow, I got soap in my eye."

I laughed all the way to the dining table. About a minute later when he walked in, his left eye was red and he was pouting, which might have made me laugh some more. He sat down in his usual seat, and I leaned right in and softly kissed the corner of his eye, then his cheek and the corner of his mouth. "Better?"

He shrugged a little. "What about where you got me with the towel?"

"I have every intention of kissing that better later tonight."

His pout twisted into an almost smile. "Just as well."

I pushed the plate of sandwiches and fruit to him first. "After you."

He picked up half a beef and salad sandwich and ate the whole thing before he spoke. "Thanks for helping me," he said, taking another half of a sandwich.

"I'm sorry for the soap in the eye."

"I'll consider forgiving you," he said with his mouth half full. "Depends on how well you kiss my towel-flicking wound later."

I laughed and shoved the rest of my sandwich in my mouth. "Deal."

"And you can help me dig the drainage lines, but then you have to study."

I might have grumbled. "I hate it. It's boring as hell."

"And you'd prefer to be diggin' in the dirt with me?"

I nodded quickly, hoping it was an invitation. "Hell yes."

It wasn't. He just smiled and changed the subject. "What's your first assessment on again?"

"Meta-analyses in agronomy or some shit."

Travis laughed as he bit into a piece of apple. "What will be your focus?"

"You."

He snorted out a laugh and chewed the last of his fruit. "I don't think your professor will appreciate your expertise on that subject."

"At least I'd pass."

"With honours."

"A high distinction even."

Trav laughed and pushed the last of the cut fruit to me. "Eat up. We have work to do."

I shoved the last of the apple in my mouth, carried the plate to the kitchen and spent the next hour running drainage lines for Travis. He stood in front of the tractor with the auger at his feet and directed me, calling out what he wanted me to do. I manoeuvred the machine as he bid, and we'd made a grid of lines, ten metres by fifteen, in no time.

The skies were rolling and rumbling with heavy clouds, and when I'd put the tractor back in the shed and was walkin' back to the yard, I could feel the change in the air. I called out to Travis, "You got thirty minutes before she hits."

He looked up at the sky, and seein' how the clouds were getting low and dark, he nodded. I jumped up onto the veranda and went inside to radio George, tellin' him to head home if he wasn't already. And knowin' I actually had to make a start on this bloody assessment, I grabbed my books and went straight back outside.

I figured if I had to read through this shit, I might as well do it where I could enjoy the fresh air and the view. And by view, I meant Travis. Because I knew damn well he'd work in the rain, and the only thing better than a hot and sweaty Travis was a wet Travis. That, and the smell of rain was purely a bonus.

So I on the back veranda, pretendin' to read but really was just watching Trav. He was shovellin' out the trenches, getting 'em perfect no doubt, then shovellin' in gravel as the first of the rains fell. It was just a light mist to start with, but the smell it brought with it was heavenly. It was a washing-the-earth-clean kind of smell that soothed and healed somehow, and the smell alone could conjure memories of childhood summers or of nights of lovemakin' and no-sleepin' to the sound of rain on a tin roof.

I watched as he laid the ag pipes in the trenches, and by the time he was backfillin' with a mix of gravel and what we'd excavated, the rain was heavier. But he never stopped. He'd run the drains to meet at the far end where I'd used the tractor to dig out what would be a filtered catch point. It was his idea, of course, so all nutrient-rich runoff could be harvested and reused. I'd seen it used on grander scales of crop irrigation, so in theory it should work.

By the time he'd lined the catch-pool with black poly tarp and put in the tub he'd requested at the co-op, he was soaked through. His hat was keeping most of the water off his face, but it was pooling on the brim, his jeans were darkened with water and his shirt was clinging to him in a way that I was most truly thankful for.

"You actually readin' any of that?" he called out.

I didn't realise he'd stopped workin' and was looking at me. I smiled at him, not even pretendin' to look at the book in my lap. "Every line."

He just laughed and kept on working. Kneeling down in the mud, he fixed elbow-joints to the pipes and started to join all the drains together.

It was only when I heard the others come back to the homestead that I started to do some actual reading. It wasn't like I could let them see me just lazing around ogling Travis while he did all the hard work. Even though that's exactly what I was doing.

Only George and Billy came up to the house, the others went to their respective homes. George gave me a nod and a sly smile as he walked past; Billy was wearing his usual grin.

It was then he saw Nara, sitting out in the rain on the huge pile of old-garden soil. She was riffling through it for the worms, throwing them into the bucket at her feet. She was covered in mud and soaked through, and when she looked up and saw Billy, she grinned. It was easy to see they were related when she smiled like that.

"Having fun?" Billy called out.

She nodded. "Yep."

Then Billy looked at me. "She been okay here today?"

I looked back out to Nara. "I think she's had a real good

day," I told him. "Travis made mention that we should have collected the worms for the new garden and she just went out in the rain and started digging." Then I told him, "She's been helping Ma all morning too."

Billy smiled and seemed a whole lot relieved. "I'll leave her to it, then," he said. "George and me will be in the shed. The others are done, I think, Mr Sutton. This rain ain't much good for workin'."

I held up the stupid textbook I wasn't reading. "Tell me about it."

Just then, George came back out, holding a baby bottle full of milk. I was gonna say something funny, but then he handed it to me. It was warm, which meant one thing. I looked up at him from my seat with what I'm sure was my best I-don't-think-so face.

"Don't shoot the messenger," he said flatly.

The back door opened and Ma held it while a certain one-foot-high, unsteady-on-its-too-big-feet kangaroo slowly made her way outside. Matilda took a few more steps, her front paws down as her back feet caught up, and she looked around. Of course she spotted me holding the bottle and headed my way.

She was no bigger than a cat, her back feet were twice as long as she was, her ears were the size of her head and her tail was barely long enough to keep her steady. I watched in horrified silence as she reached out her front paws, wobbled a bit, then put her little hands on my leg.

Oh, you have got to be kidding me.

I looked at George, who wasn't even trying to hide his smile, and a still-grinning Billy, and then Ma, who was looking at me like there was something wrong with me.

"Pick her up," she told me. "She'll get cold."

I looked out into the rain to find Travis stopped, shovel midair, looking at me and smiling that smug fucking smile.

With a this-is-such-bullshit sigh, I threw the book on the seat next to me, put the bottle at my feet and with one hand at the base of her tail, I scooped the kangaroo up and tucked her into my arm, kinda like holding a footy.

I picked up the bottle and shoved it in her mouth, ignoring the chuckles from everyone watching and the way her little paws touched my hand or how her eyes fluttered closed as she fed.

I glared at Travis, because this was all his fault, and even in the rain I think I could see that look in his eyes Ma talked about—the one of me hangin' the moon—and it made my heart beat all out of rhythm.

I shook my head at him. "Oh, shut up."

CHAPTER NINE

FIGHTING: THE STUPID KIND.

WHEN TRAVIS FINALLY CAME INSIDE, soaked to the bone and shivering, he headed straight for the shower. After dinner when everyone was gone and Travis had given Matilda another bottle, we headed to bed.

Stripped down to our underwear, we lay facing each other. Travis smiled all suggestive like, and he traced his fingers along the side of my face. I considered kissing him to the sound of the rain, but after Ma's words of wisdom of trying the whole talking thing instead of the sexing thing, I took his hand, threading our fingers, and he flinched.

Unthreading our fingers, I turned his hand over, and even in the dark room I could see the palms of his hands were red. "Your hands are sore."

"Shovelling all day will do that."

I gently traced over the swollen skin. It was hot. "You should have let me help you."

Trav smiled and closed his eyes. After the work he'd done in the rain today, I had no doubt he was tired and sore. "'S'okay," he mumbled sleepily. "Was my idea."

I slid my hand along his cheek and traced his eyebrow

with my thumb. He sighed and slipped into sleep while I just lay there watchin' him. He looked so peaceful, so beautiful. His eyelashes cast moonlit shadows on his cheeks, his lips looked silver-purple, slightly open, slightly smiling.

I pulled the blanket up to our ears, gently took his fingers under the covers and just held his hand between us. I whispered that I loved him, and the heavy ache of regret crept into my chest that I hadn't told him when he was awake.

———

DAY TWO OF THE RAIN, and it was set in, cold and miserable. It didn't stop Travis, though. Happy with the filtering and drainage system, he started to move the sleepers back into place for the borders of the new garden.

He didn't want my help, which pissed me off, and he told me to try doing some *actual* study *because that assessment won't write itself*, which pissed me off even more.

"This assessment is bullshit," I cried.

"You still have to do it."

"It not relevant. Maybe to some little farm on the coast somewhere, but out here it's not worth a pinch of shit."

"So write that."

"You can't write that the premise of the whole assignment is bullshit," I told him. "I'm sure my professor, who probably wrote the fucking question, would love some outback hick telling him he don't know squat."

Travis took a deep breath. "Charlie, that's exactly what you should tell him. Just tell him *why*. You can discredit every point he makes, as long as you can back it up and justify your reasons."

I huffed and threw my pen on the desk. "It's bullshit."

"What are you supposed to write about?" he asked calmly. "Exactly, word for word."

"We need to assess the quality of the meta-analyses carried out in agronomy with the intent to formulate recommendations, and illustrate these recommendations with a case study relative to the impact of agricultural activities on the environment or biodiversity. Use the following eight criteria defined for evaluating the quality of blah blah blah."

Travis smiled at my eye roll. "Look, Charlie, you're overthinking it. Tell me what's wrong with it."

"It's not relevant to farming out here."

"How?"

Ugh. Like I needed to spell it out. "Because everything we do is different. They're basing their *eight criteria* on regional New South Wales data only, which is not relevant to what we deal with, yet I am supposed to use that as the basis of my assessment. They use the term *heterogeneity of data*, yet the two models are, by definition, not comparable at all. They should be analyzed with random-effect models and weighted accordingly."

A slow smile spread across his face. "You need to write that down."

"What part?"

"All of it."

I huffed at him. "You're not helping."

"You don't need my help by the sound of it."

"Yes, I do."

He took a deep breath, but his nostrils flared and instead of replying, he just went back to the garden. He worked in the rain wearing one of my dad's old Driza-bone long jackets, which would at least keep him dry. His boots were caked in mud, but he only stopped for lunch. And after we'd eaten, I went back out to my seat on the veranda to find Ernie out in the rain helping him.

Which didn't exactly piss me off.

It stung.

So of course I sat out there and watched them and stewed on the fact it wasn't me he wanted to help him. In fact, it seemed like I was the last person in the world he wanted help from. I think I bounced between pissed off and hurt a good dozen times, and in the end, I snatched up my books and went inside.

I stomped a bit and huffed and puffed like a fucking brat, but threw myself into my office chair and read the stupid fucking textbook. I highlighted shit and made stupid notes, getting crankier with every-fucking-thing the longer I sat in there. I could tell it was close to dinner time by the smell wafting through the house, and I considered telling Ma I wasn't hungry but decided it would be more satisfying sitting at the table in a foul fucking mood so everyone could enjoy it, including Travis.

Especially Travis.

So what did he do? He ignored me.

And who'da thought my level of pissed off could possibly get any higher. It kinda went from a sunshiney kind of pissed to a nuclear kind of pissed.

And all the while, the rain didn't stop. Almost like it knew, like it was trying to simmer and soothe when all it was doing was making things worse.

So I went back into my office and pretended to be doing more reading, while Travis pretended that was what I wanted. I waited for him to go to bed, then he pretended to be asleep when I crawled in, and I pretended it didn't cause my heart to ache in my chest.

Morning was no better.

And it was still fucking raining. The forecast said it wasn't stopping any time soon, so I shut my laptop with more force than necessary and opened the goddamned textbook. I knew it wasn't rational to be so damn angry—I didn't even know what the hell I was mad at. Just everything. I was mad at everything. I didn't need a reason. And I didn't need to be stuck in the fucking house reading a stupid book written by some city farmer who didn't have a fucking clue what it was like.

I snatched my hat off the hook at the front door, and not even pausing at the rain, I jumped off the veranda and crossed the yard to the shed. I needed to be doing something else, something constructive, something destructive, it didn't matter. Just something else.

So I hooked up the angle grinder into the vice on the bench and collected all the tools I could find and started to sharpen them. The power, the noise, the strength of refining metal, the smell, it felt good.

I'd finished all the shovels and chisels and started on the fencing pliers when Travis spoke behind me. "You gonna throw things around in here all day?"

I didn't look up. "Yep."

He waited for me to finish the one I was doing. "Charlie? You wanna tell me what's bothering you?"

"Nothin's botherin' me."

"Yeah, right."

"You wanna tell me why you ignored me last night?"

"Are you fucking kidding?" he yelled. His anger made me turn and face him. "You wanna know why? I ignored you because you're behaving like a fucking child, that's why. Isn't that what they say to do when a toddler's having a tantrum? To ignore them? So I did. You wanna have a conversation like a fucking adult, then I'll start listening."

He spun around and walked back into the rain, and I stood there speechless.

I knew I should have chased after him. My hammering heart was telling me to call out, call him back, tell him he was right and I was sorry. But my pride-leaden feet wouldn't move.

So I added sulking to my already colourful mood of irrational anger and petulant pride. If I was bein' truthful, I could probably add childish and foolish and a whole lot of stubborn and stupid.

I didn't go after him. I didn't call out to him. I didn't want to face anyone. Considering the pouring rain outside, I could hardly take Shelby and disappear into the desert, so I did the next best thing. I went into my office, shut the door behind me and locked it, something I only did when I wanted absolute fucking solitude.

I heard Ma's hushed voice outside the door, probably telling someone to steer clear. I couldn't even bring myself to feel bad. Dinner time came and went and despite my protesting stomach, I didn't show. It was childish, and I knew it. But I figured no one wanted to see much of me right now either.

Normally when I got into moods like this, I'd pack a swag and head off to the lagoon for a day or two and the space would clear my head. Not that I'd felt like this in a long time. Not since my father...

Fuck.

I sank back in my chair and wallowed in self-loathing while I stared at the ceiling until I went to bed. Travis was asleep for real this time, his soft, even snores giving him away. He was curled into a ball on the far side of the bed, and I climbed into bed as quietly as I could.

I watched him, wanting to touch him so much, *so*

fucking much, but didn't dare wake him. I wanted to feel his skin, I wanted to hold him against me, to smell his hair, to kiss the side of his head.

But I couldn't.

I'd put this distance between us, and I had no clue how to make it right. I was being irrational, and it was like a runaway train I just couldn't stop. I didn't want to feel like this, I certainly didn't want to hurt him. I just didn't know how to stop it.

I pulled the blankets up over him so he was warm and let his sleepy-smell wash over me. I lay back down and remembered how much I'd adored seeing him in my bed when I thought it was just temporary—fleeting—and here I was taking it all for granted.

Like it wasn't the most wonderful thing in the world. Like it wouldn't kill me when he was gone.

Because it was, really, just a matter of time.

————

TRAVIS'S SIDE of the bed was empty and cold when I woke up. I felt it just to be sure.

Breakfast was quiet, everyone was wary of my mood, which just made me feel a whole lot worse.

Travis gave me a tight smile, and I tried to return it, but I guess I couldn't quite get it right. Thankfully it was everyone's weekend off, and they were all headed into town after breakfast. They needed downtime, and I needed space. I was sure by the time they got back on Sunday afternoon, I'd be out of this foul mood and everything would be back to normal.

Then George asked the inevitable. "Travis, you headin' into town?"

I froze, waiting for him to answer, waiting for the guillotine to drop.

He cleared his throat. "Nah, I'll finish up the garden today."

George looked at me. "Charlie?"

I pushed my plate away. "I, um, I have... stuff to do here." But I looked up at everyone and gave them the best smile I could muster. "Thanks, guys. It's been a good week. See ya's on Sunday."

Everyone was gone with a nod or a polite, *strained* goodbye, except for Travis. He didn't move. "Charlie," he started.

"I'm sorry," I blurted out.

Just then, Ma walked in and seeing us sitting at the table, she backed up. "Oh, sorry. Sorry." She just about tried to run out of the room.

"No, Ma, wait," I called out, stopping her. I had everyone walking on eggshells, and it was killing me. "I'm sorry," I said pathetically. "I'm sorry. I don't mean to make everyone so uncomfortable." I stood up. "This is your home too, and I'm being selfish, and I'm sorry."

I walked to the door and stopped. I looked at them both, but couldn't think of anything else to say. Well, nothing to excuse my behaviour or explain it. I tried to say sorry again, but I don't know if the words came out. I only made it as far as the hall.

"Don't fucking ignore me, Charlie!" Travis yelled. He was four steps behind me, pointing his finger at me. "If you've got a problem with something, then fucking speak to me."

"I don't have a problem."

Travis looked up at the ceiling and took a deep breath.

He was trying to stay calm. "Charlie, what's going on? Why are you pushing me away?"

"Jesus, Travis. I don't know. I said I was sorry."

"You're shutting me out."

"I'm not," I said, then amended, "I don't mean to."

"Why are you so mad at me?" he asked. It was the first time I think I'd ever seen him so unsure. "I don't know what I did."

"It's not you. It's me."

He threw up his hands. "Oh that's fucking lovely. *It's not you, it's me*. Can't think of anything more original?"

"It is me, Travis," I yelled back at him. "This is the real me. This is who I am. I'm the boss of this place, and I need to run it like I am. Sorry you don't like what you see."

"So, is it Charlie the boss speaking or Charlie the boyfriend speaking?"

"Both. I'm both. You knew that when you were so fucking adamant on staying."

He looked like I'd slapped him. "Do you want me to go?" he asked quietly. "Is that what this is?"

"Argh." I ran my hands through my hair. "No!"

"You keep saying the words, but everything else you do says yes."

I paced into the lounge room with my hands in my hair. "I don't know what's wrong with me."

"Please, Charlie," he cried, begging. "Talk to me."

"I don't know how."

He was staring at me, right into me. He looked open and raw. "Tell me what you feel, please, Charlie."

"I don't know," I said. I rolled my shoulders, like I was struggling in my own skin and tried again, "I feel... bound."

"What?"

"I don't know!" I cried. "Bound. Restricted, confined, I don't know."

"By me?" he whispered.

"No," I answered quickly, "not you. This place, the rain, the responsibility. I feel like I can't stretch properly."

He just stood there, not saying anything.

"Not you," I said again. "You're the one person who sees the real me."

"Charlie..."

"Guilty. I feel guilty." I didn't even mean to say that. I don't know where it came from. It just came out.

"What for?" he asked. He was so damn concerned, and it made me feel worse.

"I don't know," I said again. I know it was lame, but it was the truth. I didn't know. I couldn't find the words to describe it. "It's a weight. In here," I said, pushing against my chest. "I don't deserve you."

"You're not your father."

His words stopped me cold. I blinked. "What?"

"You need to let it go, Charlie. I thought you had. Or, at least I thought you were trying to."

"I'm trying! I don't know if I will ever be able to!" I cried. "I don't know, Travis. This is me. This is who I am."

He shook his head.

Then I told him, "I've changed. A year ago, I was happy being out here, being alone. It's who I was, it was how it had to be, and I was fine with it."

"Were you?"

"No, I was fucking miserable."

He smiled a little, despite the conversation.

"And now, now I can't do anything. It's like everything I do isn't good enough."

"That's not true."

"It doesn't matter if it's true or not," I shot back at him. "It's how I feel."

"Why?"

"I don't want to disappoint you. It's like a pressure, and it's not from you. It's from me. I know that. Because I don't want to let you down or make you regret your decision to stay."

"Oh, Charlie," he whispered.

I ran my fingers through my hair and huffed out a laugh. "You wanna know something? I watch you when you're sleepin' and think how amazing it is, how you gave up every-thing you've ever known to be here with me, and I can't even bring myself to say three little fucking words out loud." I shook my head. "How pathetic is that?"

"It's not pathetic, Charlie," he said quietly. "I chose to stay here, remember?"

"You didn't *just* decide to live on the other side of the planet for me," I said. "You stepped back in the closet for me, and I'll never forgive myself for asking you to do that."

His eyes narrowed. "No I didn't."

He wasn't getting it. "I can't be the person you want me to be, Travis."

He sighed, and he kind of turned to leave, but didn't. He looked... stuck. He wouldn't look at me. "I don't know what I can say that will make you..." He swallowed thickly. His voice was barely a whisper. "Sounds like you're saying it's all too hard. Like you don't want this..."

I shook my head. "I want it, too much. Maybe that's the problem. Maybe I'm holding on too tight."

Travis stood side-on to me, still looking at the floor. "If it's a problem, then maybe you need to let me go," he whis-pered and walked out the door.

I wanted to tell him not to walk away, not to leave, not to hate me. But I couldn't speak. I could barely breathe.

I stood staring at where he'd been, blinking back regret and breaking-heart tears, when a door slammed, making me turn around. It was Ma. She looked pale and pissed off, and a whole world of sad.

"I was told to stay out of it," she spoke through clenched teeth. "But I won't stand by and say nothing. You want to be alone out here forever, Charlie? You want to be just like your father, you want to push everyone away and hate and resent everyone, then go right ahead. Spend every day of the rest of your life being as miserable as he was. He was bitter, and it put him in an early grave."

"Ma," I tried to speak, and tears burned my eyes.

"I haven't finished talking," she spat. "Not every relationship is meant to last, Charlie, but what you and Travis have isn't dying. You're killing it. Like you won't be happy until you've driven him away so you can spend the rest of your life miserable, so you can what? Say that you were right all along?"

I couldn't speak. I shook my head, and hot tears spilled down my cheeks.

"You know what?" Ma said. "You should go. Take Shelby and disappear for a while, clear your head, sort out what it is you want, and when you come back, you wanna hope that man is still here." She folded her arms across her chest. "If he wants to go, I won't stop him."

"No," I said, wiping away stupid tears. "Ma, I don't know what's wrong with me."

"What will it take for you to realise, Charlie?"

I let out a shaky breath, shook my head and shrugged. "I don't know."

Ma left me with that and a resounding, hurt-to-hear silence.

————

I DON'T EVEN REMEMBER SITTING down on the sofa, and I don't know how long I'd been there staring at nothin', but two little black paws on my thigh snapped me out of my head.

Matilda.

She looked up at me with her big brown someone-please-love-me eyes and leant up on her toes so her little twitchy nose could sniff me. She wanted food.

I scooped her up and held her like Travis did and walked into the kitchen. The house was silent. Empty. No wonder Matilda came to me; no one else was here. I was her last resort, an irony I'd have probably found funny if it didn't hurt so fucking much.

When her bottle was warm, I sat back in the lounge room and fed her. It was oddly comforting, the warmth of her against me, the flutter of her heartbeat, this little living thing.

And I think I realised right then and there why Travis refused to get rid of her.

"I'm not saying he was right," I told her, my voice was croaky and hollow.

She blinked up at me as she drank in I'm pretty sure what was kangaroo for "of course you wouldn't, you idiot."

I sighed and leaned back in the sofa. The last four nights of not sleeping weighed in heavily, and I must have closed my eyes. I didn't mean to fall asleep, and I didn't mean to dream of what Ma said, but the words *what would it take for me to realise* woke me up.

Matilda was still tucked into my arm, snug, warm and sound asleep. Someone had stoked the fire, and there was a blanket over my legs. I don't know who had seen me, who still cared enough to make sure I was warm. But I felt horrible. Not in a sick kind of way, but in a what-have-I-done kind of way.

I sat my aching body up, careful not to wake Matilda, but she stirred and woke anyway. I helped her into her makeshift pouch that hung from the door handle, and that's when I noticed it had stopped raining. I could hear hushed voices from the kitchen, which I soon realised were Ma and George.

I had no idea if Travis was still here, and quite frankly, I didn't want to know. It was stupid and it was childish, but if he *was* gone, the longer I didn't know, the longer I could put off having my heart ripped out.

Instead of finding Ma and George and telling 'em how sorry I was for acting like an arse, I went into the bathroom. I avoided eye contact with myself in the reflection and almost laughed when I saw the pile of Travis's dirty clothes still sittin' on the floor.

It meant maybe he hadn't left my sorry arse.

Or maybe he didn't take them when we went. They were my clothes anyway, he just wore 'em. So maybe he only took what he came here with. Maybe Ma and George were in the kitchen trying to decide how to tell me he'd gone.

I scooped up the laundry and walked past the kitchen. And what I saw stopped me cold. Ma and George were there, and so was Travis. I should have been happy he was still here. Thrilled, ecstatic even. I should have dropped the stupid laundry and sat my arse down and begged him to forgive me, but I didn't. The looks on their faces stopped me.

Somehow I knew. Somehow, without bein' told, I knew he was leaving. Their faces told me. There was mail strewn across the table and a newspaper—I'd forgotten how just the other day, I'd organised to have them delivered for him. It's funny the stupid things you think of at times like that, but I thought, *Now I'll have to cancel it.*

"Charlie?" Ma called out.

"I'll just be in the washroom," I whispered and somehow got my made-of-stone feet to move. I dumped my armful of dirty clothes on the floor in the laundry and blindly started to sort them. My eyes burned and my chest ached and bile rose in my throat. I heard the door open behind me, but I couldn't turn around. I didn't want to hear it. If he didn't say it, then it wasn't happening, and it wasn't all my stupid fault.

I stuffed some clothes into the machine and turned it on, and started re-sortin' the clothes on the floor. I held up his red-dirt-muddy inside-out jeans. "It's bad enough you leave your shit on the floor and I have to pick up after you and sort your shit, but is it too much to ask that you can turn the fucking jeans in the right way? I mean, I'll do *all* the washing, I don't fucking care—" I sucked back a ragged breath and tried not to cry.

"Charlie," he said, just a whisper. I almost didn't hear him over the pounding in my ears.

"But could you at least try and fucking help?" I asked, wiping my eyes with my sleeve. "I mean, it's not too much to ask, but some of this shit needs soaking."

"Will you shut up?" he cried. "Just for two fucking seconds. I know it may come as a shock to you, but the world doesn't revolve around Charlie fucking Sutton."

It was really only when he stopped talking and I looked at him, I mean really looked at him, that I should have known something wasn't right. He was holding some half-folded white pieces of paper, his hand down at his thigh. He was looking kinda pale and whole lotta scared.

"Trav?" I asked, my voice was real quiet, and there was a sense of dread creeping up the back of neck. "What's that?"

"It's a letter," he whispered back. "To me. From the Australian Immigration Department."

Oh. "Oh."

He swallowed hard. "They're sending me back, Charlie. They said I can't stay."

CHAPTER TEN

IT'S NOT A REALITY CHECK. IT'S A PUNCH TO
THE HEART.

TRAVIS HELD UP THE PAPER, and I could see the
Australian Government insignia in the corner. He held it
up, and his eyes scanned as he re-read it. "They're giving me
twenty-eight days, and I need to have left the country."

I shook my head, trying to take in what he was saying.

"Actually," he said quietly, "it's twenty-one days now,
given how long the letter took to get here."

"No."

Travis looked at me then. "Actually, yes." He held up
the papers. "Says so right here."

They were making him leave. It wasn't up to me or him.
It wasn't whether he wanted to go or not, or if he'd had
enough of my stupid arse, or if he hated the desert. It was up
to some bureaucrat that didn't even know him. "No."

"You just gonna stand there and shake your head and
say no? Like that will fix anything. Is that all you've got,
Charlie?" he said, his eyes filled with tears. "Because this is
real." He held out the letter, and he started to cry. "So that's

it, Charlie. Looks like you get what you wanted, no blame on you. You must be so fucking relieved."

"No," I said again, moving to him without even a conscious thought. I pulled him against me and wrapped him up in my arms. He fell into me and sobbed into my neck. "Travis, no."

He held onto me just as tight, the letter now just crumpled papers at my back. "Charlie," he mumbled my name over and over. "I've missed you."

I pulled back just a little and took his face in my hands. I wiped his tears with my thumbs and kissed his cheeks, his eyes, his nose and his lips. "I am so sorry. I am so, *so* sorry."

His face twisted and fresh tears fell. "They're making me leave, Charlie," he mumbled, like I hadn't heard any of what he'd said.

"No," I said, clearly and adamantly. "We won't let that happen."

He smiled, still crying, and I slid my arms back around him, a mix of holding too-tight and not-tight-enough. And we stood there in the laundry like that, just all wrapped around the other, until the tears stopped and the temperature dropped. I didn't want to let him go.

Eventually he said, "So you don't want me to go?"

I ran my hand through his hair and kissed the side of his head. "Never."

He pulled back and looked at me. His eyes were puffy and sad, and he whispered, "I don't know what to do. I don't know to fix this."

"What? *Us?*" I asked. "We'll talk more. *I* need to talk more, and I promise I'll make it up to for being such an arse-hole, and I need to speak up when things get too much. I just need you to help me learn, and—"

And he was smiling through his tears. He held up the letter. "I meant this."

"Oh." I laughed. "Well, that's easy."

"Easy?" he asked, his eyes going wide. "Charlie, it's the Immigration Department!"

I kissed him, soft and sweet. "If you leave here, it'll be because I'm an idiot and I'm impossible to put up with, not because some pen pusher in Canberra says so, okay?"

He smiled now and pressed his face against mine. He whispered, "I missed you."

"I missed you too," I replied, holding his face so I could look into his eyes. "And I'm sorry for being a jerk. I really am."

"You really are a jerk, yes I know," he said with a smile. "I've seen you in all your jerk glory all week." He put his hand to my face, then looked at me seriously. "Don't do it again." The way he said it was very final. There was no or-I'll-kick-your-arse clause on the end. I knew he meant there would be no second chance.

I nodded and said something I should have said a hundred times. "I love you, Travis."

He smiled. "I know you do."

I took his hand and led him out. "Come on. We need to go call the government. Someone's gonna wish they didn't answer the phone."

We only got as far as the kitchen door. When I saw Ma and George in the kitchen, looking all solemn and sad, I stopped. Ma looked at me, then seeing my hand holding Travis's, she sighed, relieved. "Oh thank God," she said. "Charles Sutton, you and I are gonna be havin' a little chat, you hear me?"

Letting go of Travis's hand, I stepped into the kitchen, wrapped my arms around her and lifted her. "Sure thing,

Ma," I said, putting her back down. "But first I just need to make a few calls and sort out this visa mess, okay?" She kind of smiled, and as I walked into my office with Travis, I'm pretty sure I heard Ma say something that sounded like "bloody kids".

I stood at the side of my desk and straightened out the somewhat-crumpled letter on my desk and read the whole thing.

Travis's original visa, the one he came here with, was a temporary working visa. When he'd decided he wasn't going back to the States, he had it extended. The problem, as we were just finding out, was that it only renewed for six months, not two years like we'd assumed. A six-month temporary visa, in effect from the approval of the extended original visa, meant that in twenty-eight days—now twenty-one days—he was expected to leave. Actually, in twenty-one days, he was expected to be already gone.

I picked up the phone and dialled the number the letter said to call. It was a Sydney number, and after six different voice activated directions, all I got was "Thank you for calling the Department of Immigration and Border Protection. Office hours are Monday to Friday, nine AM to five PM..." I looked out the window to see it was getting dark. "What time is it?"

Travis looked at his wristwatch. "Almost six."

"Shit." I sighed. "Where the hell did today go?"

Travis shrugged. "You spent most of it with your head up your arse, remember?"

I heard George's muffled laugh from the kitchen and Ma's prompt response tellin' him to shush.

I flipped my laptop open and quickly searched up the government immigration website. "There has to be another number," I said, more to myself than anyone else. "One in

Perth. It's not five o'clock there yet." So after a bit of searching, I found a number for an office in Perth. After speaking to three different machines, I then spoke to two different people who, because I was in a different state, were probably less helpful than the damn machines, then before I could pop a vessel in my fucking forehead, I got put through to some guy who, very calmly, told me that he couldn't help me and I'd need to speak to the Sydney number listed on the letter.

To which I promptly and somewhat fucking loudly, replied with, "You can't just upend someone's life between the hours of nine and fucking five, arsehole."

He replied with a dial tone.

I growled at the phone in my hand, so Travis took it and put it out of throwin' reach. "We'll call them tomorrow."

"Tomorrow's Saturday."

"Then we call them on Monday."

I sighed, and feeling deflated and useless, I pulled him against me. I ran my hand over his back, over the nape of his neck and into his hair. It felt so good to just touch him. "I'm sorry."

"Don't apologise," he mumbled. Then he pulled back. "Actually, you need to go say sorry to Ma and George. And properly this time."

"I know."

He frowned. "Charlie, please tell me we'll get this sorted out. I don't want to leave."

"Trav." I put my hand to cup his face and softly kissed his lips. "I'll do anything. Everything. Whatever it takes."

I took his hand and walked us into the kitchen. Ma smiled a little warmer this time, though she still looked sad, and it hurt knowin' I was the reason.

"Where's George?" I asked.

"Taking a shower."

"I am really sorry," I told her again. "I should have never behaved the way I have this last week."

"No, you shouldn't have. It's not just you anymore, Charlie."

"I know," I said. "And I'll apologise to George when he comes back out."

She nodded. "Yes, you will. And to the others when they get back on Sunday."

I felt like a scolded child, and in light of how I'd behaved, it was probably deserving. "And the others."

She looked at Travis, then back to me. "Nothing like a cold slap in the face from the Immigration department to make you see reason, huh?"

I nodded. "It sure did."

Trav took a deep breath. "We need to call them on Monday."

Ma smiled sadly. "I heard."

I squeezed Travis's hand. "We'll sort it out. Surely it's just a matter of making some phone calls or filling in some forms. I mean, people come to Australia all the time, right?" I looked at Travis. "Right? Was it hard when you applied?"

"I just applied for a temporary work visa," he said. "Or maybe I filled in something wrong... I don't know." He shook his head. "What if they say no?"

I dropped his hand and put my arm around him. "I'd like to see them try. If you think you've seen me be stubborn before, then wait to see what I'm really capable of," I said with a smile, trying to get him to do the same. Which he did, kind of.

"You boys want vegetable soup for dinner?" Ma asked. I kind of forgot we were standing in the middle of her kitchen. "Wasn't quite sure if you'd be even eating, so it's all I made. You can help yourself."

"Oh, sure thing," I told her. "We can do that. Want me to make a damper?" I asked.

"That'd be nice, Charlie," she said. Then she looked at Trav and frowned. "You okay, hun?"

He gave her the best smile he could muster, and to be truthful, it made my heart hurt to see him struggle. "Actually," he said, "a quiet night in front of the TV with soup sounds kinda perfect."

So Trav sat the table and watched while I made damper, kneading out flour and water into a round loaf-looking thing. I only stopped a few times to kiss him and put fingerprints of gluggy flour on his face.

When George came into the kitchen, I apologised to him for basically being a brat. I know that me hurting Ma hurt him, and I told him for that I was truly sorry. Ma took one look at the kitchen—at the flour all over the table, the floor and all over me—and she just turned around and walked out. My hopes of having a real quick shower with Travis while the damper baked in the oven was replaced by me cleaning up the mess instead, but I didn't mind. Travis didn't seem to mind either. He kind of didn't go too far from me, and I really regretted wasting the last five days.

We all sat in the lounge room and ate our bowls of soup and fresh, steaming hot damper. It was the most familial thing we'd done in a long time, and I don't think I'd ever felt part of a family more than I did that night.

Trav put his empty bowl on the floor in front of us, hooked his arm around mine and pulled me so we were lying down—his back to my front—and then he pulled my other arm around his waist. He didn't let go.

We barely fit on the sofa layin' like that, but I didn't

dare suggest otherwise. I shoved a cushion under my head the best I could, and he snuggled back into me. We watched the footy and every so often I'd kiss the back of his head, but he was restless and withdrawn. Very unlike Travis.

With the letter from the Immigration department and the way I'd behaved these last few days, I was guessing he'd had a pretty horrible week.

I had to make it up to him.

When Ma and George had gone to bed, I wiggled out from behind him, turned the TV off and took us to bed. He pulled off his sweater, then I helped him with his shirt and jeans. While he climbed into bed, I stripped down to my underwear and slid in beside him.

It had been five days since we'd done anything remotely sexual—the longest we'd ever abstained. And as much as I wanted to remedy that, I had a feeling Travis needed something else a bit more.

"I was thinking maybe we could just talk tonight," I started.

Even in the darkened room, I could see his eyes flicker with something like confusion or amusement. "Okay."

"You're so tired," I said softly, running my fingers through the hair at his temples. "You've had a shitty week, and I'm sorry."

He smiled and closed his eyes for a long moment. "You keep apologising."

"Because I mean it."

"I know you do," he said simply. "You wanted to talk?"

I didn't really know what to say, and I didn't want to talk about his almost-expired visa, so I figured it was best to prompt him go first. "Tell me something I don't know about you."

"What?"

"Tell me something I don't know about you," I repeated. "I dunno. Something from your childhood, something you did as a kid."

"Um, okay," he said, giving me a tired half-smile in the moonlit room. "There was a kid at elementary school who used to pick on my sister, so my brother and me loosened every bolt on his bike. He only got half a block home and it fell apart underneath him. He bit pavement and never picked on her again."

I laughed. "You didn't?"

"Yep. Front wheel, forks and handlebars. Even the seat," he went on to say. "I was only in first grade, so about six years old, I think. My brother was about eleven. He took the rap."

"You got caught?"

"Found the wrench in my brother's school bag."

I chuckled. "Did you get into trouble?"

"Nah. Kid deserved it." Then he sighed. "I think my mom was kinda proud. She was always telling us we had to look out for each other."

I let go of his hand and shuffled in so he could put his head on my chest. I slid my arm around his shoulder. "Tell me something else."

"I broke my wrist when I was twelve," he said. I could tell he was getting close to sleep; his accent was thicker, his voice deeper when he was almost asleep. "We took a vacation to Colorado to go skiing. And I was supposed to go down the beginners' slope, but I wanted to down the fast slope—"

"That doesn't surprise me."

I could feel him smile against my chest. "Well, there's a reason they have beginners' slopes."

I laughed. "I guess there is."

"Broke my wrist in two places," he said, his voice even sleepier. "Doctor said I was lucky it wasn't my neck."

"I've never been to the snow."

Travis kind of pulled me a bit closer and mumbled, "I'll take you one day."

I traced circles on his back as he fell asleep and just enjoyed the feeling of him breathing against me. His body heat, his weight, his smell—everything I'd craved these last five days.

I kissed the top of his head and smiled, thinking we should do this talking thing more often.

I was just about asleep when I heard a weird husky clicking noise. It took me a minute to realise I wasn't imagining it; then it took me another minute to realise what it was.

It was Matilda.

I rubbed my hand up Travis's arm, but he was sound, sound asleep. He was exhausted and stressed, and I didn't have the heart to wake him. So I ever-so carefully peeled him off me, pulled on some shorts and went in search of the hungry kangaroo.

I was pretty sure her makeshift pouch would be hanging from the lounge room door handle, and following the noise, that's where I found her. She had her head poking out, looking around for the human bearing food. She called out louder, that weird clucky-clicky noise they make, when she saw me. I considered leaving her hanging there while I got her bottle ready, but the way she waved her little hands about was kind of cute and disturbing, so I picked her up, pouch and all, and took her into the kitchen with me.

I found three made-up bottles in the fridge, heated one up in the microwave, and sat at the kitchen table while she guzzled it. "Do you need to pee after a bottle at night?" I wondered out loud. She didn't answer, of course, just stared up at me with those big brown eyes. "Because it's cold outside and I ain't taking you."

I shivered, being only half-dressed and away from the fire. I considered taking her into the lounge room, but she was almost done. I waited for her to drain the bottle, tossed it into the sink and hung her pouch back on the lounge room door handle.

I climbed back into bed and quickly wrapped myself around a very warm Travis, and I now realised why he would put his cold feet on me when he got back into bed. I kissed his shoulder blade and closed my eyes.

I swear I'd only been asleep for a minute when that damn clicking noise woke me again. I fell out of bed and stumbled out to the lounge room, wondering if Matilda did in fact need to pee and found it was actually two in the morning. And it was freezing.

I threw some more wood on the fire, left Matilda in her pouch and went and got her bottle. This time I sat in the lounge room next to the fire and started to feed her. About a minute later, Travis walked out, still half-asleep and still just wearing his undies. He mumbled something that sounded like "bed cold you gone", and then he sat himself next to me, tuckin' himself into my side. There was a knitted blanket that hung over the back of the lounge, so I reached up and pulled it over him.

I had Matilda under one arm, Travis under the other and the next thing I knew, it was morning.

I woke up to kink in my neck and the feeling of being watched. I opened my eyes slowly, realising I wasn't in my bed, and found Ma standing there looking at me, smiling. "Look at you," she whispered.

Travis was now kind of lying across me, and Matilda

was awake but happy enough. Well, she wasn't clicking at me for food. "What time is it?" I asked.

"Five thirty."

Ugh. I tried to move my neck and shoulders, but my muscles protested.

"Here," Ma whispered, reaching out for Matilda. "Let me take her. She'll want a bottle soon."

Once she'd picked her up, pouch and all, I shivered at the loss of warmth. I tried to pull the blanket over more of me, making Travis stir. He sat up, clearly confused as to where he was or why.

"I came out to feed Matilda, and you followed me," I explained.

He frowned, his eyes not adjusted to being open yet, and shrugged. "Oh." Then he blinked until he was awake. "I didn't feed her!"

"I did," I told him.

He slumped back into the lounge and sighed. "This is not a comfortable sofa." Then he looked down at himself and peeked under the blanket. "I have no clothes on. That's not embarrassing."

I laughed. "You have undies on."

"I'm sure Ma wouldn't appreciate it like you."

I flicked back the corner of the blanket that was barely covering me. "I have shorts on at least. I put 'em on when I got up the first time."

"I can't believe I didn't hear her. Sorry."

I put my hand on his leg. "You were exhausted. And that's my fault. It was the least I could do. Why don't you go get dressed, and I'll make you some coffee?"

"Yeah." He groaned as he stood up and gave me a full frontal view of his morning wood as he readjusted the blanket around him.

"Jesus."

He chuckled as he walked off, leaving me to think of nasty things, like the smell of disembowelling a kill beast for meat, before I had to go into the kitchen to face Ma. The last thing she needed to see was me with a semi.

Shaking it off, I went into the kitchen and flicked the coffee machine on to warm up. I threw on a coat at the door, then went out to feed the dogs. The first thing I noticed was the new garden bed. Travis had all but finished it, and I had no idea. I really had missed so much these last few days.

With the dogs fed, I was coming back inside when Ma was hanging Matilda's pouch on the clothes line. "This needs some air," she said.

"He did an incredible job," I said, looking at the new garden.

"He certainly did," she said with a fond smile.

"I'm really sorry, Ma," I said again. "I made a big mess of everything."

Ma nodded. "Yep. You almost lost him, Charlie."

"I know."

She seemed pleased, be it with my answer or my sincerity, I wasn't sure. "Come inside. It's freezing out here. Let's have a hot breakfast and a little chat."

I had a feeling this wasn't going to be exactly pleasant— the chat, not the breakfast—and I wasn't far wrong.

It wasn't unpleasant like shovelling horseshit; it was unpleasant in an oh-God-I-want-to-die kinda awkward.

"Take a seat," Ma said. Travis was already sitting at the kitchen table, holding a bright-eyed Matilda in my old sweater, which was her new pouch, apparently.

"Now, I was gonna say this just to Charlie, but I think you both need to hear it," she said seriously. "Charlie, the way you treated Travis last week was disgraceful."

"I know," I agreed. "I've apologised—"

She patted my hand. "Listen, hun, I ain't finished." She took a deep breath and started again. "The honeymoon period kinda came to a screeching to a halt, didn't it?"

"The what?"

"The honeymoon period. The beginning of all relationships, when it's all new and exciting," she explained. "Then reality kicks in and takes the shine off. You two live and work together. That's not easy. Once the getting, you know, the hot and heavy—"

I cringed. "Ma, you don't have to have this conversation. Like, seriously, you don't. Please..."

She shrugged and rephrased. "Once you stop fucking like bunnies."

My mouth fell open. "Ma!"

She tried again. "Once the intensity—"

My face was burning with embarrassment. "I like intensity better than the bunny thing."

Ma sighed her losing-patience sigh. "Charlie, once the intensity wanes a bit, you need to work on the communication side of your relationship."

"I'm not very good at talking about feelings and stuff," I said, deliberately not looking at either of them. At least talking about emotions wasn't talking about sex. "I mean, I'm trying, but it's easier to spend the day out in the desert chasing cattle than it is for me to do that."

Ma waited for me to look at her before she replied. "You need to learn. Relationships are hard work, Charlie. But they're worth it."

"You and George don't need to work on anything—"

She raised her are-you-fucking-kidding-me eyebrow. "Charlie, you need to work on your heart and head, before your sex life."

We'd just nosedived into awkward again.

"Don't make a face," she chided. "And don't be a child." She was now serious. "Do you want to spend your life alone? Do you want him to leave?"

Dread and fear ran cold through me at the mention of it. My eyes were wide, and I looked at Travis. I shook my head. "No."

"Then you start putting his needs before your own. You start thinking 'what would Travis want' before you say and do something stupid. And Travis, you too, hun. You're not on my shit list like Charlie here, but you're not innocent in this. You both need to work on this, now, or there will be nothing left to fix. You hear me?"

We both nodded.

"Now go and spend the day somewhere away from here. You two need to talk, and I need a day of peace and quiet."

I stood up quickly, keen to be anywhere but there, and Travis wasn't far behind me. "We might take the horses up north," I suggested.

"Great idea," Travis chimed in. He handed Matilda over to Ma's waiting arms, and we got the hell out of there. We headed straight for the shed that joined the stables, quickly saddled Shelby and Texas, and rode up through the Northern paddock without so much as a word.

I was embarrassed and not exactly sure what to say. Everything Ma had just said was the God's honest truth, and having it said out loud, it was a bell that could not be un-rung. It was a good ten minutes before Travis spoke. He looked about as uncomfortable as I felt. "Well, that was..."

"Awkward?" I finished for him.

He exhaled, relieved. "I thought for a minute there she was going to give us the birds and the bees talk."

I snorted out a laugh. "Bit late for that."

Travis smiled, but it slowly faded. "Do you think she might be, you know, right?"

"Right about what? That we need to talk more?" I asked, not really expecting him to answer. "Because we'd kind of already agreed to that."

"No," he said with a smirk. "That we'll ever stop fucking like bunnies."

I groaned out a laugh. "I can't believe she said that."

Travis laughed. "It was almost as bad as my parents' talk with me on gay sex."

I stared at him. "They didn't?"

"They sure did."

"Oh my God. Did you want to curl up and die?" I asked. "I sure as hell would have."

Travis laughed again, looking all sorts of happier than he had all week. "I'm pretty sure my dad wanted to vomit. He was kind of green." He shook his head, smiling at the memory. "Mom started to tell me about the importance of protection and lubrication—"

"Oh man. Really?"

He nodded and grinned. "When she asked if I knew if I'd prefer to catch or pitch, my dad looked horrified. He threw the book *Joy of Gay Sex* into my lap, told me read it as he was runnin' out of the room, basically."

"Was he okay with it?" I asked. "I mean, there's just no way my dad would have ever, ever done that."

"Yeah, he was okay. Just didn't like the logistical aspects of it, ya know? Like insert tab A into slot B kind of thing.

I barked out a laugh. "The poor guy."

"Poor him?" Travis cried. "How do you think I felt?"

I laughed at the look on his face. "So what was it like?"

"I just told you. It was mortifying."

"Not the talk. The book," I clarified. "The book on gay sex."

Travis grinned. "Awesome. That book taught me more than any fifteen-year-old kid should probably know. I used it for... research." He sighed. "For years, actually. It fell apart, I used it that much."

I burst out laughing. "How did you know, you know, whether you liked to catch or pitch, as your mum put it?"

"A carrot."

"A what?"

He snorted out a laugh. "A carrot. It was a very well-endowed, well-rounded carrot. I had to heat it up a bit first."

I laughed so hard I almost fell off my horse.

He just grinned without shame. "I was alone in the house, so I thought I'd see if I could roll a condom on with my mouth like they did in porn movies, which I couldn't, by the way. My fifteen-year-old self thought the taste was disgusting."

"My twenty-six-year-old self thinks the taste is disgusting."

He snorted at that. "So I was alone, the carrot was already dressed, and I thought why the hell not. I wasn't sure at first, but was curious enough to try it. The book said it could be extremely pleasurable if done right."

"Carrots are my new favourite vegetable."

Travis laughed this time. "So I had the book, I had the house to myself and the lube my parents gave me."

"They gave you lube?!"

"And the condoms."

"Ma's conversation about fucking like bunnies doesn't seem so bad," I mumbled. "They really gave you all that?"

He nodded. "Yep."

"Jeez, and I thought most folks from Texas were conservative. Sounds fairly open to me," I said. "You're very lucky to have such open-minded folks."

"I know," he said seriously. It wasn't a biting reply, but there was something to his tone.

"So you'd come out to them already?" I asked. I had never asked the details. I knew his parents didn't care either way about his sexuality, just like he knew my father hated mine. "When did you know for sure that you liked boys?"

"I think I always knew," he said simply. "But fourteen for sure."

"For sure?" I asked. "Sounds kind of definite."

"Well, I made out with my best friend, so..."

"I guess that'd do it."

He smiled, but it wasn't strictly a happy one. "My first boyfriend. We'd kind of hedged around the subject a bit, but he was sleepin' over one time and we got to wonderin' about first kisses—our friend Jackson had kissed Louisella and she told everyone he was bad at it—and I said, 'There should be practice first-kisses before the real first-kisses,' and he said, 'Maybe we could practice,' and then he tried to run away, but I caught him and told him, 'I'd really like that,' and I kissed him."

I could just imagine a fourteen-year-old Travis doing exactly that. "So how was your first kiss?"

"I was so nervous, and everything in my head saying it was wrong, but it felt so right." He sighed and was quiet for a while. "What about your first kiss?"

"I told you already. I turned eighteen, the boys took me into town to get drunk and get laid. I ended up in the bathroom stalls with some random guy, drunk, kissing and sucking dick." I shifted in my saddle. All this talk about sex and not having had any for five days was starting to take its toll. "I mean, I was sure I was gay, but yeah, getting busted by George when I was on my knees in front of some dude pretty much sealed the deal."

Travis snorted. "So classy."

"I was eighteen! I had a lot of catching up to do."

"Some dude," he mimicked me. "Did you even get a name?"

"Nope. I was drunk. I remember looking twice at a guy, and he kinda nodded and walked into the bathrooms. I followed, he pushed me into the cubicle. At first I thought he was gonna punch me, but he undid my jeans..." I stopped at that. I figured he didn't need details. "George came looking for me."

"And he found you."

I remembered the look on George's face and cringed. "Not my finest moment," I said. "So, names. What was your first boyfriend's name?"

"Ryder Newell."

"Ryder?" I scoffed. "Did his parents not like him or something?"

I meant it as a joke, but Travis certainly didn't laugh. "Well, not in the end they didn't."

I didn't like how that sounded. "In the end?"

"Ryder's dad wasn't very—" He seemed to struggle with the word. "—tolerant. He used to make fag jokes, and he'd preach about sinners. Not just about gays, but about swearing, drinking, sex before marriage. He was very strict."

"He was a religious man?" I asked.

"Not all religious people are bad, Charlie." He frowned. "My folks are religious. They go to church and say grace before Sunday dinner, and they're not bad people."

I started to apologise. "I didn't mean that..."

Travis shrugged me off. "No, Ryder's father was a cruel

man. He used the Bible to disguise his hatred, and that's the worst kind of person."

There was a different tone to Travis's voice. One I'd not heard from him before. I decided to just shut up and listen.

"Ryder and I were kinda inseparable by this point, but he struggled with what we did. He loved being with me, and he'd talk about us running away together, but we were just kids. I didn't really know what it all meant at the time. I was just doing what felt right and good, you know? But he... struggled." He sighed, long and deep. I kept my eyes on Travis, not able to look away. I could feel it in my stomach, in the hairs on the back of my neck that this story didn't end well.

"Ryder hung himself from the tree in his own back-yard," he said. Just ever so casual, like he was describing his friend leaving for summer camp. I pulled on the reins, bringing Shelby to a complete stop, but Travis mustn't have noticed. He kept on going. "They were two ranches over, but my momma said she heard Mrs Newell screaming as the sun came up." He stopped talking when he realised I wasn't alongside him. He looked back over his shoulder, and all I could do was sit there in shocked fucking silence.

He pulled Texas around and came back to where I was. I tried to think of something to say, but my mind was swimming. Travis swung his leg over and dismounted. He put his hand up and patted my thigh. "Charlie, hop down."

Mechanically, I did as he asked. I slid down off Shelby, and he put his hands up to my face. "You okay?"

"Am I okay?" I asked him. "Never mind me. Are *you* okay? Jesus, Travis, that's... the worst thing I've ever heard. And you're just telling me now?"

He smiled. "I made my peace with it a long time ago."

I shook my head, trying to process this information. "I don't even know what to say."

Travis took my hand and, looking around for somewhere suitable, led me over to small clearing and sat down. He patted the ground next to him. "Take a seat."

I looked around. We were in the middle of nowhere. Nothing around us but red dirt, saltbush and blue, blue sky. "Here?"

He laughed. "Right here."

I sat down next to him, and he took my hand. "What happened to Ryder changed my life. I was just fifteen years old, and I took his death really hard. It was horrible. The weeks after were the worst. My mom suspected there was more to it and asked me if I *loved* loved him. She said she saw the way we looked at each other. She said she didn't mind." Travis took a deep breath. "She said she saw what Mrs Newell went through, and my momma swore to me right there she'd love me regardless. I asked her what my daddy would think of such a thing, and she said it didn't matter, she refused to lose a child like Mrs Newell did."

I didn't realise I was crying until Travis wiped my cheek.

"Don't cry," he whispered. "It was horrible, like life-changing kind of horrible, and I went through the whole *what if I had listened more* and *what if I'd run away with him* scenarios in my head. I did that shit for a long time, but you know what I realised?"

I shook my head. "What?"

"What happened to Ryder gave me my life."

"Your life?"

He nodded. "The life I have now. It let me to be true to myself, to be completely honest with who I am and not apologise for it. I often wondered if Ryder hadn't died, if my mom wasn't so petrified of me choosing the same fate, would she have been so understanding?" He shrugged. "I don't know. Even she admits she doesn't know."

"You talk about it with her?" I asked. "About her accepting you being gay?"

"We talk about everything," he said. "That's my point exactly. Would I have that relationship with my parents now if Ryder hadn't taken his own life? I'm not rationalising it or putting a price on his life, but if I can take anything good from his death, then I can see what that is."

I squeezed his hand and just sat with him for a while, processing what he was saying. "It gave you freedom."

"In a lot of ways, yes. It wasn't as easy as I'm making it out to be," he said. "I mean, I was gay, fifteen, in junior high and lived in Texas. But I never apologised for it, and I had my family... including a big brother who would have punched the shit out of anyone who gave me hell."

I chuckled at that and looked at him. He was just sitting there in the sunshine, looking like he was made just for me. His light brown hair was longer now, shaggy even, his skin looked sun-kissed and his eyes were piercing blue.

He took my hand in both of his and held on, like he was scared I was gonna run. He swallowed hard. "It's why I understand what happened between you and your dad," he said quietly. I went to pull my hand away, but he had a hold of it. "Charlie, what happened with Ryder, well, that's a bit like what happened with you. And when you were telling me what your dad said to you, it sounded familiar. And I knew I had to get you to talk about it, to try and let it go. I had to do something..."

Oh. "I, um..." I swallowed down the lump in my throat, not sure what to say.

He leaned in and went to kiss my cheek, but I caught

his lips with mine and kissed him properly. It was a slow, thank-you kind of kiss, which he returned with a you're-very-welcome kind of kiss back.

I pulled back before I got too carried away. It had been a long five days since we'd been intimate, and even the sweetest of kisses were testing my resolve.

"Ugh," he groaned, adjusting himself. "I know we're supposed to do this talking thing, but do you think we could possibly take an intermission and make out a little?" He looked hopeful. "Maybe even come a little, because you're driving me insane."

I laughed but wasted no time launching myself at him, pushing him backward so I was on top of him. I brushed the hair back from his forehead, settling my weight on him. "I want to get this right with you. This being-in-love thing. I want to make it right."

His smile faded. "I don't want to leave in three weeks, Charlie."

I leaned down and kissed him. "You're not going anywhere."

He held onto me, his arms around my back and his boots hooked around the backs of my legs. I slid my hand under his neck and held his head as I swept his mouth with my tongue. I rolled my hips, grinding our cocks between us through the denim.

But it wasn't enough. I needed more, and from the way he whisper-begged me, it was clear he did too. I'd barely got my hand down the front of his jeans, wrapping my fingers around him for one thrust before he came. He bucked and cried out as he spilled his load between us, and that was all I needed. I didn't even get my jeans undone, just rutting against him and watching him unravel tipped me over the edge. I collapsed on top of him; he wrapped his arms around me and kissed the side of my head.

And there, lazin' in the red dirt with the winter sun on our faces, we spent the rest of the day talking about all sorts of things—inconsequential things, important things—and making out and making each other laugh.

It wasn't until Shelby walked over, staring down at us and dangling the reins in my face, that we thought we should go home. We got up and dusted ourselves off the best we could and realised that Texas had wandered off a little.

And by a little, I meant a good few hundred metres. At least he was in the direction of home. Travis tried whistling to him, which of course didn't work. Texas just shook his mane in an I-ain't-listenin' kind of way.

I got up on Shelby and held my hand down to Travis. "Come on, we'll go get him."

He grumbled a bit, but gave me his hand. He jumped up and settled in behind me in the saddle, putting his arms on my hips. I gave Shelby a rub on the neck and told Travis, "Just be careful where you put your feet. She might be extra smart and placid, but she's still a horse. You kick her in the flanks, and we're both walkin'."

We headed toward Texas who, when he saw us approaching, headed toward home. "That sonofabitch," Travis cried. "He's leaving without me!"

"Leaving?" I said. "He's already gone."

About a hundred yards ahead of us, Texas was prancing in that I'm-something-special way horses do, and every time we got to within closin' distance, he'd gallop off again, pigrooting and bucking. I laughed and Travis got pissed off, but I wouldn't run Shelby with the both of us on her back. By the time we got home, Texas was already waiting at the gate, like he'd done nothing wrong.

George was at the shed, and Ma was crossing the yard to join him. She shook her head. "Thought something was wrong until we heard you laughing and we saw you coming down the yard," she yelled.

Shelby stopped at the gate, and Travis slid off, grumbling about his horse. I laughed as I got down and took the reins of both horses. Travis pointed his finger at Texas. "If you think I'm feeding ya, you've got another thing coming. How about I give double to Shelby and none for you, considering that's how we came home." Travis took both reins off me and still mumbling, lecturing Texas, led the horses into their stables. It sounded like he said, "Bastard of a thing he is. Not worth the oats to feed him."

I was still smiling at him even though I couldn't hear what he was saying, and Ma was smiling at me. "You've had a good day," she said, not really a question.

"The best." Then I added, "Thank you. We spent the entire day talking 'bout stuff. It was great."

"Glad to help," she said. Then she looked at my clothes and finally at my hair. "Talking, huh?"

I brushed my coat and jeans, then my hair and smiled as clouds of dust billowed off me. "Mostly talking, yes."

She rolled her eyes but smiled warmly. "Go and help him settle the horses, then clean up. The others will be home soon."

I nodded and turned to leave, but she stopped me. "Charlie?"

"Yeah?"

"It's good to see you smile."

I'm sure I blushed before I walked in to where Travis was still swearin' at his horse.

CHAPTER ELEVEN

FIGHTING: THE DEFINING KIND

I INSISTED TRAVIS SHOWER FIRST, knowing if we ran out of time before dinner, Ma would be scowling at me and not him. It also helped that he was naked and wet in the shower in the bathroom, and I was fully clothed in the kitchen with Ma. Because I'm pretty sure if I went in there with him, neither one of us would be eating dinner.

As it happened, everyone was back from their weekend in Alice Springs, and there was the usual chatter about what went on coming from the dining room. It all fell silent when I walked in, though, and I was reminded of how poorly I'd behaved the week before. I had them walking on eggshells because I'd been in such a pissy mood.

I gave them a smile and took my seat at the head of the table just as Ma was bringing in the last platter of food. I figured there was no time like the present for getting sorries out of the way. "Before we start, I just wanted to apologise for my behaviour last week. I was out of line, and frankly, I'm a little surprised you all came back to work for me."

You could have heard a pin drop.

I looked around the table. "Unless you've all come back to tell me you're not workin' for me no more..."

George laughed, and Travis hooked his foot around mine under the table.

"Nah, takes more than that to get rid of me," Ernie said, though I think he just wanted to start to eat. He was eyeing the food like he hadn't eaten all weekend. He probably hadn't.

"Please, eat," I said. "Don't disrespect the cook by letting it go cold."

There was the usual clanging of serving spoons on crockery, but before anyone had had one mouthful, Travis said, "Um, I suppose I should tell y'all that the Immigration department is kicking me out of the country." There was absolute silence, and every pair of eyes at the table was on him. "They've given me three weeks to leave."

Almost comically, every one slowly turned from lookin' at Travis to lookin' at me.

I gave them the best smile I could manage. "He's not going back." Then, because that sounded a little psycho, I added, "Unless it's his choice."

No one moved. Hell, no one even blinked. So Travis said, "Charlie seems to think it's just a mix-up or something. We'll call them tomorrow to sort it out."

"Can they make you leave?" Trudy asked quietly.

Travis shrugged. "I guess."

"'S'okay, Mr Travis," Billy said, wearing his usual half-face grin. "I can hide you. If someone comes lookin' for you, you come with me. Ain't nobody find you. Not even a Tracker'll find you."

Travis looked at him seriously. "Would I still be alive? Because that's sounding very much like I wouldn't be alive."

Billy laughed, and it was the type of laugh that made

other people smile. So with the mood somewhat back to happy, I said, "Please, everyone, eat."

They didn't need telling twice. The food was devoured in no time, and while they talked of their weekend, conversation generally came back to Travis. It was pretty clear they didn't want him to go as much as I didn't want him to go either. Well, maybe not *as* much, but close. These people were his friends, his Australian family.

When everyone had gone for the night, instead of sitting with me, Travis sprawled out on the floor in front of the fire. I didn't mind one bit. It meant I could sit on the sofa and watch him instead of the stupid television. He had a wide-awake Matilda with him. She was out of her pouch, wobbling, still unsteady on her too-big feet, kinda trying to climb onto him. She would put her little front paws on his chest or face, and he'd laugh when her whiskers tickled his nose.

She was a cute little thing, not that I'd ever tell Travis that.

We hadn't talked any more on what would happen with Matilda. And now with this whole immigration mess looming over him, I didn't want to bring it up. I didn't want to fight with him, I didn't want to upset him, because there was that miniscule flicker of doubt—that sinking, couldn't-even-contemplate feeling that he might need to leave before her.

"What's up?" Travis asked, looking up at me from the floor. He was on his side with his back to the fire, Matilda now curled up at his chest.

"Nothing, why?"

"You were frowning."

"Was I?" I asked. "I was just thinking, that's all."

Travis's eyebrows knitted together. "About?"

"Tomorrow."

"The immigration department?" he asked.

"Nah," I lied. I scrubbed my hand over my face and sighed. "We should get a shade cloth over that garden so the frost doesn't kill your seedlings. And we need to start running the fencing in the first southern paddock for when we bring the cattle down. We muster in two weeks."

Travis grinned at the mention of it. "Cool."

I checked my watch, and given it was a Sunday, it was almost time for his weekly Skype session with home. I looked at how cosy he and his kangaroo were, and stood up. "I'll just get the laptop. You need to call your mum."

When I brought the laptop into the lounge room and plugged it in, Travis was pointing his finger to Matilda, making E.T. voices about phoning home.

"You're such a dickhead," I said, shaking my head.

He put his hands up over her big ears. "Don't use that language in front of the kids," Trav said.

I shook my head at him and opened the laptop. "Fair dinkum."

"Fair dinkum?" Travis said. The look on his face was a cross between confused and concerned. "What the hell is that?"

I double-clicked on the Skype icon, and while it was loading, I said, "I dunno. Just something we say. It's like 'oh, bloody hell' or 'are you serious?' Maybe a bit of both."

"Don't ever hassle me for the things I say," he said, shaking his head. "Fair dinkum."

"Exactly. That was a good one." I clicked on his mum's profile and hit dial.

He narrowed his eyes at me. "I wasn't using it, I was taking the piss."

"You're getting this Aussie dialect down pat."

Travis growled just as his mum came on screen. He didn't even say hello. "Oh thank God, someone who speaks American."

"What's that, honey?" his mum said.

"Charlie's using words like *fair dinkum* and *crikey*."

"I never said crikey," I cried, defending myself. Then I stuck my head in front of the screen. "Hello Mrs Craig. Nice to see you."

There was a two-second time delay, and then she smiled. "Oh, hello, Charlie. How've you been?"

"Very well, ma'am. You?"

Travis pushed my head out the way. "Oh, I'm fine, Mom, thanks for asking," he said sarcastically.

"Oh my sweet Lord," she cried. "Is that the baby kangaroo? Look at her! She's not in her thing."

Travis laughed. "She's not in her pouch, no."

"Michael, come quick and see Travis," she called out to Travis's dad. There was a shuffling noise, then, "Look at them."

A moment later, I heard his father's voice, a deep Texan accent. "It looks like a mutated squirrel."

I laughed, and Travis grinned. His whole face kinda shined. "Hey, Dad."

"How you doin', son?"

I stood up from the floor and left him to have some quiet family time with his folks. His story earlier about that kid Ryder explained a lot about him and his family, and it made my heart hurt a little knowin' he missed them so much, but wanted to be with me instead.

I straightened up our room, put clothes away and generally made myself busy while trying to give Travis some privacy. When he was done, he found me in my office.

He was holding Matilda in her pouch again, feeding her

a bottle. He looked at the desk and saw the letter in front of me. It was crumpled and kinda dirty, a little tattered. "Rereading it won't change the words on it."

"I know," I said. I gave him a small smile. I stood up, walked around my desk and leaned my arse against my desk, then held out my arm for him. "Come here," I whispered. He walked over and stood between my legs, and I pulled him in even closer, careful not to squash Matilda. "How's things back home?"

"Good. Everyone's well. My brother's having a barbeque dinner. Everyone's going around to his place," he said. I could tell he was trying not to sound disappointed that he wasn't there. It was, I'd imagine, the little things like that he missed the most. "I told them about the visa issue."

"Oh? What did they say?"

"Momma just said it would work out the way it was supposed to." He shrugged. "That's her motto about most things."

"Was she a bit excited at the mention of you coming home?"

Travis pulled back. "I thought you said I wasn't going back?"

I gave him a tight smile. "Didn't you hear Billy? He said he'll hide you out in the desert," I reminded him.

"Did you notice he didn't answer me," Trav said seriously. "When I asked him if I'd still be alive, he didn't answer. I've seen *Wolf Creek*, you know."

I snorted out a laugh and pulled him in close again and held on to him a little bit too tight. All I could see was material, a bottle, a kangaroo tail and two big ears. "Is she almost done?"

"Almost," he said quietly. The words rumbled in his chest against my ear. "Then it's bed time for this little one."

"Bed time for us too, yeah?"

Travis leaned back in my arms so he could see my face. He had that look in his eyes, the one that was a mix of want and need. He nodded quickly, before looking at the joey in his arms. "I'll just get her settled."

Knowing he'd need a little time in the bathroom to get ready, I stood up. "Here, I'll take her."

He handed the warm bundle over and kissed me, a taste of what was to come, before disappearing down the hall. I waited for what felt like forever for her to finish her bottle and wondered errantly if this is what parenthood was like: sex, intimacy, daddy/daddy time being hindered by a hungry little thing who just wouldn't wait.

I shook that fucking ridiculous notion out of my head, hung her pouch on the lounge room door handle, threw some logs on the fire and rinsed out the bottle, leaving it on the sink to deal with later.

I had more important things to do tonight.

I had only just stepped into our room and pulled off my shirt when Travis came out of the bathroom wearin' only a towel and shut the door behind him. Then he was on me. His lips were on my neck, his hands were all over my back and then at the fly on my jeans. "I want to take my time with you," I said gruffly.

"Charlie, if you're not *in me* in the next five minutes, I'm pretty sure I'll die." I laughed, and he stopped and pulled back. "I'm being serious."

I took his face in my hands and kissed him. He smiled against my lips, knowing he'd won, and in the darkened room he slid onto the bed. I stepped out of my jeans, took the lube bottle from the bedside table, and threw it onto the bed beside him. I crawled across the mattress after him. "We can't have that now, can we?"

———

WAITING for nine o'clock to come around was torture. I'd been up since five, despite the late hour we actually got around to sleeping. I was restless but did my best not to let Travis see it. I didn't want him to know I had any doubt this whole visa mess couldn't be sorted out with a simple phone call. I didn't want him to know how terrified I was. I know we were supposed to be working on the whole honesty thing, but if I told him I was scared, if I admitted I had one ounce of doubt, then I was admitting he *could* be leaving.

And that was something I just couldn't bear thinking about.

When nine o'clock Sydney time finally, *finally*, rolled around, which was eight o'clock Territory time, we sat in my office—and I'm pretty certain Ma stood in the hall, listenin'—while Travis made the call. He dialled the number and got the stupid voice activation robot I spoke to the Friday before. After being on hold for for-goddamn-ever, and just before my nerves split my skull, he spoke to an actual person.

I could only hear his side of the conversation of course, but he went through the time-wasting particulars like reference numbers, visa numbers and then they finally got down to the reason for his call. "I think there's been some kind of mistake," he said. "I'm sure I filled out the subclass 887..."

The person on the other end of the call did a fair bit of talking, and Travis bit his lip and listened. He got quieter and seemed to shrink in his seat a bit, and he most certainly wouldn't make eye contact with me. He wrote some numbers down, thanked the person for their help and hung up the phone.

"So?" I asked, clear out of patience.

"I have to call this number," he said, tapping the paper he'd just written on. "It's an Outreach Officer." He shrugged. "It's local. It's in the Alice, which is a good thing. Be more understanding, I guess."

"What else did they say?" I pressed. "I mean, they spoke for a long time, they had to say more than just that. What was that subclass thing you said?"

He did that sigh-and-smile thing, but it seemed like more of a trying-to-breathe to me. "That guy seems to think I'll need to reapply. Said it was just a temporary visa extension, not a permanent one. I mean, I don't remember thinking anything about it when I filled it in, to be honest. I just wanted more time here. I didn't think it mattered..."

He wasn't sounding very hopeful.

"So we just have to call this person?" I said, looking down at the number. "Then we'll call them. They'll sort it out, and you can reapply."

He whispered, "I don't think it's that easy, Charlie..."

"Why? What did they say?"

He shrugged. "He said if we couldn't change it, then I'd probably still have to leave while a new application was being determined. Just because it's being processed doesn't mean I can stay."

I shook my head, and then I shook it some more. "No. We'll call this other person, this local guy, and they'll fix it." I looked at my watch. It was only half past eight here in the Territory. We had half an hour to wait.

It was quite possibly the longest half hour of my life.

Trying to stay positive, I suggested we pull out the old shade cloth from the back shed. "We'll see what shape it's in," I said. "We might be able to use it over your garden."

He looked at me like I'd lost my mind, or more to the

point, like I didn't care about the pending phone call he had to make. He glanced at the clock on the wall. "Um, okay."

"It'll fill some time," I told him, already walking out the back door.

He took a few quick steps and caught up to me, but he never said anything. Even when I was climbin' up on top of old boxes and pulling stuff out all over the place, he was quiet.

I finally found what I was looking for. "I knew it was in here somewhere," I said, throwing the folded up shade cloth at his feet and climbing back down. "We used to have this over the round yard for when we broke the horses in during summer. But it wasn't much good for that, so we built the more permanent one that's out there." I figured talking was better than silence. "Anyway, my old man didn't like to throw much of anything away." I unfolded the shade with not much help from Travis. "Dunno what condition it's in, but even if it's no good, it'll do until we can get something better."

Travis nodded, and I handed him one corner. "Here, hold this and we'll take it outside. It'll probably fall apart as soon as it sees daylight."

"Is anything likely to jump out of this?" he asked, taking the end of the folded up material.

"Well, it's likely, yes," I said with a smile. "But it's not the *jumping* that you have to be careful of. It's the *biting*."

"You're still not funny," he deadpanned and walked out of the shed.

We dropped it on the ground and started to unfold it. There were no nasty surprises, of the slithering variety anyway, but there were a few redback spiders. Travis just stomped his boot on 'em all casual-like, and I laughed.

"Remember when you freaked out over seeing one of them?"

He narrowed his eyes. "I didn't *freak out*. And they're deadly!"

"Oh, please. No one's died from a redback bite in sixty years," I said, straightening out the shade cloth. "Anyway, now you're just stompin' on 'em like a true local."

"Yeah, great," he said, kicking at the corners of the shade cloth, trying to flatten it out. "I wonder if the immigration department will take that into account. Maybe I should write that on my application."

"Trav," I said quietly. "We'll get it sorted out. I promise."

He huffed and mumbled something under his breath, then putting his hand through his hair, he looked out across the far paddock. "You can't promise me. It's not up to you."

I lifted my end of the large square of shade cloth. "Come on, pick up your end and we'll carry it to the house," I said. I waited until he did as I asked, and when we dropped it on the ground near his new garden bed, I said, "And I can promise anything I like."

He shook his head at me. "You know, some days I just don't get you at all. One day you're all bitchin' that you can't do anything, then the next day it's like nothing can stop you."

Ma, who was now standing on the veranda holding Matilda, snorted out a laugh, and when I turned to look at her, she was still smirking. "You know, as far as descriptions go, that wasn't accurate at all," she said, rolling her eyes.

I lifted my chin defiantly. "Never claimed to be perfect."

This time it was Travis who snorted and rolled his eyes.

Ignoring my glare at him, he looked over the shade cloth. "One rainstorm and this will be ripped to shreds."

"Well, we ain't expecting rain for a few weeks now, so it'll get through the coldest part of winter," I said. "Then if we need to, you can just order some new stuff."

He nodded and gave me a sad smile, but he had I-won't-be-here-in-a-few-weeks written all over his face, which of course made him look at his watch. He exhaled through puffed-out cheeks. "It's five past," he said.

"Well, come on," I said brightly. "Let's get this cleared up once and for all."

We sat in my office just like we had earlier. Travis sat in my seat with the phone, and I sat on the spare chair, hanging on every word. Ma stood in the doorway this time, still holding the pouch. There was a long tail sticking out the end and two bright brown eyes keenly waiting for the bottle Ma was swirling in her other hand.

Figuring I needed to do something with my hands other than fidget or sitting on them, I held them out toward Ma. She smiled and handed Matilda over while Travis dialled the number he wrote down earlier.

He gave the same details as before and when he was put on hold the first time, he looked like he was about to be sick. "Charlie, what if they say no?"

I gave him the best reassuring smile I could. "Then we go to Canberra or Sydney or where-the-fuck-ever we have to go. We do whatever it takes until the answer is yes, that's what we do."

He smiled then, just as the person on the other end of the line picked up. He did the whole spiel again, giving visa numbers and reference numbers and explained all he could over the phone, and then he listened. "Ah, yeah, hang on.

I'll find out," he said. Covering the mouthpiece, he asked me, "When could we go to town? They need to see me."

"Whenever," I answered. "Today. We could leave now if you want."

He smiled and spoke back into the phone. "Earliest would be one o'clock today. We're three hours out of town..." He frowned. "Oh, okay. Excuse me for asking, but is that a little late? I'm running out of days..." He nodded. "Oh, I see. No, that's fine. Thank you. I'll see you then."

He put the receiver down quietly and shrugged. "Monday after next. Two o'clock."

"What? But that's forever away!" I cried. "That's, what —" I did the math "—sixteen days away. You've only got twenty!"

"I told her I was running out of days," he said quietly. "She said it wouldn't matter. She said she'd know a day or two after the interview." Then he gave me the saddest fucking smile I'd ever seen. "At least we should be done mustering by then. It'll be cutting it fine, but I guess it's something."

I wanted to tell him I didn't give a flying fuck about the muster. I didn't care about anything else right now. But I needed to keep my head. The last thing he needed was me going off the fucking deep end. No, he needed me to be strong and to act like it was just a minor detail.

I gently bounced a still-drinking Matilda on my lap and smiled at Travis. "Then we go to this meeting, and we sort it out. If she, or whoever, decides you can't stay, then we invite them out here and hide their bodies where no one will ever find them."

Travis's mouth fell open.

"What?" I cried. "I've seen *Wolf Creek* too, you know."

Okay, so maybe threatening psychopathic homicide

wasn't keeping my cool, but he managed a small smile, so it was worth it.

"I mean it, Trav. We will sort this mess out," I told him softly, confidently. "Like I told you before, if you leave here, it will be because I'm impossible and infuriating and you can't stand to be near me one more minute. Not because some arsewipe in a suit sitting in some city skyscraper gets to tick some boxes on his to-do list."

Ma gave a soft rap on the door. She gave me an apologetic smile. "Ernie's out the front. Wants to know about running those fences for the muster. I told him you were busy, but he said George told him to check with you..."

"It's okay," I said, then looked down at the still-bloody-feeding kangaroo. "Um..." I went to hand her over to Travis, but he stood up.

"It's okay, I'll go," he said. He clapped his hand on my shoulder. "It'll help to keep me busy, and you need to finish that assessment anyway."

"I ain't doin' no bloody assessment" I said. "Plus, you don't know how I want the fence lines run."

He looked at me from the door. "I know exactly how you want them done, and I'm sure Ernie does too. He'd be just double checking out of courtesy. You want 'em run just like last time, separatin' lines for yearlings, heifers, bulls and steers in the first west and south paddocks, yes?" he asked, all smug and certain.

I glared at him, maybe huffed a little too. Instead of answering him—because he knew he was right—I looked down at Matilda, at her big brown blinking eyes. "This is all your fault."

Travis chuckled down the hall, only pausing to put his coat and hat on before I heard the door close behind him. Then Ma was back in the doorway. "I didn't mean to be listening," she said. "But it was nice, what you said to him about staying. And Charlie, I can see you're putting on a brave face for him."

"I have to. I can't even think about him going, Ma," I said quietly. "So I have to stay positive, yeah? Though I'm sure he probably sees straight through me."

Ma smiled and walked over to me. "Here, give her to me," she said, taking Matilda off me. "You'll find a way to make it right, Charlie."

"I don't know what I can do," I admitted. "I mean, what does any government agency do for me? In this country, if it doesn't happen in a major city, it doesn't happen. Half the politicians in this country think their meat comes from a supermarket. They don't have a clue what it takes to get it there: the hours, the sweat, the blood. All they want to know is that I pay my taxes on time." I shook my head. "And now they think they can just dictate this shit to me? It's bullshit!" And then because I was on a roll, I kept on ranting. "You know, I'd like to see any one of them come out here and do what he does. He has worked his arse off since the day he got here. You know, only a handful of people can survive out here, let alone love it. I'd like to see a pen-pushin' politician do one freakin' day out here. They'd be crying for a private jet to come get 'em before smoko." I took a deep breath and tried for a little calmer. "He deserves to be here. He's earned it."

Ma was trying not to smile. "You done?"

"I ain't nowhere near done."

"Good. Then put that thinkin' cap of yours on and figure out a way for him to stay. Like you told him, it'll be because of your stubborn hide that he goes, not because they tell him."

"I didn't call myself stubborn," I said lamely.

She patted my shoulder and took Matilda out of my office. I stared at the pile of textbooks I had no intention of reading and opened up my laptop instead. I went straight to the Immigration and Border Patrol website, clicked on visas and started to read.

The next thing I knew, there was another knock on my office door. It was Nara. "Mr Sutton," she said quietly, "Ma told me to tell you that lunch is almost ready."

I looked at my watch. Shit. It was near twelve. I'd been reading for three hours. I gave Nara a smile. "Thanks. I'll be out in a bit." I closed down the six tabs I had opened and went to my email, looking for one in particular. After double checking dates and times, I pulled out my mobile phone, just as Travis stood in the doorway. He looked a little windblown, a bit dirty and a lot of cute. I gave him a smile when my neighbour answered his phone.

"Charlie?"

"Yeah, hi, Greg, it's me."

"What can I do for you? Everything okay?"

"Yeah, everything's just fine," I said into the phone. Travis was still staring at me, and I looked right back at him when I said, "When did you say that Farmers Association meeting was on?"

"Weekend after next," he said. "Will you be there?"

"Yeah," I said, smiling at Travis. "Travis and I both will be."

CHAPTER TWELVE

THIS WON'T BE TRAVIS'S LAST MUSTER. HE HASN'T SEEN THE DESERT IN SPRING, SO HE CAN'T LEAVE YET, OKAY?

"TRAVIS IS DOING WHAT?" Travis asked when I'd clicked off my call to Greg.

I grinned at him. "Travis is going to the Northern Territory Beef Farmers Association as an agronomist, who not only understands the science of what we do, but how to do it out here."

"Why am I doing that?" he asked. Then he cocked his head. "*When* am I doing that?"

"Not this weekend, but the next."

He looked at me for a long, confused moment. "But we're mustering, and then I have that meeting in the Alice on the Monday after." He shook his head. "Charlie, I don't have time, and believe me, if that's my last week here, I ain't spending it somewhere else, and I certainly ain't spending it somewhere you won't be..."

I put my hand up. "But that's why you have to do it," I said. "I've been reading up on it. I read the visa website, and it said there's a subclause for skilled workers in regional areas. So then I read up on that, and it turns out that agricultural sciences qualify, which is great, right?" I asked. He looked more confused, so I explained, "I still didn't really know what that meant either, so I kept reading and found some forum pages where other people talked about their visa conditions, and how some were kicked out, and others talked about what helped them stay."

He was listening now. "And what did they say?"

"A few different people said they were active in the community with what their skill was. One guy from Canada who's based in Tasmania said he was granted a permanent visa because of his qualifications in some aquaculture thing about some kind of fish. And there was a teacher guy from India who was helping other people from India assimilate and learn English, and there was a woman from Argentina—"

"I get the picture," he said, interrupting me. He sat down in the spare seat. "So you think if I talk to a bunch of farmers about soil, they'll grant me a permanent visa?" He sounded sceptical.

"Not a speech as such," I clarified. "More of a one-on-one consulting gig. If we can get a few farmers to say that they've consulted with you on business matters pertaining to agronomy, then that should be enough."

"But I haven't."

"But you will."

"When?"

"At the Beef Farmers meeting."

"Isn't that too little, too late?"

"It can't hurt," I said. "And anyway, it doesn't matter what the farmers think. All that matters is that the lady in Alice Springs, the Outreach immigration woman, knows you're doing it."

Ma walked past the office door carrying a tray of food. "Boys, lunch."

So we had a quick lunch of soup and sandwiches. They all talked in between mouthfuls of food about football or something, but I was making mental lists of stuff I had to do. Travis was right about one thing: we were runnin' out of time.

I looked at George and asked, "If we were to bring the muster in a week sooner than planned, could we do it?"

People suddenly stopped talking about football.

George gave it some quiet thought. "We'd need to leave tomorrow to get across Arthur Creek before she comes down. Three horses and two bikes at least. Once she floods, it'll be a week's wait. We'll hafta bring 'em down home east of the ridge anyways, because we won't get across the creek."

I knew all of that. I guess he was just thinkin' out loud. "Yeah, but can we do it? Have we got the gear? The fuel? The supplies? Physically, can we do it? Can we ride out tomorrow?"

George gave a nod. "Yep."

I looked around the table, at everyone watching us. "Let me make some phone calls first. I'll need to check with the transport company. If the trucks can't pick up the cattle until the week after, then we'll stick to the original plan."

Havin' that many head of cattle in confined yards for too long was dangerous and costly. I wouldn't risk it. If it couldn't happen, then I'd have to think of something else.

But I didn't have to. Apparently being Charlie Sutton counted for something, because when I rang the trucking company—who were sending out three road trains to collect my cattle—they then made some calls, phoning me back fifteen minutes later saying it was all okay.

I sat back in my seat and sighed, and after a few minutes of collectin' my scattered thoughts, I went out to find George.

He was in the shed taking inventory of fuel. "Have we got enough?" I asked. "I can call in a delivery, but they won't get here 'til Wednesday at the earliest."

"We should be right for tomorrow," he said. "Might wanna order it anyway. We'll need it regardless, I guess." Then he asked, "So we heading out early?"

"Yep," I answered. "Transport'll be here four days earlier than planned. If we're bringin' the herd east, it'll take an extra day at least, but that still gives us a good pace, yeah?"

George nodded. "Sounds right to me."

"I'll go tell the others," I said.

"Already did," George said in the slow and steady way he did. "Figured it involved Travis stayin' somehow, so you'd make it happen. I told 'em all we'd be leavin' tomorrow."

I snorted out a laugh. "And if the transport company couldn't change their dates?"

The corner of his lips curled upward. "You don't think they'd say no to you, do you? You'd be one of their biggest contracts." He shook his head. "Anyways, you'd have just told 'em to make it happen or you'd find a new truckin' company."

I shrugged. "I've never asked 'em to change before."

He started checking the dirt bikes like I wasn't even there. "You never had so much to lose before either." Then like he hadn't just said something profound, he added, "Might wanna go tell Ma you're bringin' the whole muster in a week early. I didn't tell her. I wasn't *that* game." I smiled and sighed and headed for the house when he called out, "Might wanna offer her some help too. If you know what's good for you."

I laughed, because it was true, and when I walked into the kitchen, Ma was just sitting down with a cup of tea and a sandwich. I cringed. "Hey," I said, taking a seat next to her.

She eyed me dubiously. "What have you done?"

I cleared my throat. "Well, I might have brought the muster forward."

She didn't blink. "How soon forward?"

It always scared me when she spoke quietly like that. "Um, maybe like a whole week?"

"Charles Sutton..." Her stare was like steel. "I'm not ready."

I cringed again. "We leave tomorrow."

I'm pretty sure she was trying to bore holes into my head with superman-burning-ray-vision or something. This was why George was bein' busy in the shed.

"Um, I will help, so whatever you need me to do..."

"I need you to get out of my kitchen, that's what I need," she said quietly, calmly. Scarily. "I think I'll be bit busy tonight, cooking a week's worth of food, don't you?"

I nodded. "I said I'll help. How about I start making a list or something?"

She took a deep breath, pursed her lips and seemed to calm down a bit. "You will help, alright. You can go get Nara for me—she's more helpful than you—and then you can sit out on the veranda and peel a bucket of potatoes."

I made a face. "I'm better at lists."

She raised her say-one-more-word-Charlie-and-so-God-help-me eyebrow.

I stood up. "Right, then. Potatoes, it is." I went and

found Nara, and then, because I was bringing the muster forward—only to help Travis, the absolute love of my life, so he didn't get booted out of the country, and I would do anything to help, because I think it would kill me if he left—I sat on the back veranda and peeled a fucking ton of potatoes.

It was around three in the afternoon when the said love of my life walked up to the house with Ernie. They all just kinda stood there awkwardly, not knowing what to say, and Travis was grinning at me. I was sitting with one tub of water in between my feet for the clean potatoes and a still half-full bucket of dirty potatoes to my side. I also happened to be wearing bright yellow washing up gloves. I glared at him, and his grin got even wider. "Anyone laughs," I warned, "and they're fired."

So of course, Travis fucking laughed. "Nice gloves."

"The water is freezing!" I said, because that explained the gloves. Well, it did to me. "And I have twenty kilos of potatoes to peel, and I swear to God, you lot better enjoy every last one of them."

Travis was still chuckling, and Ernie kind of didn't know where to look. Apparently he wasn't used to me ranting like Travis was. Travis, on the other hand, seemed to think it was funny. I'll admit, it was good to see him laugh, but I threw a potato at him anyway, which he caught like it was some baseball or something.

Ernie cleared his throat. "Um, we're done with the southern paddock," he said. "Thought if we all got in and did it, we'd get it done quicker. The others have started on the western side now, but I wondered if you needed anything else done."

I smiled at him. Ernie had been on my staff for years, one of those quiet achievers who just got in and got his work done with minimal fuss. And it was great to know he could step up and be in charge if needed.

"Bikes are serviced, George's checked the fuel and oil—"

"He was putting crates into piles when we walked up just now," Travis added.

"So all that gear is ready, then," I said. "We'll still need to pack bags of kibble for the dogs and then fill all the water tubs. All the horse gear, the spare saddles, the spare swags and all that. We should bring the horses in tonight too," I told them.

Travis gave a nod. "I'll go," he said. "Texas is just by the fence. It'll only take me a minute to saddle him. I can bring the others in before dark." He didn't wait for approval of any kind, he just turned on his heel and walked away.

Ernie waited until Travis was out of earshot. "He's a goer," he said, kind of smiling and talking to the ground. Then he looked at me, still nervous but determined to say something anyway. "He's a hard worker, and I'll be sorry to see him go. I mean, if he has to go, that is. If they make him go." He swallowed hard, looking a dozen shades of awkward. "Guess what I'm just tryin' to say is that none of us want him to go. If we have to work longer hours so he can get done what he needs to get done so he can stick around, then we ain't got no problem with that."

Jesus. That was the longest, most personal thing I'd ever heard out of Ernie's mouth. I don't know who was more shocked, me or him. But I was moved by his words and ever so grateful. "Thank you," I said. "I really appreciate you sayin' that."

———

"YOU KNOW I'm kinda glad you brought the muster forward a week," Travis said. The room was dark and cool, and we were all intertwined in bed keeping each other warm. His head was in the crook of my neck, his thigh over mine, and my arms wrapped tight around him.

"Why's that?"

"I mean, I'm really looking forward to spending a week out riding," he explained, "but I think a week around here twiddling our thumbs and waiting would have driven me insane. At least this way, we're busy all this week with no time to think about that meeting and then you have me doing that stupid speech, which I should make you write, by the way." He sighed. "I dunno. It's just good to be busy, that's all."

I ran my hands over his back. "Busy is good. But don't get too excited about sleeping out this week. It'll be freezing."

"I have you to keep me warm."

I snorted. "It's not like we can share a swag with the others just a few feet away."

"You'll find a way to make it happen," he said simply. "If I'm counting down days, I'm not spending one night away from you."

"You're not counting down days," I replied.

He leaned up on his arm. I could make out the concerned look on his face even in the darkened room. "Can you at least act a little worried that I might be going?"

I pushed his hair off his forehead. "No," I said softly. "I can't even bring myself to think it."

He frowned, sadness etched in every line. He shook his head and put his face back into the crook of my neck. "Yeah, I know" was all he said.

I tightened my hold on him once more and fell asleep trying not to think of anything else but him.

When I woke up, I rolled over so I could snuggle into him, only to be met by something that distinctly wasn't Travis. I opened my eyes slowly, and right in front of my face were two big ears and bright brown, wide-awake eyes. I leaned up and gave Travis my one-eyed half-asleep glare.

"She didn't want to go back to sleep, and I was cold," he mumbled.

"So she's in bed with us?"

"Yep."

"Well, put her on your side."

"Aw, she's not that bad."

"No, I want to cuddle you, not her."

"Oh."

He gently picked her up, pouch and all, and put him on the other side of him. I quickly took her place. I wrapped my arm around him, he snuggled his back against me and Matilda only fussed a little. "Too bad," I told her.

Travis pulled the cover over her so she'd think it was a big pouch or something, and the three of us lay in bed until we couldn't put the day off a minute more.

———

THE PLAN WAS—ACTUALLY it was Travis's idea, but it was a good one—that three horses, two bikes and the old Land Rover would go north. I would take the chopper and head off the far north cattle and close the gates that would otherwise lead them south, because we needed them to head east first. George would finish the holding yards at the homestead, and Nara would stay at the house and help Ma and look after Matilda.

All we needed was to get everything across Arthur Creek before it flooded, and then at the end of the day, George would fly me over the creek to join up with the rest of the droving party.

I'd been thinking about how he said I'd find a way for us to be alone when we were mustering, but I also couldn't help but think of what Ernie said either. As much as I wanted alone time with him, he needed to spend some time with his friends as well. If the worst-case scenario were to come true, if he were to leave, they'd miss him too.

So the first night when we were setting up camp, I put our swags a few yards apart, off to one side, but still kinda near the others. He gave me a questioning look, so I told him, "We'll spear off from them tomorrow so you have tonight with them."

I think he got the message.

We made a campfire, heated fresh stew and damper, and we all laughed as Bacon told us stories from when he went barramundi fishing up the Top End and of what wankers the crocodile cowboys were. Travis laughed until he was holdin' onto his sides like they hurt at Bacon's impersonations, which were somewhere a cross between Steve Irwin, Crocodile Dundee and Gordon Ramsay. I didn't find the stories as funny as Travis did, but it sure was good to hear him laugh like that.

It wasn't too long until it was too damn cold to stay out of our swags, and when were all lying down and quiet, Travis did that just-lying-there-starin'-at-me thing that made my heart go beat itself all out of rhythm.

He mouthed the words, "Thank you."

I replied, just as silently, "You're welcome."

Then I watched him for as long as my eyes would let me.

I WAS UP BEFORE EVERYONE, had the fire going again and the smell of eggs and bacon woke everyone up. I boiled water for hot tea, but made sure I had enough granulated coffee for Travis to survive for a few days without his new coffee machine.

As early and as cold as it was, everyone was still excited about the coming days. One thing was for certain, I wasn't the only one who loved bein' out in the middle of nowhere. It made me smile, even more grateful for these people who stood by me, who belonged out here as much as I did, Travis included.

I wished the immigration department could see him out here. It'd all make sense to them if they could just see how he gelled with this place, with its people.

I was starting to think he needed to be here, a part of this red dirt landscape, as much as I did.

He saddled Texas and Shelby and burdened Billy's horse with our gear while I packed our supplies and helped load everything back into the Land Rover. The plan was Travis and I would go on horseback on the quickest, most direct route north, while everyone else—on bikes and in the Rover—would sweep west, bringing in any stragglers, and we'd meet at the top northern paddock.

We'd cut the water in the tops last month so the herd would come down on their own. There was always some who needed persuading, which is where the helicopter came in handy. But by day three we should be ready to start heading 'em home. With roughly two thousand head of cattle, the trip down east of the ridge line to avoid any swollen waterways would take an expected four days.

It'd be four days of hard work, stress and bone-tired

sleepin' on frozen ground, but there was a familiar buzz of excitement as we got ready to go.

But what I couldn't wait for, what had me smiling and itching to ride out, was I had two days—two uninterrupted, just-us days—in the desert with Travis.

I had to bite my smile as the others drove out. But as Travis and I rode north, side by side, it was Travis who laughed.

"When I said you'd find a way for us to have some alone time out here, I wasn't thinkin' two days," he said, shaking his head at me.

"You could have gone with the others if you wanted," I told him, knowin' damn well he didn't want to.

He snorted. "Not likely." He took a deep breath of the cold morning air and sat higher in his saddle. "This is what's it's about, right here. Open desert, flat to the horizon, blue sky, red dirt and you."

I grinned at him. "I was just thinkin' the same thing."

He smiled and looked out over the desert that surrounded us, and he sighed a sound that was as close to content as could be.

"I never understood people's fascination with the ocean," he mused. "I get that there's a power and beauty to it, I guess. But it's nothing like this." He smiled as he spoke. "I mean, look at it. There's a peacefulness to this place, and no doubt it's as dangerous as it is beautiful. The colours change, the air changes, everything in the desert changes every hour of every day, but yet it somehow stays the same." He sighed again. "Does that even make sense?"

He'd just described what I'd failed to put into words for years. "Perfect sense."

"I guess I'm preaching to the choir telling that to you," he said, shaking his head.

"Are you kidding? Not many people understand..." I tried again. "Not many people see it the way I do."

Trav smiled at that. "You finally starting to believe that I like being out here as much as you do and that I'm not just saying it to make you happy?"

I rolled my eyes. "Maybe."

Shame it's too late, I thought.

Shame you have to leave.

"Just in time for me to go, huh?" he asked, no doubt seeing the change on my face.

"I don't believe that," I told him.

"Don't or won't?"

I didn't answer him. He knew the answer. He just wanted me to say it aloud. So instead I said, "For the next two days, we don't talk about it, okay? For the next two days, it's just us, a million miles from anybody and anything, with not a worry in the world, okay?"

He seemed to consider it a while before giving me a smile. "Okay."

"Good. Now tell me," I said, changing subjects completely, "if you could have any superpower, what would it be?"

"What?"

"It's the what-if game. Superpowers. Pick one and only one."

"You didn't get out much as a kid, did you?"

"Not at all, so shut up." I ignored him laughing at me. "Okay then, if you could have one luxury item out here, what would it be?"

He was just about to say something, but then narrowed his eyes at me. "Just 'cause I'm saying it, doesn't mean I actually want you to buy it, okay?"

I snorted out a laugh. "Depends on what it is."

"A pizza oven."

"A what?"

"You know, those big stone furnace-lookin' things. We could cook pizzas any time we wanted."

"You miss pizza?"

"Well, it's not like we can just dial Domino's out here."

"True," I agreed, then wondered how I could get one delivered. The oven, not the pizza.

He rolled his eyes. "No, no, no. I said you can't buy one just because I said I want one. We're just playing a game!" He glared at me for a while, then sighed, resigned. "I know that look," he said. "You're totally figurin' out how to get one."

I laughed and totally lied. "No, I'm not."

"I'm not playing this game with you," he said. But he couldn't help himself, because for the next few hours, we played what-if question and answers about everything ranging from politics and ending world hunger to stunt doubles in movies and spaghetti westerns.

True to our word, we never mentioned him leaving. Even though the whole leaving-and-breaking-our-hearts topic was like its very own presence riding along with us, we just never talked of it.

Finding a sheltered place to camp isn't exactly easy on the very flat, very open Outback desert. But as the sun began to get lower, we found a cluster of shrubs that would at least provide a windbreak for the horses. We tethered them to the branches, fed and watered them and went about setting up camp.

I started a small fire while Travis laid out our swags. I was busy getting the brush, kindling, flame and oxygen ratios right and hadn't really been paying much attention. But when I looked behind me, not only had he zipped our sleeping bags together to make one bigger one, he'd put our two swags together, opened them both up, had the covers overlapping and had effectively made us a double bed.

He grinned proudly. "This is gonna be so much fun."

I looked down at our bed. "Did you learn how to do that in Scouts?"

"Summer camp."

"You made double beds with other boys at summer camp?"

"I was joking, Charlie." Then after a second, he laughed and started to riffle through our supplies for dinner.

"What's so funny?"

"Oh, I was thinking," he said, seemingly pleased with himself, "that I'm pretty sure Scouts didn't give out the badges I'll earn tonight."

"For making two swags into one bed?"

He looked at me like I'd missed the obvious. "For what I'll do in that bed tonight."

Oh. I laughed at that. "Badges, huh?"

"Yep, you could sew them onto your hat," he said, looking up at my Akubra. "It might hold it together a bit longer."

"Hey, don't knock the hat."

He walked over to me and pulled the hat off my head. Then he grabbed my chin and lifted my face, planting a kiss on my lips. It was a brief kiss, because he started to smile. "Now hurry up with the fire. I'm hungry."

So I made a fresh damper in the coals of the barely started fire and heated some stew. I radioed in to the other camp, who were settled in and eating dinner, and then I radioed the homestead. When George had me convinced everything was fine, Travis stoked up the fire, stripped out of his coat, boots and jeans and got into the swag.

"You'll get cold without wearing something," I warned him.

"Body heat's the best kind," he said. Then he patted the thin mattress. "Hurry up."

I sat down on the canvas bed and took off my boots and jeans as quick as I could. It was gonna be a cold night, and I knew we'd be waking up covered in frost in the morning. I covered our coats and boots the best I could, then grabbed Travis's jeans from the crumpled mess in the dirt where he'd left 'em and shoved both our jeans down into the swag with us.

"What are you doing?" he asked.

"So they're warm when we get into 'em in the morning," I told him, finally settling down in our bed for the night. I was shivering a bit and turned to face him, to put my arm around him, and Travis didn't hesitate. He was rubbing his hands all over my thighs, the friction warming my skin.

"It's cold," I said, stating the obvious.

"You need to warm us up," he said, pulling me across and on top of him. We shuffled a bit in our joined-together sleeping bag until I was fully on top of him, between his legs, and he had his arms around me. He ran his hands down my back, pulling our shirts up so our bare chests touched. Then his hands were under my briefs, pushing them down over my hips and gave my arse a squeeze. "I'm getting warmer already."

"Your hands are cold," I said, my voice squeaking.

So he rubbed them all over, hard and fast, the friction warming us both. "Better?"

"No," I said, trying to pull his briefs down to free his hard on. I needed to feel him, skin on skin.

He laughed as he lifted his arse and we slid the cotton

down the best we could. As soon as my cock touched his, hard against hard, he moaned. "Oh, shit."

Resting on my elbows, I hooked my hands under his arms and shoulders and kissed him. The kiss was slow at first, but then it got a little deeper and then it got a lot more. It wasn't long until our lips were swollen and our breaths were heavy, and I still wasn't close enough, deep enough.

He held onto me so tight, and his legs were hooked around my thighs. We were grinding against each other, rubbing and thrusting, and then his breathing got all ragged and his fingers dug into my skin. He pulled my hips against his, pushed his head back, and his eyes rolled closed as he came.

He spilled hot between us, his whole body writhed and shuddered, but he never let go of me. He snaked his hand around my neck, pulling me in for a kiss, and that was all it took: the sight of him by the light of the fire, his touch, his taste, his smell.

I slid my hand between us and gripped myself as my orgasm erupted through me.

I collapsed on top of him, out of my mind and out of breath. "Jesus."

He chuckled, a throaty sound in my ear, his breath warm on my neck. He kissed the side of my head. "Did you survive?"

I could barely form words. "Not sure yet."

His chest vibrated underneath me as he laughed. "We're a mess," he murmured, kissing the side of my head again. "Roll over." He pushed me off. He didn't let me go too far, though. He reached over to his carryall and pulled out something. It was his shaving bag, though there were no razors or shaving cream in it. He handed me a bottle of lube to hold, then pulled out the soft wipes we'd bought the other weekend. They were wet, which was great, but they were also fucking cold. He wiped us both clean. "All better."

I looked at the lube. "You sure are prepared. You know, when I said pack for anything, I was talking about the weather."

He laughed, threw the discarded wipes into the fire, took the lube, zipped up the shaving bag and grinned at me. He put his head in the crook of my arm, pulled up the sleeping bag and snuggled in. He was quiet for a moment, but then he sighed. "I'll never get over how the sky looks out here. Look at the stars. I think we can see every single one of them."

I tightened my arm around him a bit and kissed his temple. "It's pretty amazing, isn't it?"

He made a contented sound and hooked his arm and leg over me.

"You warm enough?" I asked.

He took a second to answer, and when he spoke, it sounded sleepy. "I ain't never felt better."

———

THE MORNING WAS A DIFFERENT STORY. It wasn't just cold. It was freezing. Well, in our swag we were as warm as toast, but the getting out wasn't anywhere near as pleasant.

We slid on our jeans, still in our sleeping bags. "I'll never think throwin' our clothes into bed with us is stupid again," Travis said.

"Stay here," I said. Then as quick as I could, I climbed out of the swag. I shook out my boots, in case any little eight-legged buggers thought they'd found a warm spot for the night, and pulled them on. Then I shook out my coat and slipped it on. I think every cell in my body was shaking as I got the fire going again. It didn't take much convincing —a good supply of kindling and a dash of diesel was all it took.

I had water boiling and Travis's coat near the fire warming up in no time. Travis stopped laughing at my fire-lighting skills when I handed him a cup of hot coffee while he was still cocooned in the sleeping bag.

He didn't say any actual words, but his smile and his eyes said something that looked a lot like "you're so awesome and I love you."

To which I answered, "I love you too." I didn't really mean to say those words out loud.

He was just about to sip his coffee. "Huh?"

I was gonna say something like *shut up and drink your coffee*, but something stopped me. I'd told him before that I loved him—it made my chest all tight and flood with butter-flies, but I said it. I figured if there was ever a time when I *should* tell him again, it was now. "I said, I love you," I mumbled before I lost my nerve. Then I corrected myself. "Too. I said, I love you *too*. Sometimes the say-it-in-my-head voice comes out my mouth."

He grinned one of those heart-stopping, steal-my-breath kind of smiles, looking all kinds of perfect with his sleep-messed hair. Before he could say something smart, or equally as sappy, I added, "Shut up and drink your coffee."

He laughed and sipped his coffee. I made myself a cup of tea and put the pan on the fire. While the bacon started to cook, I picked up Travis's now-warm coat and held it out for him.

Still smiling and without putting his coffee down, he peeled himself out of the sleeping bag and stood up. I was expecting him just to take the coat, but no, I had to help him into it. "Oh my God, it's so warm," he said. "That's the most romantic thing you've ever done."

I blushed, of course, and looked down at where his boots were. "If you think I'm helping you into those, you're dreaming."

He just smiled and held out his coffee, which I stupidly took. He pulled his boots on and laughed when he took back his coffee. I grumbled at him and went back to the fire, turning the bacon and sipping my tea. He came up behind me, pulled down my coat and pressed his lips to the back of my neck. He whispered, "I love you too, Charlie."

My breath caught and my heart felt like it was about to hammer right out of my chest. He turned me around and kissed me softly, on the lips and the cheek, before he hugged me. And just when I thought he was about to say something sweet, he said, "Please don't burn my bacon."

And the day kind of only got better as it went on. He teased me about being the most unromantic romantic ever while we ate breakfast, and then we packed up camp and kept heading north.

The morning's topic of conversation was the stupid assessment I was supposed to be doing, which now was the very last thing on my mind. I had much more important things to worry about first, but if I told Travis it didn't matter if I finished the stupid degree now that he could be leaving, then he'd know I had my doubts about him staying.

And I couldn't have him thinking I had doubts.

It was stupid, I know. I should have talked about it, I should have told him I was scared they'd make him leave, but I just couldn't. I couldn't tell him how petrified I was, because that would make it real.

It made much more sense, in my backward thinkin' brain, that I ignore it or pretend it was no big deal. I wanted him to believe he was staying, and I wanted him to never think for one second that I doubted him.

So that's exactly what I did.

We talked about agronomy and the science of soil and how he had to write a speech on something to give the old farts at that meeting. "Do you really think it will make any difference?" he asked.

"Sure," I said, going for nonchalant. "Well, it can't hurt."

"I thought he wanted you to give a speech or something."

"He did," I admitted. "But it makes more sense for the lady you're having that meeting with to think it's you."

"Surely I'm not the only agronomist out here."

"Well, probably not. But you're the only one I want out here, so that should be reason enough."

He kind of got a bit quiet after that, so I suggested we stop for lunch and give the horses a break. We ate cold beef sandwiches, and instead of eating my apple, I cut it up and gave it to the horses.

Travis shook his head. "And people think you're a tough boss."

I snorted. "Don't go tellin' anyone anything."

He just shook his head at me, and we sat down on a bit of a rise and watched the sun change the colours of the land. I promised him that, when this whole thing had blown over and we had some time, I'd take him to any part of the country he wanted to go. He'd travelled halfway around the world and been here not quite seven months, yet hadn't seen much more than the Outback. "We could go fly fishing for trout in Tasmania or deep-sea fishing off the Barrier Reef. Or barramundi fishin' up the top end."

"I'm starting to think you wanna go fishing."

I ignored his sarcasm. "I could take you to Kakadu or Sydney. Apparently Melbourne is great—lots of great restaurants, or so I've heard. I've never been, so I wouldn't really know."

"Uluru," he said.

"Uluru?" I repeated. "Seriously? I offer to take you *anywhere*, and you pick something that's just down the road?"

He rolled his eyes. "A six-hour drive is hardly *just down the road*."

"Well, it's more like nine hours, but really? Of all the places and you pick somewhere else in the desert?"

"I want to see it."

I shrugged. "Fair enough."

"Though Kakadu sounds pretty cool."

"Yeah, but I must warn you," I told him seriously. "The dirt up there ain't red."

He gasped dramatically. "Oh, the horror."

"Yep. It's a travesty."

He smiled, looking out across the horizon. It was mostly red with patches of green saltbush and a scatter of trees. The sky was a pale winter blue and the air was cold. The sun felt good on my face.

He took it all in, like he was storin' it to memory, like he didn't ever want to forget. What he was thinking I didn't dare ask. He had a leavin' kind of sadness written all over his face.

I stood up quickly, wanting to put some distance between me and that train of thought. "Come on, we better keep moving."

We were about three-quarters to our rendezvous point when we started to see the first signs of cattle, which meant one of the bores wasn't too far away. Travis gave Texas a nudge and headed left, canterin' off with a grin. I hung back and let him have his fun, kinda just enjoying watchin' him ride, to be honest, and waited for him to bring about twenty head of cattle back on his own.

By the time we were at the southern end of the northern paddock, we had close to a hundred herded into where the fence corners met. Not long after that, Travis pointed west. "What the hell is that?"

I looked out to where he was pointing and grinned. It looked like a hazy river of white and red, moving in from the west. "It's the others."

Travis started to smile. "Jesus. It looks like something out of the movie *The Mummy*. You ever seen that? Where the dust storms in the desert move in shapes," he said. "It looks just like that. Well, not as big and there's no skulls in it."

"Huh?"

He snorted out a laugh. "Never mind." Then he nodded pointedly to the herd moving in. "How far out are they?"

I gauged the distance with a shrug. "About four k's."

"How many head is that?"

"Looks like about a thousand."

He grinned and sat up higher in the saddle. "Wow."

He was obviously itchin' to go. "You wanna go meet 'em?"

"Can I?"

I rolled my eyes at him. "I'm pretty sure I can manage this mob here on my own. They're not going anywhere." Then I told him, "Listen to Billy. He knows what to do."

I watched him ride off, and then as they got closer, I watched my team spread out in a line about a hundred metres adjacent to the fence and watched as the cattle walked 'emselves in. Just like a well-oiled machine.

We set up camp before nightfall. I laid our swags out, kind of near each other but separate, of course, and Travis gave me a quick snarly-pout when he realised we weren't having a joined bed. I didn't mind that Bacon and Trudy had their beds closer together, but it was just something I wasn't comfortable in doin' in front of the others. It wasn't a gay thing. It was a boss thing.

We put out salt blocks for the cattle, I spread the working dogs out on the boundary, and the mob was settled in for the night.

By the time dinner was cooking, it was pitch-black and biting cold. We sat around the fire and the others talked of their two days bringing in 'em from the west. Everyone was kind of huddled in a bit, so sitting with mine and Travis's legs touching didn't seem so weird.

It was the closest I think I'd ever been to him in front of the others. We'd never touched or done anything remotely couple-ish in their company. I just couldn't do it. It was a private/professional line-crossin' that just didn't seem too proper in my mind. They knew we were together. We didn't need to advertise it.

But jeez, it sure was nice.

When we finally called it a day, my bed was cold, my sleep was restless, and even though he was just a few feet from me, it seemed a mile too far.

───────

WE HAD a wakeup call from George. And by wakeup call, I meant a helicopter flyover. He kept left so as not to disturb the mob of cattle too much, but it was enough to get us all up and moving.

He put the chopper down in a clearing and walked the

few hundred metres back, which I was pretty sure was enough distance to give someone enough time to make him a cup of tea.

He had fresh supplies of stew, breads, milk and fruit, enough to last us two days. He smiled at me in particular. "The cook"—meaning his wife—"said she weren't so mad at ya anymore. She made some biscuits, and there's even scones and jam."

We carried the crates of fresh food from the chopper to the Rover. He also had more water, dog food and another crate of chaff for the horses. He traded the full crates for our empty ones, and with a nod of his head and tip of his hat, he took the chopper up and took her north.

"We've got about two hours," I told everyone.

"Before what?" Travis asked.

"Before George brings the rest of the mob in from the north. We'll head this lot through the eastern gate here, and by the time we cross the ridge, he'll have the others coming down."

It was all hands on deck now. Trudy, Bacon and Ernie took the bikes, Billy was quick to claim his horse back, I saddled up Shelby, leaving Texas to be the supply horse and Travis to drive the Rover.

"I hate driving," he moaned.

"Oh, quit your whining," I said with a smile. I knew he hated driving. "You need the practice."

"You sit on the wrong side of the damn car," he bitched. We'd had this discussion a few times, and he had no qualms in telling people what he thought of right-hand-drivin' cars.

"There's no roads out here," I said, getting up on Shelby. "So you don't have to worry about driving on the wrong side of the road."

"Changin' gears with my left hand is stupid."

I sighed, the longest out-of-patience-if-you-weren't-so-cute-I'd-kick-your-arse kind of sigh, and got down off Shelby. "Fine. I'll drive." I walked over to the ute, then pointed at Shelby. "You look after her. If you fall off and bust your knee again, you're walkin' home regardless."

He grinned, because he fucking won, and when he walked over to my horse, she near nudged him off his feet. "See?" I called out from the Rover. "She's not happy about it either."

Travis swung himself up into my saddle and gave Shelby a pat on the neck. "She loves me."

I was too busy glarin' at Travis, and kind of forgot the others were still there. They found something funny, all trying not to smile—except for Billy, who just grinned without shame. I watched as Trudy, Bacon and Ernie rode the bikes north to round up the herd George was gathering, and without so much as a look back at a still-grinnin' Billy or a smug, not-even-mildly-embarrassed Travis, I threw the old ute into gear and drove out.

I grumbled to myself for a while, but as we moved the herd through the eastern gates, we got busy musterin' and the hours just slipped on by. I heard the chopper coming before I saw it, and then heard Bacon, Trudy and Ernie on the bikes, and the two mobs merged into one.

Everyone crowed their excitement as we headed toward home and I couldn't help but laugh at how we all felt that buzz. There weren't anything like it on the planet, I didn't reckon. I could still make out Travis's smile through the haze of dust, and he had Shelby turnin' on a dime for cattle that tried to stray from the herd. It was like watching poetry, watching him on my horse. I could have watched him all damn day.

And for the next three days, we crawled homewards.

The nights were cold, and as much as I wanted to pull our swags together, I didn't. We did that just-layin'-and-starin'-at-each other thing until we fell asleep every night, and as much as I wanted to get home, shower and shave, sleep in our bed with him in my arms all night, I also didn't want this muster to end.

Because once we got home, reality would kick in. We had to leave the day after the transport trucks took our herd to sale, for that meeting with the visa lady. We were literally down to days. And the closer we got to home, the closer we got to maybe having to say goodbye, and that was something I just couldn't even bear to think about.

I think Travis was even worse than me.

On the third and final evening of the muster, we'd settled the herd and were about to start setting up camp, when Travis called me over. He'd been a bit quiet all day, but now he looked worried, even a little scared. "I can't do this," he said quietly.

I was immediately concerned. Travis couldn't not do anything. "Can't do what?"

"I thought I could just lay down next to you one more night in separate swags, but I can't," he whispered. "I need to be with you."

I'd never seen him like this. "Trav, are you okay?"

He shook his head. "No. I'm leaving, Charlie. I know you don't seem to think so, but there's a very good chance this is it for us, and I can't stand—"

"Hey," I said, trying to soothe him a little. He didn't want me to tell him he wasn't leaving; he didn't want words at all. "Go get Texas. Head south to the front of the herd."

I left him standin' there and headed straight for Billy. He was my second-in-charge. "Billy, Travis is..." *Travis is what? Not feeling well? Freaking out?* I didn't really know, so I didn't say. "Me and him are gonna set up camp at the front of the herd tonight. You okay to man this lot here tonight?"

Billy nodded quickly. "Sure thing, Mr Sutton." He looked over my shoulder. I didn't have to turn around to know who he was looking at. "Is he okay? He ain't done much talkin' all day."

So I wasn't the only one to notice. I gave Billy a nod and tried to smile. "He's okay." I told him I'd radio in later, loaded our gear onto Shelby, and ignoring the others who were silently watching me, I walked beside my horse and followed Travis.

By the time I'd caught up to him, he had a fire started. He stood up. "I'm sorry."

I was quick to touch his face. "Don't apologise."

He wrapped his arms around me and buried his face into my neck, and for the longest time he didn't move. It was like he had three days' worth of hugging to catch up on, or maybe he was trying to compensate for the next-however-long in case he did actually have to leave.

Maybe it was a bit of both.

Either way, I didn't mind. I think I held on just as tight.

Eventually, I pulled his face up and kissed him softly. "You okay?"

"Better" was all he said.

I'd never seen him look so sad. "You hungry?"

He shook his head, and whispered, "No."

"Trav, tell me, what can I do?"

He gave me a sad smile. "Just being here with you is good. I feel like I can breathe now. Don't get me wrong, I have loved being out here with you, and rounding up cattle is the most fun ever. But..."

I finished for him. "But you're counting down days in your head, and you don't want to waste one more minute?"

He nodded quickly, and his eyes shone with tears. "I knew you'd understand." He shrugged one shoulder. "I didn't mean to make a big deal of it. The others are probably wondering what's up."

"Don't worry about them. Anyway, I care more about you bein' okay than what they're thinkin' right now," I told him. "Plus, they'd just be worried about you, that's all. You're their friend, Trav. They think of you as one of them." He smiled, more genuinely this time, so I kissed him again, soft and sweet. "Feel better?"

He nodded and smiled and went back to hugging me, and he never quit havin' some part of him touching me for the rest of the night. He made our swag into a double bed again, and I made him eat some food. When the horses were fed, I radioed to the other camp and then to the homestead to let George know we were separate from the others, stoked up the fire and got into bed. We'd only taken off our coats and boots; it was just too damn cold to undress any more.

From the look in his eyes, I knew what Travis wanted before he'd even said the words, before he'd grabbed his shaving bag and handed me the bottle of lube. "Charlie," he started.

"Let me guess," I said. "You'll die if I'm not inside you in the next five minutes."

"The most excruciating of deaths," he said, making me laugh. Then squirming in the sleeping bag until he was on his front, he lifted his hips and pulled his jeans and briefs down over his arse. "Please, just do it."

"Oh God, Travis."

"Charlie." He sounded desperate.

I poured a trail of lube down over his arse, making him moan and squirm. I warmed it with my fingers, pushing in and out of him, prepping him. He slowly rocked back on my fingers and he moaned. "Charlie."

I undid the fly of my jeans, and the sound alone made him breathe quicker. As I slid above him, he spread his thighs as much as the sleeping bag would allow.

I pressed myself against his hole. "I'm not gonna last," I told him. "I'm too turned on."

He made a laugh-groan sound into the mattress and raised his arse. "Charlie," he snapped at me. "Goddammit. Just fucking do it already."

Going by feel alone, I lined myself up, nipped my teeth into his shoulder and sunk my cock into his arse.

He groaned like I'd never heard him before. His whole body flexed and jerked underneath me—he came as soon as I entered him. I followed not long after, and we lay still and unmoving, trying to catch our breaths.

I rolled off him, and he turned quickly to burrow himself into my neck. I wrapped him up tight in my arms until my heart stopped its hammerin' in my chest. "I should get you cleaned up," I murmured into his ear.

"Mm mm." He shook his head. "Again," he said. I snorted out a laugh, thinking he was joking, but he was serious. "You can go slower this time."

"Trav, I don't want to hurt you," I said, planting a kiss on the side of his head.

This time he snorted. "Believe me, that's not hurting." Then he slid his hand around my spent cock, and with teeth-scraping kisses over my neck and the slowest tongue-tastin' kisses in my mouth, he brought me back to life.

He somehow got his jeans and undies all the way off by just using his feet, and when I tried to do the same, he stopped me. "Leave yours on," he whispered gruffly. "I like 'em around your thighs." This time he was on his back. He pulled me over him, and when I was right where he wanted me, he spread his legs and lifted his knees up to my sides.

He was still ready from last time, welcoming and wanting, slick with cum and lube. I breached him slowly, kissing him as I sunk as deep as I could go. He held me there, right fucking there, gasping for air around our kiss. All I could feel was the pulse of our heartbeats where we joined, throbbing and pounding through every fibre in my body.

We rocked back and forth, always kissing. And on the cold, cold ground by the flickering warmth of the fire, we made love. The way he held me, the way he looked at me, it was the closest to heaven I'd ever get without dyin'.

————

TRAVIS WAS HAPPIER in the morning. Still not his usual jokin', laughin' self, but he seemed not so out of sorts at least. When we started to move the herd homeward, he rode off with Ernie to round up some steers that tried to make a run for it, and he came back grinning.

I figured the best thing for us both to do was keep busy. So as soon as we'd funnelled the cattle into their holding yards, I told the others to get everything unpacked while I started work on separatin' the bulls from the steers and the weaners from the heifers.

We only stopped for lunch because Ma had that Charlie-Sutton-you'll-do-as-you're-told tone to her voice, and by the time the sun was going down, we'd made a good start on tomorrow's work.

With enough time to shower, shave and feel halfway human, we ate the nicest roast meat dinner Ma ever put up and everyone called it a day. Travis fed Matilda, and too impatient for her to go back to sleep on her own, I told him to bring her along with us. The three of us got into bed, and too bone-tired and body-sore after too many nights on the hard, cold ground, we snuggled in and slept like the dead.

If I was countin' down days, it wasn't strictly a bad way to end one.

CHAPTER THIRTEEN

WHERE I CAN'T KEEP MY DAMN MOUTH SHUT. TWICE.

THE NEXT TWO DAYS, we sorted cattle. We tagged and treated the ones we were keepin' and waited for the three big old road trains to take the rest to sale. It was always a mix of excitement and relief to see 'em go, and as they drove down the driveway in a cloud of dust, musterin' was done for another winter.

Talk at the dinner table was all excited and joking about leaving for their week off. They always had a week after every muster. It was always slow after the cattle had gone, and they all usually headed to the Alice the morning after. Because I'd brought the muster a week forward and screwed up the roster, I told 'em to take this weekend, next week and the weekend after. It was eleven days all up, and they more than deserved it.

Their plan was to head out in the morning and not be back until the following Sunday. Trudy and Bacon were thinkin' of going to the Gold Coast, and Ernie was gonna head to Darwin. Billy said he'd only go as far as the Alice, and Nara wanted stay at home. They were all smiles until

Trudy asked what our plans were. "Well, there's that Beef Farmers meeting this weekend that Charlie and Greg are making me go to," Travis answered. And then he dropped a bombshell. "Then I have that appointment with the immigration lady on Monday to see if I can stay or not."

Everyone kinda went from smilin' to frownin' and the mood took a nosedive. With drovin' all week and then the prospect of a week in town, I guess it made sense they'd forgot.

But it never left my thoughts, and it certainly never left Travis's either.

"We can stay," Trudy said. I'm presuming she spoke for the team because they all gave a nod. "If you need us to," she added. "I'm sure we can take our days off another time."

And the truth be told, as much as I loved my team and as much as I appreciated the gesture of 'em offerin' to stay, I didn't mind too much that they'd be gone this week.

I needed time to decompress, to get my head on straight, and to have some quiet time with Travis. He'd been distracted during the day when we were separating the cattle, and he was clingy at night. He'd always have to be near me, some part of him touching me, and he even did Matilda's night feeds in our bed. I didn't complain. I didn't want him too far gone from me either.

I wanted to spend lazy movie-watchin' days around the house and maybe even a little sleepin' in, and I couldn't do that with them around. I couldn't be curled up on the couch with Travis during the day in case someone walked in.

I gave 'em a smile. "Thanks for the offer. I appreciate it, I really do. But take your week. Enjoy it." I hooked my foot around Travis's under the table. I cleared my throat and tried for a conviction I most certainly did not feel. "This meeting'll be no big deal. We'll go in on Saturday morning for the conference and be home Monday evenin'."

I'm sure they saw through me. But thankin' God for small mercies, none of them called me on it. Travis just kind of looked up from his plate of no-appetite, half-eaten dinner and gave one of those heart-hurting smiles. I wanted to take his hand. Hell, I wanted to hug him right then and there, but I didn't. There was no way I could.

When they'd all gone for the night and the house was quiet, Travis was lying in front of the fire with little Matilda, and Ma sat down on the lounge next to me. "It was nice of you to give everyone that many days off, Charlie," she said. "Very generous."

"It wasn't just for them," I said quietly. When my eyes caught Travis's, Ma understood.

She gave me a smile and a pat on the leg. "Did you want George and me to take off? If you want some alone time, you know you just have to say."

"No, Ma. I don't want you to take off somewhere," I told her. "Unless you want to go. I can book that motel again for you. You can go out for dinner, go dancing."

Ma smiled warmly. "I was going to suggest you and Travis do that. You'll have a few extra days in town with no interruptions."

I shrugged one shoulder and looked at Trav. "It's up to you. What did you wanna do? We could head in tomorrow with the others if you want, or we can just hang out here."

He had his hand held out, and Matilda had her little paws on his arm, tryin' to keep herself steady. "I wanna stay here."

I looked at Ma and smiled. "We'll stay here."

So for the next two days, we removed ourselves from the world around us. We spent the days on Shelby and

Texas in the desert, just us, like we didn't have a worry in the world.

The sun was shining, the sky was a showing-off shade of blue and cloudless but the air was still cold. The desert always looked clean after the rain, everything was fresh and reborn, and I'd be lyin' if I said it didn't make me feel a bit the same.

We rode out both days, just enjoying being together in the vast, unforgiving red desert. I loved being able to ride out on Shelby, and having no destination in particular was my favourite frame of mind. I loved it even more when Travis was with me.

We talked all day. Travis talked of home, and I got to thinkin' that maybe tellin' me stories didn't mean he wanted to go there. It didn't mean he was about to leave me and go home. I think I finally realised he just wanted to share it with me. He was sharing stories of his past, not because he was homesick, but because he wanted me to know the real him.

There wasn't much I could tell him he didn't already know about me; my life's story was in the desert around us. But I was starting to realise I had barely scratched the surface that was Travis. He knew more, he'd done more, he'd seen more than I ever could.

Of a night, we'd curl up in bed, make love and talk some more. He was always near me, forever touching me. And I think what killed me the most was that we'd just reached perfect and now he was going to leave.

I tried to be strong for him, tried to act like I had it all under control, but the truth was, I was falling apart.

The morning we were leaving for Alice Springs, Ma made us a pot of tea, which I didn't drink, preferring to torture myself by sitting around watching the clock announce every minute. When Travis excused himself to go to the bathroom, Ma kicked me under the table.

"What?"

"You're making it worse," she hissed at me. "Even I can feel the nervous energy coming out of you."

"I'm trying to keep a lid on it," I whispered back to her. "I can't help it. I'm nervous as hell."

A short while later, Travis appeared in the door holding a bundled-up Matilda. She had her trademark big ears and eyes poking out the top. He looked at me. "You ready? I can tell you wanna get this over with."

I stood up and looked from Travis to Matilda and back to him. "What are you doing with her?"

"Figured now'd be as good a time as any to take her into town. That guy from the kangaroo rescue shelter said we could take her in anytime."

I shook my head. *No. No, no, no.* "You're coming back, Trav."

He cleared his throat. "You always said she couldn't stay here forever."

"Well, she can't, but she's not going yet," I told him. "And neither are you." I walked over and took her from his arms. I held her up near his face. "Give her a kiss and tell her you'll see her in three days."

Trav looked at me with and-you-wonder-why-I-love-you in his eyes. He leaned in and pressed his lips to Matilda's head. "Be a good girl," he said.

I rolled my eyes and repeated, "And you'll see her in three days."

Travis chuckled and said, "And I'll see you in three days."

"See? That wasn't hard," I said, handing the bloody kangaroo over to Ma.

She wasn't even trying to hide her don't-pretend-you-don't-love-her-too smile. "You boys drive safe, you hear?"

———

WE GOT TO THE HOTEL, and when I suggested going out, Travis said no. He didn't want to go out, not for drinks, not for dinner. He wanted to stay in, take full advantage of the spa bath and order pizza to be delivered.

Like I was ever gonna say no to that.

He was quiet and restless, even after round one of aquatherapy in the spa, and I think it probably pissed him off that I was so dismissive about his visa worries. "I'm telling you, Trav, it'll be an easy fix."

His brow furrowed and he huffed. "What if it's not?"

I figured wearing him out was a good tactic so he didn't have time to get stressed. I pushed him back on the mattress and pinned his hands above his head and kissed him instead of answering. Then I wore him out all over again.

The next morning, after sleepin' in, we went out for a lazy breakfast, had coffee and read the papers. Then to add to my Operation-Distract-Travis, I said, "Come on, let's go shopping."

"For what?"

"Clothes."

"Who for?"

I laughed at the confused look on his face. "For you."

"I don't need any clothes. I wear all yours."

"I know you do," I said, giving him a just-joking stink-eye. "But you need new clothes. Fancy clothes for your meeting. That woman'll take one look at you all dressed up and sexy, and she'll just tick all the boxes."

Travis rolled his eyes so hard I wondered if it hurt.

But he relented, until we walked into the expensive men's clothes store and he saw the price of the shirt I was holding.

"Shut up and try it on," I said, handing over the blue-and-white chequered button-down shirt.

"It's a hundred and twenty dollars," he hissed at me, "for a shirt!"

I sighed and handed him a plain blue one as well. "This one too."

Travis looked at me with "did you not just hear what I said?" written clear on his face.

I shrugged and pretended it was no big deal. "It'll match the colour of your eyes."

Travis blinked and looked like he was about to say something, but he must have decided against it. He took the shirt almost timidly.

Before we could have a complete mushy moment in the clothes store, I held up a t-shirt, batted my eyelashes and in the girliest voice I could do, I said, "And this one. It's almost as pretty as you."

He snatched the shirt from me. "You're such a dickhead."

A saleslady came up to me and asked, "Can I help you, gentlemen?"

Travis said, "Change room for me, sense of humour and some dignity for him."

I laughed at that. The lady smiled politely and led Travis to the change rooms, and when she came back, I said, "He'll need jeans and boots too."

So with no more jokes, we got down to picking out clothes. The lady went straight for the Wranglers, which most stockmen wore, but I suggested a pair of RMs. It's not like I could just tell her it was because I liked the way they hugged his arse and thighs. I was holding up a pair of blue jeans when Travis walked out of the change rooms wearing the blue shirt I'd picked out. I was right about one thing: it matched his eyes perfectly.

Travis knew it too. He grinned and raised one like-what-you-see? eyebrow, and before I swallowed my tongue, I threw the jeans at him. "Try those on."

He protested about the boots—well, he protested about the price of them.

"You can't wear the poxy American ones forever. You need real boots, like mine," I said.

Travis, the saleslady and I all looked at my well-worn, scuffed, dirty and moulded-to-my-feet boots. "Have you *ever* cleaned them?" Travis asked.

I shrugged one shoulder. "Wore 'em in the river once, but I don't think that counts."

Travis ignored me. "And my boots aren't *poxy*. These are adjustin'."

"How long you had 'em for?" I asked. "They should be adjusted by now."

He laughed at me. "Not ad-justing. They're Justin boots."

"Who's Justin."

He took a God-give-me-patience breath and exhaled slowly. "Never mind. I don't need boots."

"You need Aussie boots," I told him. "If you're gonna live here for the next-however-many years, you need real Aussie boots."

He looked at me then with I-won't-be-here-for-years-Charlie-they're-kicking-me-out-next-week sadness in his eyes. I handed him the boots, like me buying 'em would somehow make a difference in whether or not he could stay. "Please."

He took the boots, and whether the saleslady who was still standing next to us thought there was more to us than just friends, I didn't care.

Travis tried the boots on, and I think he let me buy them for him because it made me feel better or something. I don't think he had it in him to argue over stupid boots, or the winter coat I picked out for him after that, or how much the lot cost.

About a grand later, we collected our bags and walked outside. He was back to bein' quiet, and I knew without asking what was weighin' on his mind. I nodded up the street. "This way."

"What's up here?" Travis asked.

"Barber shop."

He raised an eyebrow. "Seriously?"

"Yep. Ma does a pretty decent job at cuttin' hair, but you need a proper cut for Monday." Then, because I figured it was something he might like, I said, "Did you want 'em to wash it too? You know how they do that head-massage thing? Ma says it's the best thing ever."

He stepped in close and eyed me cautiously. "First shopping, then the hairdresser? Exactly how gay are you?"

I spoke low so only he could hear. "You can have the shopping and hairdresser, but on the account of loving dick and arse, I'd say very gay."

Travis burst out laughing, and thankfully, the sullen mood was gone. I don't think it was ever too far from the surface, and maybe he was just as good at hiding as I was, but either way, we had a great afternoon.

Haircuts done and lunch eaten, we went back to the hotel. I suggested a trip to the reptile centre as a touristy thing to do. "I've seen enough desert snakes to last a lifetime, thanks," he said.

"What did you want to do?" I asked. "We've got a few hours before the Beef Farmers Association meeting starts."

Trav looked at the freshly made bed, then looked at me. His eyes were darker and his voice was gruff, and he palmed the front of my jeans. "Sex, sleep, maybe some more sex..." He trailed off as his lips met mine.

His suggestion of how to fill in an afternoon was so good, we almost didn't make the meeting.

————

THE CLUBHOUSE WAS HUGE, bigger than I ever remembered. It was a returned serviceman's club, the place where people spent Friday and Saturday nights drinking and dancing, bands played and community meetings were held. There was a restaurant and bar—something I had every intention of finding first.

"You ever been to one of these meetings before?" Travis asked as we walked in.

"Nope. My old man went to 'em. Said they were important, but I always thought they sounded boring as hell."

We signed in, and the guy at the reception desk told us the function was upstairs. Bein' nervous never crossed my mind, but when we walked into the auditorium and there were about eighty people in there, I near turned around and walked out.

I figured there'd be ten or twelve old-time farmers sitting around talking about the good ol' days and bitching about the cost of fuel. But it wasn't like that at all. The room was full, people were talking and laughing, there were product sponsors and salesmen doing the rounds. The entire room was dressed like an R.M. Williams catalogue vomited in there, and I was thankful Travis made me buy some new shirts too.

Travis was behind me. "You okay?"

"Um, yeah?"

He laughed. "You can't lie for shit," he said, walking toward the bar. "Let's get you a drink."

We didn't get too far. Travis had just ordered two beers when Greg met us at the bar. "Charlie!" he said. He had a smile a mile wide and his hand out. I shook it quickly, glad to see a familiar face. "So glad you could make it."

Then he turned to Travis and shook his hand as well. "Good to see you in a bit better shape than last time I saw ya," he said. "How's the knee?"

"Good as gold," Travis said. "Never did thank you in person for comin' looking for me."

"Don't mention it," Greg said. Travis handed me a beer, Greg looked me up and down, then turned to Travis and grinned. "Jeez, Sutton here scrubs up alright, doesn't he?"

"He sure does," Travis answered.

"Oh, Jesus Christ," I mumbled, taking a swig of my beer and trying not to die of embarrassment.

Greg threw his head back and laughed. "Come on, there's people I want you to meet."

He introduced me to his wife, Jenny, who I hadn't seen since I was a kid. She must have thought the same because the first thing she said was, "Shit, you grew up." She was just as I remembered her, though, light brown hair, blue eyes, sun-worn skin and a no-nonsense mouth. I liked her immediately.

"Jen, this is Travis, the American kid I was tellin' you about," Greg said to his wife. I was wondering just what exactly he'd told her and whether that entailed just how close me and Trav were. But then he said, "The one who spent a night out in the desert with a busted-up knee."

She shook his hand and there was small talk for a while, none of which pertained to gay farmers, for which I was eternally thankful. Whether she knew and didn't say outta bein' polite or if her husband never told her a word of what he saw, I don't know.

Jenny smiled kind of sadly and said, "Charlie, I was very sorry to hear of your father."

Oh. I hadn't even thought of that topic of conversation being raised here tonight. I wasn't even real sure what to say to that. Thanks didn't seem wholly appropriate. So I said, "I'm very grateful for all the help Greg gave me at that time. It wasn't easy."

Greg just smiled and gave a pointed nod to someone behind me. "Well, I hope you're prepared to do the rounds tonight. There's some people who'll be real interested in seein' you here."

Well, that sounded ominous.

And by people who'd be interested in seein' me here, he meant the ten or twelve old-time farmers I'd assumed were here.

Despite the last day of being very much boyfriends, Travis and I were back to playing the single, straight, just-workmates game. Along with Greg, we took our seats at a table of eight older-than-middle-aged, all fourth and fifth generation Territory farmers. I only recognised their names, not the faces. But they sure as hell recognised mine.

They all knew my father and proceeded to spend the better part of an hour reminding me of what a good man he was. Jack Melville, the oldest, most pompous-looking of them, did most of the talking. He spoke about my dad like he was he was his best friend, and for all I knew, he probably was. It struck me as odd, and I was beginning to wonder if we were all talking about the same man. They were recalling a man I simply never knew.

All I could do was smile and grit my teeth and test every ounce of self-control to not say anything. When I started to stab at the label on my beer, Travis seemed to realise I was close to snapping, and he slid his foot around the back of mine under the table.

No one could see it, no one could possibly know. And I don't know if he did it to calm me or to reassure himself, but either way it worked.

Travis helped me say a final goodbye to that ghost six months ago, and I'd been trying to finally let the cold words of my father go. It was a work in progress—it would take longer than six months to get rid of a lifetime of guilt, I knew that, but after so many years, I was finally starting to let it go.

And then I came here and was reminded by everyone I met that I'll never be rid of the ghost of my father. The man that was Charles Sutton Senior, the man who hurt his own son terribly, would forever be etched in my looks, his name, his home.

I still smiled and was polite and friendly, but I could feel the cold stab of disappointing my father every time someone said something like *you're the spittin' image of your dad,* or *your father'd be proud, son* and just how sorry they were to hear of his passing.

"So," Greg said over the table, changing the subject. "Travis here is staying at Sutton Station." He succeeded in turning the attention at the table to Travis. Then Greg recounted for them how the horse Travis was riding got spooked and threw him, and how he spent a night lost out in the summer desert with a busted knee. But in what was one of the smartest things Greg had seen, instead of trying to walk back to the homestead, Travis deliberately headed in the other direction. "A lot of other men would have died trying to go home, but you survived by following a change in soil colour." He shook his head. "I ain't heard nothing like it."

Travis smiled, but I could tell he was a bit embarrassed, and he kind of gave the other men at the table a nod. "I'd seen the eastern ridgeline from the helicopter when we were mustering," he explained. "There's a yellow limestone that runs through it, and after I came off the horse, I could see the red dirt wasn't so red. I remembered Charlie saying that ridge was the only shade for miles and I knew there was water farther up, but my leg was pretty torn up." Then he added, "Plus, I knew Charlie'd come lookin' for me, so I needed to buy myself some time."

There were some wide eyes and disbelieving looks, and Travis just smiled and sipped his beer. But then the questions started about his accent and what in God's name was he doing in the middle of the desert at Sutton Station. He explained his studies in agronomy and soil sciences and how he'd come for one month but knew not long after he'd got here that he'd be staying longer than that.

Of course, he didn't say anything about me being the reason for that, and he never mentioned his visa trouble and the possibility of going home. Instead, Travis just said, "Red dirt, blue sky," as an explanation for staying, and they all kind of nodded like they knew what that meant.

I guessed they did.

I offered to buy the next round of drinks and made my way to the bar. And that wasn't much better. "Young Charlie Sutton?" some guy beside me asked before I could order. He looked more surprised than anything. "Jeez, look at you!"

"Well, I guess that's me, but you'll have to excuse me for not remembering..."

He smiled then and stuck out his hand. "Allan Stilton," he introduced himself. He looked maybe forty-five, which was younger than most here. "Greg told me you might be coming. It's good to see you."

Well, I figured any friend of Greg's was an okay sort of guy. "Nice to meet you."

"Well, you look about as comfortable here as I feel," he said.

I barked out a laugh. "Is it that obvious?"

He smiled, and we ordered our drinks in turn. "I manage Ardale Downs," Allan said. "North of Greg's place."

"Ah." I took a sip. "I'm west of him."

Allan kind of smiled like I'd missed an inside joke. "I think there ain't a person here tonight that doesn't know who you are."

I took a mouthful of beer. "I'm starting to get that impression, yeah." Then I corrected, "Well, my father's reputation and name precedes me."

Allan smiled at that. "Don't sell yourself short. From what I hear, you're doing a better job."

"Shhh," I pretended to whisper. I gave a pointed nod to the table of old-time farmers, where Greg and Travis were still sitting. "Don't let the eighth battalion from 1942 hear you say that."

Allan laughed loudly. "Greg likes to stir them up."

Greg must have heard Allan laugh, because he looked over. Seeing us two talking, he made excuses for himself and Travis and they joined us.

I handed Travis his beer while Greg made introductions. "So that conversation looked riveting," I said lightly.

Travis scoffed. "I believe they have the collective opinion that agronomy is nonsense. There's nothing they can't learn from farmin' that can be taught from a book." Travis shrugged and sipped his beer. "Or so they said."

Allan laughed. "It's like the Wright brothers trying to tell NASA no thanks, that they know all there is to know about flying. The fundamentals are there, but times have changed."

Travis and I both laughed at the analogy. "See?" Greg cried. "This is why we, us three"—he indicated to himself, Allan and me—"need to shake these guys up."

Allan groaned and rolled his eyes. "Has he been buggin' you about this too?"

I laughed. "Yep," I said, looking around the room at the dozens of people, most of who were my father's age. "Though I have to admit, I wasn't expecting this many people. Seriously, I think I should be sitting at the kids' table for dinner tonight."

Greg smiled, but it was more of an aww-hell-kid kind of smile. "You'll get used to it."

"I don't belong here," I said, though not to anyone in particular. It was just a general thinking-out-loud statement.

Greg looked at me seriously. "You belong here just as much as anyone else. All the big station names are here, yours included."

"If one more person tells me they're sorry to hear about my dad, I think I'll—"

"Charles Sutton?" some older guy I probably should have recognised but didn't interrupted.

"Yes, that's me," I said, waiting for it, waiting for it...

"Very sorry to hear about your father. He was a

great man."

I could almost feel my teeth crack, my jaw was clenched so tight, but I forced a smile. "Thanks."

Greg dismissed the other guy politely enough, then pulled on my arm and led me, Travis and Allan around the corner of the bar. It was darker, more private. He ordered a round of bourbons for us all. "Sorry about that," Greg said to me. "Guess you're sick of hearing it."

"I wasn't exactly prepared for it from every person here, that's all," I admitted. "Nor the fact that most of 'em know who I am just by lookin' but I haven't got a clue who they are."

"There's quite a buzz that Charlie Sutton's son is here," Greg said, handing me a bourbon and dry. "Drink that. Won't make them go away, but it will make you care less."

I risked a glance at Travis, and I could see the worry in his eyes. He was keeping his hands busy with his drink, and I wondered how much self-control it took for him to not touch me. I could tell he wanted to, maybe as much as I wanted to feel it.

I sipped my bourbon instead. "Let me guess, though. My dad would have been at the table of old men, talkin' about how good the eighties were."

"Every meeting," Greg said with a laugh. "He only missed one or two. I think some kid took a spill off an unbroken pony when he was ten and broke his wrist."

I held out my right arm, the one I broke. "And two ribs," I amended. "And I was twelve." Greg and Allan laughed, and Travis shook his head. Then I added, "It was the day before he was supposed to leave. I remember that much because he yelled at me for a week about missing it."

Everyone was called to be seated as dinner would soon be served. I was kinda glad, because two beers and a bourbon on an empty stomach was starting to make my head spin. We sat at a table with Greg, Jenny and Allan and ate our meals. Afterward, there were a few formalities to go through, a few boring speeches and one product sponsorship spiel. We even had our photos taken, but all in all it wasn't too bad.

After that, we moved back to the bar and traded stories of last week's muster, which led to talk of farming and soil. Travis and Greg were debating the pros and cons of fertilisers and acidification, when I noticed a small crowd near the doors to our left watching us.

And then I saw who it was.

It was Fisher, the same guy who used to work for me, who helped find Travis in the desert and saw the love bites all over my chest when I'd taken my shirt off to secure a splint to Travis's leg. The same guy who called me a faggot and a queer.

That Fisher.

He had a too-much-rum kind of lean and a sneer on his face, looking at me. This wasn't going to end well. He had a grudge to bear, a secret to tell and nothing to lose.

I could see him talkin' but couldn't make out the words. The way the others around him looked over at me left little doubt to what he was saying. "Oh Jesus," I whispered, turning toward Travis and Greg, turning my back to Fisher.

"What's up?" Travis said.

"Remember Fisher?" I asked quietly. "Used to work for me? The one George punched off the veranda when... you busted your knee?"

I didn't have to elaborate. Travis knew exactly who I was talking about. "Yeah."

"Well, he's here."

Travis looked over my shoulder, and I could tell the

moment he saw Fisher. His eyes hardened. "What does he want?"

"I can have a guess," I said.

Greg frowned. "Everything all right?"

"Just a disgruntled ex-employee," I said, trying to make light of it, when the truth was it made me feel sick to my stomach.

Greg saw who we were talking about. "Ah. Well, he shouldn't be in here. You can have him kicked out if you want?"

I shook it off. "Nah, I'm sure he'll go soon enough."

He did go, but not before he got talkin' to some older guys I didn't know, and from the way they all looked over at me, once again, I didn't have to wonder about his subject choice.

"You know what?" I said. "I think I might call it a night."

"Charlie," Greg said softly. "It doesn't matter what he thinks."

He was saying he knew. I had assumed he did, but sure as hell wasn't gonna bring it up. Greg knew, and he didn't care. He had continued treating me like he always had. He was never any different. Greg shook his head. "No one here will listen to a word he says anyway."

If only that were true.

Because Fisher's rumour of Charlie-Sutton's-a-fag spread pretty quickly. Whether they believed it or not didn't matter.

It was my worst fear coming true, whispered around the auditorium, one rumour at a time. I could tell by the leaned-in whispers and wide-eyed stares. Some tried to hide their conversations, some didn't. Hell, some even made it a point of open discussion.

RED DIRT HEART 2   215

Like the table of old men, who called me over.

I should have left. I should have just walked out and gone back to Sutton Station and minded my own business for the rest of my life.

But I didn't. I went over to the table and the ringleader of the group, or maybe just the most self-righteous, Jack Melville, gave me a smile I didn't like. "You should know, Charlie, that Jason Fisher is telling unholy lies. You might want to clear a few things up."

"Well, Mr Melville, if you'll beg my pardon, but I don't care what that man says," I said as politely as I could manage. "His employment was terminated at Sutton Station, and if he has a grudge to bear, the weight is his alone."

That answer seemed to be to their liking, because they all smiled. Mr Melville nodded slowly, approvingly. "I like you, son. I can see much of your father in you."

I laughed, because he had no clue just how wrong he was.

But then one of them said, "See? Told you all it wasn't true. No nancy boy could run a station like that. I've seen the sales figures from across the state. Sutton's are quite impressive."

I clenched my teeth. "Nancy boy?"

He seemed embarrassed to have to have to explain. "You know," he said, making a face. "A poofter."

I started counting to ten in my head and only got to four when someone else said, "Don't be silly, Jim. There ain't no men out here like that. They're all in the cities where they should be."

Those were the words of my father. It was like he was saying them. I could hear them in his voice; I could see the anger in his jaw and the disappointment in his eyes.

Jack said something that sounded like *sodomy* and

disgusting and *queer*. He said they'd never have any staff member who did that because they were manly men, and then the whole table laughed because it was funny, but I couldn't really hear because the blood was pounding in my temples.

Travis pulled on my arm. "Come on, Charlie," he whispered.

I shook Travis's hand from my arm and stayed put. "Wow," I said, running my hand through my hair. "And here I was thinking my father came to these meetings to talk business, not gossip and giggle like a Country Women's Association meeting. Actually, I bet those women talk more on the issues of farming than you lot. I could probably have a more productive conversation with them."

That shut them up. Each and every one of them had their stunned-mullet faces on. I didn't fucking care. I didn't care if they were my father's friends, I didn't care if they thought I was a smear on the *Charles Sutton* reputation. I *was* Charles Sutton, not my old man, not even who he wanted me to be.

I was *me*. I worked just as hard as him, ran a better station than he ever did. I understood more about the land we worked, I had higher profit margins in a tougher economic climate than he ever did. I was better at it all.

And I was fucking gay.

And in that split-second life-defining moment, I could see the difference in myself. From seven months ago to now, I was a different man. And I was proud of who Travis had helped me become.

"You know what?" I asked the table of gob-smacked, you-can't-talk-to-us-that-way men. "I *am* a fucking nancy boy. And I can *still* run a better farm than any of you." Not one of them could argue, because they saw the stock sales; they knew it was true. "I came to this meeting because I thought we were here to discuss diversification and sustainability of one of the harshest environments on earth. But if you wanna sit here like a bunch of old women and talk about sex lives, then I'm all for it," I said, lifting my chin, looking at Jack Melville. I sneered at him. "Let's start with yours. You married? You been married for what? Forty years? You still enjoy a good old romp in the bedroom? I bet you're a missionary man, never done it in the shower? In the hall? On the kitchen table? Doggy style?"

The man's face went an immediate high-blood-pressure red. "You have no right—"

"And you've no right to talk about anyone else!" I snapped back at him. I had quite the audience now, pretty much everyone in the auditorium was staring at me. So I addressed them too. "Now if *anyone* here is interested in filtration properties and water cultivation, high salt content and water tables or beef stock ratios—if you want to network and make our industry stronger—then I'm all ears. But if anyone else here thinks it's their business to discuss my sex life or that of my staff"—I looked back at Jack Melville—"I don't care how old you are, I will knock you off your fucking chair."

I figured then was a pretty good time to leave. I made my way through the stunned-into-silence crowd and down the stairs, but had only got to the lobby when Travis caught up to me. "Charlie, wait!"

I turned to face him, because, well, because it was Travis. He looked shocked, to say the very least. "Charlie, that was... um..."

"You know what?" I asked, throwing my hands up. "I'm not even sorry."

He scrubbed his hand over his face and looked back up the stairs, then at me. "Don't ever apologise for that."

Greg came down the stairs, into the foyer and stopped when he saw us there. He grinned the biggest fucking grin I'd ever seen him wear. "You okay, man?" he asked. "Because that was incredible! Do you know how long I've wanted to tell that sonofabitch what I thought of him? And you just nailed it." He shook his head. "Nailed. It."

I took a deep breath and tried to calm the fuck down. It didn't work. I think I growled. "No wonder my father sat at that table. I ain't surprised one bit."

"They're a bunch of whingin' old bastards," Greg said. "They'd complain of the sky being blue if you listened too long. They've never liked me because I insisted Jenny sit in on the local meetings. They reckon it wasn't her place. But I tell ya, she works just as fucking hard as I do while schoolin' our kids at the same time. They had no right to say her opinion wasn't as valid as mine. I told 'em that," he said, "just not as spectacularly as you just did."

"Yeah, well, fuck them," I said.

Greg laughed. "Now you see why I wanna get rid of them?"

Maybe I was still too mad, and maybe I wasn't thinking entirely clear-headed. "I'll do it," I told him. "Nominate me for the Board. It'll be my pleasure to piss them off every chance I get."

Travis shook his head, but at least he was smiling. He told Greg, "I hope you're good with stubborn."

Greg laughed. "It's my favourite kind."

And then, because the night couldn't possibly get any worse, who should walk out into the foyer? None other than Fisher and a few of his deadbeat friends.

His eyes widened, as did his sneer. He laughed obnoxiously and came toward us, stumbling drunk. "Well, look who it is," he slurred loudly, then took a mouthful from his Bundy rum can.

"Fisher," I acknowledged him. "How's unemployment treating you?"

He laughed, though it wasn't a happy sound. Then he spotted Travis. "And look who's with him. S'prise, s'prise." He laughed again, lookin' at me. "You brought your boyfriend along."

There was dead silence. Everyone in main area of the club would have heard what he said. As if I didn't have enough adrenalin running through my veins. I closed my fists and took a step toward him. I was in the mood to punch the shit of something. Travis put the drink he was still holding down on the reception desk and stood beside me, but it was Greg who spoke. "I think you've had enough, Fisher."

"What?" he said with a laugh. "Didn't he tell ya? Sutton's a queer, and the Yank's his fudge-packin' boyfriend."

I don't really remember what happened after that. I remember grabbin' him by the throat, and I remember the blood poundin' in my ears. That fucker could say what he wanted about me, but there was no way I was lettin' him talk about Travis like that.

I pushed him outside and he swung at me, collecting me in the corner of my eye. He was too drunk for it hurt me, but I was hardly gonna let him have another chance. I closed my fist and punched him right in his good-for-nothin' fucking mouth. He fell backward to the ground and I got in a few more punches before I got pulled away.

It was Travis. He grabbed me by the arms and dragged me off Fisher, and then some security guys were there, keeping a distance between me and him. Greg told them that Fisher had been an unwanted guest upstairs at the function, causing trouble. They told Greg it wasn't the first time Fish had been involved with fighting, and then they told Fisher his trouble wasn't worth his business. He wasn't welcome back.

Fisher's face was bloodied, his nose smashed, and he was missing two of his teeth. I snorted out a laugh. "Nice dental work. And there I thought you had nothing to lose."

"Fuck you," he spat as he was escorted away.

"Not even if you were the last man on the planet," I yelled after him.

Greg roared laughing and clapped me on the shoulder. "You are too much fun." Then, still chuckling, he told Travis, "Get him home, and get some ice on that eye." Before he got to the door, he turned and said, "Good luck tomorrow. Remember what I said."

Ugh. Tomorrow.

I didn't want to think about tomorrow.

"Come on, Rocky," Travis said. "Let's go." We got into a taxi, and Travis didn't speak the whole way to the hotel. My behaviour hadn't been great, and by the time we got into our room, I was fairly sure Travis didn't like the side of me he'd seen tonight.

I wasn't a violent person by nature. I could count the punch-ups I'd had in my whole life on one hand. But maybe a fist-throwin' boyfriend wasn't on his toleratin' list. I sat on the bed and fell back onto the mattress and dug the heels of my hands into my eyes. "I'm sorry," I said quietly. "I don't know what got into me tonight. I ain't got no excuse for fighting. I'm sorry, Trav."

I felt the bed dip, and gentle fingers pulled my hand away from my face. Something cold pressed against my already-swelling eye. I opened my eyes to see Travis holding a can of lemonade against the side of my face. "We had no peas." His smile faded just a fraction. "And don't apologise. If you didn't punch him, I was gonna. But I'm pretty sure you did a better job of it than what I could have."

"I couldn't let him talk about you that way," I told him. "But I was pissed off before he even opened his mouth. I should have walked away."

Travis leaned in and gently pressed his lips to mine. "Tonight was a mixed bag of everything, wasn't it?" He studied me for a while, like he was searching for the right words. "Your dad was mentioned a lot tonight..."

I nodded. "I wasn't expecting that," I whispered.

Trav moved the cold can against my eye. It felt good against the heat of the swelling. "It must have been hard to hear that," he said. "It was hard for me to hear it—I can only imagine what it was like for you."

I tried to smile for him, and taking a deep breath, I tried the whole talking thing we'd been working on. "At first it was like they were talking about a man I didn't know, and I dunno—" I shrugged. "—maybe they were. They were telling me how great he was, what a good man he was. I started to wonder if I knew him at all..."

"They knew the farmer," Travis stated. "Not the father. There's a huge difference."

I nodded. "Exactly. I mean, he worked hard, I know that. And he was a good farmer. I never said he wasn't. But I saw him through their eyes tonight, and I wondered if my view of him was from a confused and lonely kid, ya know?"

Then Travis did the best thing ever. He just listened.

"And I felt guilty for not seeing that sooner, and you know, maybe he was just doing the best he knew how. But then that Jack Melville and all those other old guys started talking about how disgusting poofters were, and you know what?" I asked rhetorically. "I realised I didn't misunderstand anything. Because if my father were alive and sitting at that table, he would have laughed with the others. He'd have rather seen me hurt than his reputation. What they said tonight wasn't anything I haven't heard before from him. He said those words. All of them.

"And then I got mad, because I shouldn't have felt guilty. I did nothing wrong."

"No, you didn't," he agreed quietly.

"I guess I said those things kinda wishin' I'd said them to my dad."

Travis smiled. "I wish he could have heard them, especially the part where you asked Melville if he still banged his wife on the kitchen table."

I laughed then. "I said that, didn't I?"

"You sure did," Trav said with a chuckle. He sighed and studied my eyes again. "Then you basically told them all you were gay and they could all fuck off."

I snorted out an oh-fuck-what-have-I-done kind of sigh.

"And you told Greg to nominate you for the Board of Directors," Travis reminded me, "so you could piss those old farts off every chance you got."

"I said that too, didn't I?"

Travis leaned in and kissed me again. "You were kind of awesome tonight."

"I was a whole lot of stupid."

Travis smiled and moved the can of lemonade, turning it so the still-cold part pressed against my eye. "Your eye's gonna be a pretty shade of black tomorrow."

Ugh. Tomorrow. I still didn't want to think about tomorrow. "Oh, man. I totally forgot! You were gonna talk to Greg about that agronomy services thing." Now I felt even worse. "I fucked that up too."

"No you didn't," he said. "I spoke to Greg. He said it was fine."

I sighed, long and loud. "Remind me to send him a case of beer or something."

"It's been a pretty monumental night for you," Trav said. "Charlie, you kinda came out tonight to every farmer in the Territory."

"I did, didn't I."

"How do you feel?"

"I have no clue," I answered. I searched for the dread and the fear of realising my worst nightmares, but I couldn't find any. "Actually I feel okay. Tomorrow might be different though. When it's sunk in, I mean."

"Tomorrow," he said. "We have enough to worry about tomorrow."

My head was swimming, my eye hurt a bit and so did my knuckles. I pulled the can of lemonade off my eye and took Travis's chin between my thumb and fingers of my not-sore hand, pulling him in for a soft kiss. "Everything will go fine tomorrow," I whispered.

He nodded. "It has to."

I fell asleep not sure which of us was trying to convince the other anymore.

———

THE OFFICE where we had to go for the meeting was in the centre of town. It was a typical government office, and I felt out of my depth as soon as I walked through the door. The waiting time was bad, lots of sitting around in silence and there wasn't any doubt in my mind why they had no clocks in waiting rooms. I think it would have driven me mad.

A lady came to the door. She was maybe midtwenties, of Aboriginal heritage and dressed like a lawyer. She had long black hair and pretty eyes. She smiled at us. "Travis Craig?" she asked.

"Yes, ma'am." Travis stood up, and I'd have probably done the same, but my body wouldn't seem to move.

"I'm Nerida Martin. We spoke on the phone." She smiled and showed her hand toward a door. Trav took off his hat, and with uncertain steps, he walked inside.

And if I thought the waiting with him was bad, the waiting without him was just downright insufferable.

I was just about to start pacing when the door we'd come through opened and some familiar faces came in.

Ma first, all dressed up nice and pretty, with George behind her, and then Billy.

I found myself standing, shocked to see them, and so fucking relieved. "What are you guys doing here?"

"We came to support Travis," Ma said. Then she noticed my eye. She put her hand to my face. "Charlie! What happened?"

"We ran into Fisher last night," I said, automatically touching my eye. Ma gasped and George growled. Billy's eyes narrowed. I gave them a bit of a smile. "You should see him, though."

There was head shaking and quiet cussing, but eventually George asked, "Where's Travis?"

I nodded toward the door. "In there."

"How long's he been in there for?" Ma asked.

"Only about five minutes." Then something occurred to me. "Um, who's at home?"

"Trudy, Bacon and Ernie," George answered.

I couldn't hide my surprise. "I thought they were headed across the country." I shook my head. "I didn't expect 'em to give up their holidays for me."

Ma gave me one of her warm-smile-specials. "They all wanted to be here," she said. "But someone had to stay."

Just then, the door behind me opened and I turned to see Nerida go to say something but stop when she saw the four of us waiting. "Charles Sutton?"

"Yes," I said, but my voice was all croaky. I tried again. "Yes, that's me."

"Oh." She seemed surprised by something. "Have you got a minute?"

I have my whole life, I thought. She held the door open and I walked through, taking a seat next to Travis.

"A bit of a waiting party out there, I see?" Nerida said. She was smiling and seemed pleasant enough.

I wasn't sure how to explain what the people in the waiting room were to me. They were my employees, but they were so much more than that. "They're my folks."

Travis gave me a questioning look. "Ma, George and Billy are here."

He looked genuinely shocked and a whole lot touched. "What for?"

"Said they wanted to come and show support," I said quietly. Travis looked back toward the door and smiled.

"Right," Nerida said, taking control of the interview. "Mr Sutton? You're the sole proprietor of Sutton Station? Travis's employer?"

"Yes, that's correct." I knew what she was thinking. I was too young. "My father passed away two and a half years ago."

"And Travis has worked for you in fulltime employment for the last seven months?"

"Yes, that's correct."

"Were you aware that all temporary visa holders are not supposed to be at any one permanent employment for more than six months?"

I shook my head and looked at Travis. "No. I didn't know that."

She nodded, but just moved on. "And Mr Craig originally came to Australia for what was supposed to be a four-week period, to work and learn about the local farming."

"Yes."

She tilted her head. "He stayed longer because..."

Because he wanted to. Because he was too damn stubborn to get on the plane. "He felt his work wasn't done. He had more to learn." I looked at Travis and kind of shrugged. Jesus, I didn't know what to say. "I'm sorry, I wasn't aware I was being interviewed today." I tried to comb my hair a bit with my fingers. I smiled nervously at her, which hurt my swollen eye. "Ignore the eye makeup," I joked, pointing to my eye. "Musterin' cattle last week and a Brahman wasn't too happy about it." It was a blatant lie, but an explanation for the bruise. It wasn't like I could hardly tell her the truth. "So, what can I help with?"

Nerida gave a tight smile, but didn't really offer any explanation to my question. "Mr Craig is here on a temporary work visa," she said. "There was a specific non-secondary term clause, which means it can't be extended. He's already breached one condition."

What? "What?"

Nerida tapped her pen on the desk, going over what must have been Travis's file. "The first temporary visa was extended after the first four weeks. It can't be extended for a second term."

I'm pretty sure I could feel every drop of blood drain

from my face. I looked at Travis, who was now staring at Nerida.

"What about the subclass 887?" I asked. "A skilled regional worker. He fits into that category. If he's lived in a regional area of Australia and worked fulltime, then he qualifies, yes?" I looked from her to Travis and back to her. "An agricultural consultant is on the skilled occupation list on the immigration website."

She looked surprised that I knew what I was talking about. But she wasn't smiling. "Agronomy isn't an isolated skill in this area."

"What does that mean?"

"It means there are other agronomists. Local people," Travis said. His voice sounded so distant.

"I don't want anyone else working on my farm," I said. "Sure, I can hire some academic from the college here, but they'd just be some scientist, not a station hand. Travis can do both. And that's something that I can't get anywhere else." She looked so indifferent, and I wondered how someone so young and pretty could be that way. Maybe she was good at her job, but she had no idea what it was like on a working farm. "Do you know what it's like to find staff?" I asked, rhetorically, because she obviously had no fucking clue. "We're three hours out of town. Three hours from a shop, a cafe, a doctor. Do you know how hard it is to get and keep good staff when we're that isolated?"

"Have you sought the local employment offices here?" she asked. "There's always lists of people who are capable."

"Capable, maybe. Willing, no. We work twelve-fourteen hour days, week in, week out. They last two weeks," I told her. "We're too isolated. But Travis loves it."

She turned her attention to Travis. "Mr Sutton mentioned consulting."

"I have consulted with another station, Burrunyarrip. It's situated over the Queensland border. Not as big as Sutton Station, but still twice the size of anything the States has. Greg Pietersen is the owner, and I've had a few meetings with him," Travis said. None of it was technically a lie. It just wasn't a whole truth. Greg had told Travis last night to use him as a reference for his agronomic expertise and he'd happily tell some government official, who never stepped a foot outside city limits, what it took to make it out here. "I was at the Northern Territory Beef Farmers Association meeting just last night."

"And you've done consulting work with them?"

"I'm lining it up," Trav answered. "I spoke with a lot of different people who were interested, I just couldn't confirm dates... you know... because of this." He waved his hand a little toward the file on the desk.

"Well, I will need a number for the Mr Greg Pietersen you mentioned," she said.

"I have his number in my phone," I said, pulling out my mobile. I scrolled through my contacts and slid the phone onto the desk so she could write down the number.

While she was writing it down, I said, "I'm not sure how these things work. I didn't think it was such a big deal, to be honest. I mean, people move to this country all the time. And you can't tell me they all work. And they certainly don't work sunup 'til sundown in the Outback summer or sleep outside on the ground in the middle of winter, mustering cattle, I can tell you that much."

"Their applications must be for permanent visas?" Travis offered quietly.

"Well, why can't you apply for one of those?" I asked him, then turned to Nerida and asked her the same. "Why can't he apply for one of those?"

"It's not that easy," Nerida said. "The Australian government takes immigration very seriously."

"I get that," I agreed. "And so it should. But if he fits the criteria, if he ticks all the boxes, then it should be okay, yeah?" I looked at Travis, and it stopped me. I'd never seen him so utterly uncertain. He looked beaten already.

"It's the government's point of view that Mr Craig's skills are not unique to this area."

This interview wasn't going how it was supposed to go. I could feel blood thumping in my ears. She was saying no. It wasn't supposed to go like this. I was starting to feel all tight in the chest, like I couldn't breathe or something, and the sick feeling in my stomach tasted a lot like anger and desperation.

"The government's point of view?" I asked, not even trying to keep the bite from my bark. "Is that how to you displace blame? No responsibility, no care, *it's not personal*, that kind of thing. Do you they teach you how to remove yourself from personal liability? Tell me, are there classes for that?"

"Charlie," Travis warned quietly.

"No. No, Trav," I said. "This was supposed to be easy. You were gonna come in here and just fix up some paperwork, and that'd be it. It was supposed to be easy."

"Mr Sutton," Nerida said calmly. "Thank you for your time this afternoon."

I was being dismissed, and not only that, but I'd probably just screwed any chance Travis had. It was all going wrong. I answered every question wrong, and she was going to say no. They were going to make Travis leave. In one week, he'd be boarding a plane back to the States, taking my heart with him. My eyes burned and I shook my head. My voice was just a whisper. "Please don't do this."

Nerida stared at me, and I could feel Travis's eyes

burning into the side of my head. I didn't dare look at him. All I could do was shake my head and ignore the stupid burning in my eyes and chest. And maybe it was the emotions of the past weekend or maybe it was the sinking realisation that they were really making Travis leave, but I had to say something. "I love him."

Travis gasped beside me and Nerida's eyes widened, just a fraction, before she composed herself. "Mr Sutton—" she said.

I shook my head again. "Do you know what the odds are that I would ever find someone? I live and work in the middle of the desert, and he gets on a plane from the other side of the planet and arrives at my doorstep." I took a shaky breath. "The most perfect guy, and for some reason I will never understand, he chose me. I'll tell you what the odds are." I raised my pointer finger. "One. One chance in a life-time. That's all I get."

"Charlie," Travis whispered beside me.

I turned to face him then and fought back tears. "I can't do this without you."

His face fell and his lip trembled. "Yes, you will," he murmured.

"It will kill me," I told him, trying not to cry. "If you get on that plane, a part of me will die."

"Mr Sutton, Mr Craig," Nerida said. I'd almost forgotten she was there.

I stood up. "I'm sorry. I didn't mean... I ruined every-thing. I'm sorry. I should go."

Travis stood up and took my hand so I couldn't leave. "You didn't ruin anything."

I looked at the woman behind the desk. She looked sad, but also like she'd heard it all a hundred times before. I took a deep breath and tried to compose myself. "Think of me what you like. I guess it doesn't matter. But it's not about me, and it's not about the government hatin' on gay people. If you take into account anything I say, let it be this: Travis is one of the hardest workers I've known. He understands the land like he was born and raised here. He understands the desert, and he doesn't just love it, he respects it. Do you know how rare that is?" I looked at Travis. "He deserves to be here. He's earned it."

Travis was looking at me with a whole lot of sadness and thank you in his eyes. I pulled my hand from his. "I'm sorry."

"Don't be," he said softly.

I walked out of the room. Ma was quick to her feet, but she stopped when she saw my face. I needed to leave. I needed to walk outside and get some air. "I'll be outside," I said to no one in particular and kept on walking until there was sunlight on my face.

"Charlie," Ma called out behind me.

I turned to her. "I fucked it up, Ma." I ran my hands through my hair and looked around. We were out front of the local council building. There were cars in the street and people walking past, and I didn't care. "I shoulda stopped talking. Why the hell did they wanna speak to me anyway?"

She put her hands on my arms and face. "Oh, love."

I blinked back stupid fucking tears again. "I can't believe I did that."

Ma's eyes were all sad. "I'm sure it wasn't that bad."

"I told her that I loved him, Ma, and that if he leaves it'll kill me," I admitted. I leaned against a handrail and put my head in my hands. "I totally just blew it for him."

"Well," she compromised, "sometimes the truth is best."

"And sometimes the truth will get you kicked out for sure when the government don't like hearing about a bunch of gays, Ma." I'd gone from upset to pissed off, and I guess Ma knew me well enough to give me silence. She leaned against the handrail with me and never said a word.

Eventually George walked out to meet us. "Travis and Billy are coming out now."

I exhaled through puffed-out cheeks. I had no idea what to say to Travis and doubted I'd even be able to look him in the eye again. I didn't have to. He walked outside with Billy. He looked okay, not too upset, but I looked away when he got closer. He didn't even hesitate. While I was workin' on how best to say sorry, he just walked right up to me, and in front of everyone, for all the world to see, he threw his arms around me.

And I didn't mind one bit.

"That was the best thing you've ever said," he said. He pulled back, and he was a mix of grinning and wonder. He looked to the others. "Oh my God, you should have heard what he said."

"What I said?" I repeated. "Travis, I was so out of line. I bet you anything you like she's in there now stamping a big fat red 'denied' on everything she can lay her hands on."

Travis surprised me by smiling. "Maybe she is." He shook his head and looked right at Ma. "It was the most romantic thing ever."

I groaned, and we started to walk toward the car park. "What else did she say?"

"Not much. We just talked some more, she asked a few more questions. Then she said she'd have an answer for us in twenty-four hours."

Twenty-four hours. Jesus, we were now countin' down hours.

Then Travis said, "Then Billy spoke to her, but I couldn't really follow what they were saying..."

Billy? We all stopped walking and turned to look at Billy, and he just grinned his half-a-face grin. His unruly curly hair was stickin' up all over the place, and his eyes smiled against his dark skin. "We talk in the language of the Eastern Arrernte people, my people. I tell her that Travis is a good fella. I told her that my cousin Nara was in a bad place, but she is now safe at Sutton Station, and how Travis show her how to make garden and teach her like our people, how to be good to the land."

I couldn't believe what I was hearing. I had to swallow so I could speak. "You told her that?" I asked.

"'Course I did," Billy said. "Told her too, that you a good fella, Mr Sutton. A *kake* to me and my people."

Oh. He just called me *brother*.

And again with the tears. Fucking hell, I was an emotional ball of crazy. I couldn't even speak. Billy laughed and clapped his hand on my shoulder. "You okay?"

I laughed, wiped away my tears and shook off my embarrassment. "Yeah, I'm good."

Travis put his hand on the back of my neck and pulled me against him, just for a second, before letting me go. He looked to Ma and George, who were both smiling at me. "Have you guys had lunch? I'm starving."

"We did eat, yes," Ma said. "But you should go get something."

Travis hugged Ma, and then, surprising George, he hugged him too. "Thank you so much for coming in. It really means a lot." Then he looked at Billy and held out his hand. Billy grinned at him and they did some weird handshake thing. "Thank you, Billy. I thought I was happy to see you when you found me in the desert that day I came off Shelby, but it was real good to see you here today."

Billy just grinned and looked at the passing cars in the street. "We go home now. Too many people here for me."

They left me and Travis standing on the footpath, just kind of looking at each other. "Are you okay?" he asked.

I swallowed. "I will be. In twenty-four hours," I said. "When we get that phone call to say it's all good, then I will be just fine." He smiled and took a deep breath. "Are you okay?" I asked him.

"I will be, in twenty-four hours," he said with a smile. "But right now, I need food."

"What do you want?"

"Pizza."

I rolled my eyes. "I shouldn't have even bothered asking."

He grinned and started walking to the ute. "Nope, you shouldn't have."

CHAPTER FOURTEEN

WHERE MY WHOLE LIFE CHANGES IN TWENTY-FOUR HOURS.

TRAVIS HAD the three large pizza boxes on the seat between us and had already devoured two slices in the barely two blocks we'd been driving when he said with his mouth half-full, "Oh! Can we stop at the co-op?"

I swung the ute around and headed for the store. "Sure thing. What did you want?"

"I need some lime and potassium of sulphate."

"Of course you do," I said. "Wait. You're not planning on making another stink bomb."

He laughed and swallowed his mouthful of pizza. "That's ammonium sulphide. God, didn't you study chemistry in college?"

"I was gonna say, after three pizzas you won't need any help with making a fart bomb," I said, pulling into the co-op. I laughed at Travis's face as I got out of the ute.

I'd almost forgotten the events of the night before at the Beef Farmers meeting, and I certainly forgot that I'd seen Brian there. He certainly didn't look too pleased to see me now. Brian had run the co-op for forever, and up until the look on his face just now, I'd have called him a friend.

When Travis and I walked in, he looked about as uncomfortable as he could get. He took a small step back and couldn't even fake a smile.

So this was how it was going to be.

This is the exact reason I had never wanted to disclose my sexuality in the first place. It was the attitude of men like this, of business owners like this in small-town farming communities that could make life so much harder than it needed to be.

"Brian," I said maybe just a bit too cheerfully.

He straightened up some brochures on his sales counter. "Charlie," he said, not quite looking at me.

"Trust you had a good night last night?" I asked. "Entertaining... informative..."

He stammered, "It, ah, was, yes."

Gone was the warm conversation, the friendly chats of news and sales. He was bein' a whole lotta homophobic quiet. I figured I had two ways I could deal with this. I could either apologise for making him uncomfortable and leave or I could watch the bastard squirm.

I smiled at him. "Brian, tell me something," I started. "You got a problem with me? You know, being gay." I was getting used to sayin' that out loud. It just kind of rolled off the tongue.

"I, um, I..."

"You got a problem with the amount of money I spend in your store?" I asked him. "Because, well, I ain't sure on the exact figures off the top of my head, but it's at least two hundred, maybe two hundred and fifty thousand a year, isn't it?"

He blinked quickly and swallowed. He wasn't stupid. He knew where I was going with this.

"So here's the thing, Brian," I said calmly. "We're gonna continue to do business, because it's convenient for me and it's a financially sound decision for you. But if you're happy to never see another Sutton dollar again, I'll cheerfully pay to have my gear transported from Darwin or Adelaide."

His voice squeaked pitifully. "Look, I don't think it needs to come to that."

"I don't either," I said. "But if you're going to be disrespectful to me or to Travis, then I will return the favour, along with any other stations in the Territory who I can convince not to spend another cent here either."

Then he finally grew some balls and cleared his throat. "Charlie, I don't have a problem at all."

"Good," I said with smile. "Because it'd be extremely unprofessional of me not to do business with you because of what you do in your bedroom, wouldn't it? It doesn't affect how you do business at all, does it?"

He got my point. He shook his head. "No, I guess it doesn't."

"Then we're on the same page," I said brightly. "Now, Travis needs lime and sulphate for Ma's garden."

"No problem. This way," he said, walking off toward the back wall. "What size?" he asked.

I think Travis was stunned into silence. He was staring at me. "Trav, what size bag?"

"Oh." He shook his head. "Um, maybe twenty pounds?"

"Can you talk in kilos?" I griped as we followed Brian. "One word for you, Trav. Metric. The rest of the world uses it."

"Shut up," he said and pushed me into an aisle of cane mulch.

Brian was lookin' at us like we were an old bickering married couple. "Ten kilos is close enough?"

Travis looked at the bags of fertilisers. "Perfect."

"Oh," I said as I remembered. "I'll need to order in new teats for the poddy feeder. We're expecting calvin' two-to-one this spring."

Brian's eyebrows rose. "Busy."

"Always."

"Teats come in packs of ten."

"Gimme three. If I need more, I'll let you know."

We paid for the fertiliser, and I made a point of shaking Brian's hand to show him goodwill. I meant no harm before, sayin' what I did, I just had to prove a point. And by the time we left, I think he was okay with it.

I'd barely got us back onto the main road when Travis said, "Um, Charlie, you were kind of awesome and a little bit scary back there."

"Scary?"

"Yeah, like *The Godfather* scary." He made a gun with his hand and spoke in a low, husky, poorly done Italian accent. "The contract. Your signature or your brains."

I laughed at him. "And you know what I reckon scared old Brian the most?" I asked.

"What's that?"

I blew out through puffed cheeks and shook my head. "Jeez, I sounded like my father."

Travis looked at me for a long few seconds. "Is that a good or bad thing?"

I smiled at him as I drove. "I'm okay with it. Today, back there, telling him I was gay and he could deal with it or lose one of his biggest clients, it felt good."

Travis smiled. "Charlie, I think you're officially out."

I snorted out a laugh. I was grinning. "And you know what? I've never felt so..."

"Good?" he offered.

"I was gonna say free."

"Free is good."

"Free is awesome," I said with a laugh.

When Trav had eaten as much pizza as he possibly could, he put the boxes down where his feet should be, leaned against my arm with his feet up by the window and pulled his hat down over his eyes. He slept while I drove, and for an hour or so, I tried to put a name to what felt different.

I couldn't put my finger on it exactly, but something felt... different.

Better.

We still had a whole day to wait until the Australian Immigration department delivered their verdict, but even under that dark cloud of waiting, I still felt something shift inside. Something got lighter, less of a burden, and as I pulled into the Sutton Station driveway, I almost reckoned I had it figured out.

Now I know most people's driveways are kinda short, some just a few feet long. My driveway, from mailbox to homestead, was thirty-two kilometres. I dunno whether it was the ute slowin' down to make the turn off the road or if something in Travis's sleeping mind told him he was close to home, but he woke up. I pulled the ute to a stop.

"What's up? What's wrong?" Travis said, looking around, still half-asleep.

I smiled at him. "Nothing's wrong at all."

He picked up the pizza boxes so he had somewhere to put his long legs. "Then why'd we stop?"

I took a deep breath and thought, *what the hell?* This talkin' shit out seemed to be workin' out pretty good. "I think I figured it out."

Travis made a face. "Figured what out? Charlie, could you cut the cryptic? I need to take a piss."

I laughed at him. "See? That's why I like bein' gay. We don't have to mind our manners in front of a lady."

"Is that what you figured out?"

"Well, no, I was just sayin', you know, 'cause it's true."

"Alright," he said slowly. He looked around outside, probably trying to figure out why I stopped where I did. "Charlie, you okay?"

"I'm very okay," I told him. "I just wanted to tell you something before we get home and play two hundred questions with Ma." Then I told him what I thought I'd figured out. "Remember the other week, when I was all out of sorts and being a stubborn shit?"

"Um, you're gonna have to narrow that down for me, because well, there's been a few..."

I laughed at that. "When I told you I felt caged in, or something like that."

He nodded. "You said you felt bound. You used the word bound," he said. The word had obviously stuck with him. I didn't realise it had hurt him. "Not by me, apparently, but by this place."

"Not by you," I said quickly. "And that's what I figured out. It's not this place either. It was me."

He frowned, confused. "What do you mean it was you?"

"It was me. And since we left town, I've been trying to figure out what feels different, and that's what it is."

"You feel different?"

"I do, kinda. Somehow. I dunno. I feel better. You said

the word free, and I reckon that's what it is. I'm free now. I always thought bein' known as a gay farmer would kill me or my farm, but you know what? I think maybe the opposite is true."

A slow smile spread across his face. "You don't feel caged in anymore?"

"I didn't even really know I did feel that way until I wasn't anymore," I tried to explain. "I think I got all antsy over the last few weeks because I had you here every day and it should have been perfect, but I still wasn't able to, you know..." I shrugged. "I still wasn't free to be out. I don't know if that makes sense..."

Trav leaned across and kissed me. It was a pepperoni kind of kiss. "It makes perfect sense."

"And it's not that it's just because I 'came out'," I said, using air quotes. "I think it's because I'm not ashamed. I always figured if the local farming community knew I was gay, it'd be something to apologise for." I shook my head and suddenly found the steering wheel interesting, looking at it instead of him. "But I'm kinda proud of who you let me be."

He never said anything back, and when I looked at him, he was just sitting there, stunned. "Charlie, I don't know what to say," he said quietly. "I think that's the best, most perfect thing you've ever said to me. That anyone will *ever* say to me."

I smiled, then kind of laughed. It was a relief to have said all this out loud. "I just wanted you to know." I started the ute again. "You ready to go home?"

"Nope," he said, opening his door. "I really need to pee." He got out, walked over to the fence and peed the Todd River on a post. There were a few cattle about a hundred metres away, and I laughed when he waved to them. When he finally finished, zipped up his fly and got back into the ute, he grinned. "Now I'm ready to go home."

———

I WASN'T FAR wrong from the two hundred questions I presumed we'd have to answer. But it wasn't just Ma. Everyone was there and they all wanted to know every detail, especially about my black eye.

Travis, who'd picked up Matilda as soon as we got home and hadn't put her down, told them about the Beef Farmers meeting and my subsequent altercation with Fisher. "He got in one swing at Charlie," Travis said, nodding to me and the evidence that was my black eye. "But holy shit, you should have seen Fisher. Broken nose for sure, missing teeth. Rocky Balboa here sure as hell didn't miss."

I held up my right hand, showing the cuts on my knuckles. "He said some things that weren't strictly polite," I told them. "And this was after he'd told every business owner there that I—" I searched for better way to phrase it. "—didn't fancy girls." I had always avoided this subject with my team. They knew I was gay, of course, but I never, *ever* talked about it.

Until now.

"So chances are, if you're in town, someone somewhere's gonna say something to you about it," I told them. This was the shitty part. "Brian, at the co-op this morning, tried to act like I wasn't welcome."

Everyone's eyes widened, and Ma gasped quietly.

Travis was completely unfazed. He was all animated when he told them, "Then Charlie proceeded to tell Brian that he will keep doin' business as per usual or he'll see to it that everyone pays extra haulage to buy their stuff from

Darwin." Travis laughed. "You should have seen Brian's face."

I shrugged. "Ain't no one gonna tell me my money isn't good enough," I said. "And if anyone says anything to you guys, just let me know."

"Oh," Travis added, "Charlie also told that old guy..." He looked at me. "What was his name?"

"Jack Melville," I answered. Everyone here knew that name.

Travis snorted. He was talkin' like he was proud of me. "Yeah, well, Charlie told him too—and everyone else there —that this is how it is, and you can like it or deal with it."

I sighed long and loud. "I can guess there's gonna be some repercussions. I didn't really hold back any. I told 'em exactly what I thought of 'em. But I don't care. I won't bend to breakin' just because they say so. It ain't written anywhere that I have to play to their rules, and if it comes down to that, then it's an easy fix." I said, with a smile. "I'll just change the rules."

Ma smiled, all proud-like with tears in her eyes, and George gave me a knowin' nod. I think he saw a glimpse of my father in me, laying down the law like that, and if that was the trait I took with me, that was fine by me.

It was Bacon who spoke next. "So, Travis, when do you hear back from that lady?"

"She said twenty-four hours," he answered. "So tomorrow, I guess. Maybe after lunch?" He tried to keep up the confident smile, but it didn't quite work. "She said she'd try and put forth a good argument in my favour, but she said she wasn't too confident."

No one really knew what to say to that. Except for Trudy. She summed it up perfectly. "Well, that sucks."

I laughed, and all eyes turned to me like I'd lost my

mind. I told 'em, pure and simple, just like Travis had said seven months ago, "He ain't getting on that plane." I clapped Travis on the shoulder and looked at Matilda. "Put that overgrown rat down. We got work to do."

For the rest of the day and even during dinner, I pretended I wasn't waiting for the axe to fall. It was coming, I knew it was. I just wanted the rest of my time not knowing to be as normal as possible.

I barely slept a wink, and I guessed Travis didn't sleep at all. I must have dozed at some point, because when I did wake up, it was just after four and Travis was layin' next to me, whispering to an bundled-up, wide-awake Matilda.

When he saw I was lookin' at him, he stared at me for a long moment. He looked all pale and sad in the moonlight. "I was just telling Matilda that if I do have to leave, that you'll look after her," he whispered. Even in the darkened room, I could see his eyes well with tears. "You'll look after her, won't you, Charlie?"

I pulled him close, kinda squishing Matilda in between us. I was gonna tell him I wouldn't have to because he wasn't getting on that plane, but that wasn't what he needed to hear. So instead, I kissed the side of his head and whispered, "Of course I will."

The both of them slept for a while, snuggled into my arms, and I stared at the wall until it was time to get up, wishin' hard and prayin' harder that this wouldn't be the day that broke my heart.

———

I MOVED through the morning on autopilot. I barely ate my breakfast, and I had to force down lunch. We stayed close to the house, as did everyone, waiting for, dreading the ringing of the damn phone. We had a few other calls, and every time, my heart leapt into my mouth. As the hours crept on, it felt like every minute put a weight on my chest.

I was helping fix the shade cloth over Ma's garden, and Travis was pretending I wasn't bein' a pain in the arse. No one really said much, the whole day seemed eerily quiet, so when Ma yelled, "Travis! Phone!" from the back veranda, it was so loud I dropped my pliers.

Travis wiped his hands on his jeans and looked at me with wide, this-is-it eyes. I gave him a nod and a smile, when truly, I felt like I wanted to vomit and it was getting harder to breathe.

We walked inside and into my office, one mechanical step after the other. Everyone kinda followed us in, kinda pretending not to be listen, but all waiting to hear. Travis didn't sit down. He stood at the desk, took a deep breath, and put the call on speaker.

"Mr Craig?"

"Yes?"

"It's Nerida Martin speaking," she said. "Thank you for meeting with me. I know you're very keen to know the outcome, so I'll just cut straight to the chase. Your case has been reviewed."

"And?"

I don't know how he could even speak. I was standing to his side at the desk. I felt sick. I couldn't look at anyone. I couldn't let them see me on the verge of losing everything.

"In light of the contribution you've been making to the community, your application for a permanent visa has been granted."

And just like that, with those simple words, my world was righted. My eyes stung, and I had fucking air for the first time in weeks.

He was saying something back to her and laughing, and his eyes were the brightest blue I think I'd ever seen them. I couldn't really concentrate on what they were saying because my head was starting to spin and I still couldn't quite get enough air. Everyone was smiling and happy, and I had to leave. Needed to. I had to walk outside. I couldn't deal with the room of people, and I sure as hell didn't want them to see me fall apart.

Because as I stumbled to the door, my eyes burned and I refused to let any of them see me fucking cry.

Travis was about two point four seconds behind me. "Charlie?"

I turned to face him, and the look on my face must have shocked him. He threw his arms around me like he was holdin' me together. I let the stupid fucking tears fall and sucked back the deepest breath I could. "I feel like I've been breathing through a straw for weeks."

He pulled back and put his hand to my face. His lips pulled down in a twisted smiley-frown. "Oh, Charlie."

I scrubbed my face with my hands, my voice barely a whisper. "I was so scared."

Travis took my face in his hands. "I'm staying. For as long as I want."

I sighed and leaned my face into his touch. I couldn't speak. I was still just trying to breathe. All I had was more stupid fucking tears.

Travis just pulled me against him again and held me so fucking tight. So tight. "You okay, Charlie?"

I nodded into his neck. "Yeah."

"Happy tears?"

I laughed at that. "Very."

"So you weren't so confident that I'd be staying?" he

asked. "You've been acting like you knew I would be all along."

I shook my head. "God no. I thought you were going for sure. I didn't want to deal with it. I couldn't even bear thinkin' about it."

"So you let me worry all by myself?"

I pulled back so I could see his eyes, so he could see mine. "I'm sorry I've been such an idiot. I guess it's just how I deal with stress." I shrugged. Then I word-vomited. "I dunno. I just push everyone away. I don't mean it. I'm so used to bein' all caught up in my head and used to it just bein' me. Bein' alone, yeah? And then you came along and changed all that, and now I kind of can't live without you. Well, then I very nearly had to because you were gonna have to leave and I didn't know how to deal with that. I'm sorry. But I've been workin' hard at trying to talk to you about stuff. I just couldn't talk about you leaving. I just couldn't..."

He held my gaze for a long, quiet moment. Maybe he was searching for something, maybe he was savouring the moment, I didn't know. "You don't have to, Charlie," he whispered. He rested his forehead on mine and ever-so-softly nudged my nose with his. "You don't have to."

"Do that again," I whispered with my eyes closed.

"What? This?" he asked, softly nudgin' his nose to mine.

I smiled at the butterflies it gave me. "That's the best thing ever." I pressed my lips to his in a silent, perfect moment. I wiped my face and took a deep, thought-collecting breath. Sliding my hand over his, I led him back inside. Everyone was still in there, in the lounge room now, but they were quiet, waiting... I still had Travis's hand, and I had no intention of letting it go. I didn't care if they saw it, I didn't care if it weirded them out.

"Sorry," I told them. "I, uh, I just needed a minute."

"So, Travis," Billy said. He was grinning his half-face smile. "How long you stayin' for?"

He squeezed my hand, but he smiled right at me. "For as long as Charlie will have me."

Everyone's eyes went to me, waiting for me to reply. I dropped Travis's hand, but only so I could put my arm around his waist. I pulled him into my side. For the first time ever, my staff, *my family*, saw me touching Travis. I was smiling like some lovesick teenager. Hell, I think I even blushed. "I'm pretty sure I'll piss you off somewhere between now and forever."

Travis laughed. "I'm sure you will."

CHAPTER FIFTEEN

FOUR WEEKS LATER. FOUR BLOODY LONG IT-
WASN'T-LIKE-THIS-BEFORE-HIM WEEKS LATER.

THE THING WAS SO bloody big, the only place it could truly go without burning the house down was outside. "Jesus," Ernie said. "You startin' a Domino's franchise or something?"

I stood back and looked at the pizza oven. "I didn't realise it was gonna be this big."

"Didn't you read the specifications before you bought it?" he asked.

"Of course I didn't."

Ma laughed. "Well, they'll be back soon, so you might wanna get it fired up."

Travis had gone with Bacon, Trudy, George and Billy up to the northern paddocks. He'd been gone five days. We had agreed that time apart, as much as it sucked, was critical. Travis had reasoned that working, living, and playin' together, day in and day out, without any kind of time apart wasn't conducive to staying together.

And he was right.

So a few days campin' out, whether it was fixin' fences or herdin' pregnant cows into a separate paddock like they'd been doin' this week, whether it was him or me that went, would do us good.

It also gave me time to do some secret stuff, like buyin' and settin' up a pizza oven. He said he wished he had one, so it seemed the logical thing to do.

I just didn't realise it was so big.

It kinda looked like a stone igloo with a chimney, and truth be told, I should've realised it wasn't exactly small when it took a truck to get it here and forklift to get it moved into place.

But he was gonna love it.

Well. He fucking better.

"Load her up with wood," I said. "Let's see how she cooks."

It had been an interesting four weeks. I'd given everyone a week off. They were supposed to have time off when Travis and I went into the Alice, but the stubborn folks they were decided to stick around and show him some brotherly support.

And then when they got back, Travis and I went into Alice Springs. It was his idea, and in fact, I tried to talk him out of it. But he said it was time.

We took Matilda to the Kangaroo Rescue Centre.

Travis held her in her pouch the whole way into town. He carried her like a baby, like he always did, and for about a hundred kilometres I asked him if he was sure. He told me to shut up, I was just making it worse. "She needs to go," he said quietly. "I've done all I can, and she should have a new home before she gets any bigger."

The truth was he couldn't release her. If she did manage

to find another mob of kangaroos, they'd likely kill her for smellin' like a human. She certainly wouldn't survive on her own, and he knew she certainly couldn't stay at home.

"You saved her life," I told him.

He'd nodded and gone back to bein' quiet. The guy at the centre had devoted his whole life to savin' these baby critters, and he told Travis he'd done a real good job with Matilda.

It was a heartbreaking kind of horrible watching him say goodbye.

But even as he fought tears, he knew it was the right thing to do. She'd have a long, safe life in her new home, and he said as sad as it was, he was happy to leave her there.

That was two weeks ago.

The last five days had dragged their sorry selves forward, and I missed him like crazy. I kept busy enough. I finished my assessment, I even submitted it. I did some PR work with Greg on getting elected to the Board of the Territory Farmers Association next month, and Ma took it upon herself to yell at me if I got sulking without him.

It was just goin' on late afternoon when we heard the utes and bikes come into the yards. The pizza oven was raring to go. Ma was trying some practice strips of bread, wanting to leave the first pizza honours to Travis.

I guessed they saw the smoke from the oven, because George and Billy came around the back first, looking to see what was happening. When Bacon and Trudy came around next without him, I asked, "Where's Travis?"

"Oh, he's coming," Bacon said like he knew something I didn't.

Before I could ask what that meant, Travis came through the back door of the house instead of walking around the side like the others. He stopped dead, his mouth open, his eyes wide.

He was holding something.

Something in a bundle.

Something in a wrapped-up sweater.

He was staring at the pizza oven, I was staring at him. We both spoke at the same time. "What the hell is that?"

"You bought a pizza oven?" he cried, walking down the back steps.

I ignored his question. "Is that another kangaroo?"

He ignored mine. "Seriously? That thing is huge! I don't even wanna know how much it cost," he mumbled to himself. "Jesus, Charlie. Did you buy that for me?"

"Travis," I said as calmly as I could. Everyone was watching us. "Are you holding another baby kangaroo?"

He looked down at the bundle of sweater and shook his head. "No," he said simply. Then he started to smile and walked over to me. He gently peeled back the sweater and a big flat brown nose and two tiny little eyes peeked back at me.

It was a baby wombat.

Jesus.

Fucking.

Christ.

"Oh, Travis," I said. "No, no, no. Do you know what damage they cause?" I asked. "They dig holes. Big holes. The kind of holes that wreck the foundations of houses. And they bite."

"But his momma was dead," Trav said, all blue eyes and disarming smiles. "And he's really cute. I named him Nugget."

Oh, no. He'd named him already.

"Here," he said, handing the bundled-up baby wombat over to me. "Hold him. I wanna check out this oven."

I looked down at this Nugget. His little nose twitched, and he blinked. "Don't look at me like that," I told it. It. Him. Whatever.

George laughed beside me and patted my shoulder. "Yep. That's what I thought."

I looked up then and saw everyone smiling at me. "This isn't funny," I told them.

I could tell by their faces they thought it was. Ma called out from the veranda, "Come on, you lot. You can all make your own pizzas. I don't cook outside."

Everyone followed her in, excited about this new pizza thing. I stood there holding a bloody baby wombat. Travis walked up and kissed me. "Did you miss me?"

"I did," I said. "Until you got home."

He laughed and poked his finger into the sweater at the wombat. "See? He's the cranky daddy, I'm the funny, handsome daddy."

"Boys!" Ma yelled at us this time. "Come in and get your dinner organised. I ain't your slave."

Travis grinned and took the stairs two at a time while I stomped after him, still carrying the newest Sutton addition.

I walked into the kitchen, where everyone was buzzing around. Life in this house used to be quiet and boring. Now it was loud, busy and filled with talk and laughter, not to mention the occasional baby freakin' animal. I looked at Travis as he was laughing at something Ernie said, and it made me smile. I'm pretty sure once upon a time, the noise, the lack of space and solitude would've driven me crazy.

Now I kind of loved it.

It was hectic and busy. It was in my face and loud.

I guessed it was a little like family.
And a whole lot of perfect.

~THE END

The Spencer Cohen Series, Book Two

The Spencer Cohen Series, Book Three

The Spencer Cohen Series, Yanni's Story

Blood & Milk

The Weight Of It All

A Very Henry Christmas (The Weight of It All 1.5)

Perfect Catch

Switched

Imago

Imagines

Red Dirt Heart Imago

On Davis Row

Finders Keepers

Evolved

TITLES IN AUDIO:

Cronin's Key

Cronin's Key II

Cronin's Key III

Red Dirt Heart

Red Dirt Heart 2

Red Dirt Heart 3

Red Dirt Heart 4

The Weight Of It All

Switched

Point of No Return

Breaking Point

Spencer Cohen Book One

Spencer Cohen Book Two

FREE READS:

Sixty Five Hours

Learning to Feel

His Grandfather's Watch (And The Story of Billy and Hale)

The Twelfth of Never (Blind Faith 3.5)

Twelve Days of Christmas (Sixty Five Hours Christmas)

Best of Both Worlds

TRANSLATED TITLES:

Fiducia Cieca (Italian translation of Blind Faith)

Attraverso Questi Occhi (Italian translation of Through These Eyes)

Preso alla Sprovvista (Italian translation of Blindside)

Il giorno del Mai (Italian translation of Blind Faith 3.5)

Cuore di Terra Rossa (Italian translation of Red Dirt Heart)

Cuore di Terra Rossa 2 (Italian translation of Red Dirt Heart 2)

Cuore di Terra Rossa 3 (Italian translation of Red Dirt Heart 3)

Cuore di Terra Rossa 4 (Italian translation of Red Dirt Heart 4)

Confiance Aveugle (French translation of Blind Faith)

A travers ces yeux: Confiance Aveugle 2 (French translation of Through These Eyes)

Aveugle: Confiance Aveugle 3 (French translation of Blindside)

À Jamais (French translation of Blind Faith 3.5)

Cronin's Key (French translation)

Cronin's Key II (French translation)

Au Coeur de Sutton Station (French translation of Red Dirt Heart)

Partir ou rester (French translation of Red Dirt Heart 2)

Faire Face (French translation of Red Dirt Heart 3)

Trouver sa Place (French translation of Red Dirt Heart 4)

Rote Erde (German translation of Red Dirt Heart)

Rote Erde 2 (German translation of Red Dirt Heart 2)

CPSIA information can be obtained
at www.ICGtesting.com
Printed in the USA
BVHW081328270819
556814BV00003B/319/P

9 781925 886375